Duncan's early life was largely about hardship and measured poverty in Jamaica. Going strongly in his favour was his ambitions, determination to lift himself to greater heights. Duncan took the first opportunity to follow in his parent's footsteps and migrated to the United Kingdom in the early 1960's. Now the obstacles were racial, but he circumvented them, acquired a string of academic degrees, entered the Teaching profession and in just over thirteen years, established himself, in West Yorkshire as Britain's first Black Headmaster of a secondary school: a feat that Duncan would repeat four years later when he was appointed to the headship of one of Birmingham largest schools.

To my beloved children, Yvette and Kyme Duncan

To the wonderful Venecia Johnson who kept me nourished as I toiled the pages

To my grandson, Jordan, my great-grandchildren, Jessica and Joshua

Carlton Duncan

THREE LITTLE BOYS

AUSTIN MACAULEY PUBLISHERS™
LONDON * CAMBRIDGE * NEW YORK * SHARJAH

Copyright © Carlton Duncan 2024

The right of Carlton Duncan to be identified as author of this work has been asserted by the author in accordance with sections 77 and 78 of the Copyright, Designs and Patents Act 1988.

All rights reserved. No part of this publication may be reproduced, stored in a retrieval system, or transmitted in any form or by any means, electronic, mechanical, photocopying, recording, or otherwise, without the prior permission of the publishers.

Any person who commits any unauthorised act in relation to this publication may be liable to criminal prosecution and civil claims for damages.

This is a work of fiction. Names, characters, businesses, places, events, locales, and incidents are either the products of the author's imagination or used in a fictitious manner. Any resemblance to actual persons, living or dead, or actual events is purely coincidental.

A CIP catalogue record for this title is available from the British Library.

ISBN 9781035844593 (Paperback)
ISBN 9781035844609 (ePub e-book)

www.austinmacauley.co.uk

First Published 2024
Austin Macauley Publishers Ltd®
1 Canada Square
Canary Wharf
London
E14 5AA

Much thanks and appreciation is well due to Miss Venecia Johnson without whom I would not have found the time to produce this book.

Chapter 1

Mr Austin had not even the slightest idea how restive this May Day's visit to the school's administrative office would turn out to be for him. Imagined not that a significant part of his remaining existence from here on would be impacted so unimaginably by this visit to the admin office; but who can predict how any day in the life of a headteacher would turn out to be?

How was he to know that before the week was out, a murder would be announced on his patch? Restive horses have a way of taking you uncontrollably into unknown territories.

"Oh my God, Mr Austin! The heat is so unbearable over these last few days," she said amid the clattering constancy of computer keyboards and of typewriters whilst she reached for the multiple-coloured straw fan that had been resting on the right-hand corner of her cramped desk.

The odd teacher and parent dropping by; and pupils on errands, created a scene that typified the regular atmosphere in that office on most days. This brightly coloured black, gold, and green fan was not just an instrument for breezy comfort as it seemed it was right then, but to Bianca, it was a constant reminder of romantic dreams that she held and cherished most dearly.

Bianca's loquacious character led her to completely ignore the possibility that the headteacher might have dropped by the office for a purpose and, so, she continued her commentary about the atrocious weather and its effects.

"And yet there are politicians and others who want to convince us that there is no truth in the science of global warming and its disastrous effects on people's lives and their comforts," she remarked amazingly whilst staring in loving admiration at her exotic fan.

"Actually, this was a present from a very special person," she said whilst referring to the fan with amorous twinkles in her eyes.

The headteacher knew of Bianca's marriage of a year ago because school management had made special dispensation to accommodate her leave of absence for the special occasion; inevitably then, but fleetingly, he pondered whether this 'special person' was her now sixty-seven-year-old husband, Carlos. Carlos who was born on July thirty-first 1953, according to Bianca's marriage certificate which she proudly hangs in her shared office, had been married before but things went bitterly wrong and had signalled a divorce.

He had waited a long time before asking Bianca to marry him. Just as quickly as he had come to this thought, the headteacher abandoned it and quickly moved on to why he was at the admin office in the first place. This headteacher was adept at closing down irrelevant conversations without seeming to be impolite: a skill which he developed over many years in teaching and school leadership; and so, Bianca's persistent attempt to make her fan the central issue of the day was decisively steered to the headteacher's main purpose without her even realising it.

"Bianca, I just had a call from the Department of Education and Science. Our school has been identified as one, among others, that is reflecting good and sound exemplary standards in multicultural and anti-racist educational practice across the country. The Secretary of State requires a statistical reflection of our ethnic staff and pupils to be presented at an upcoming educational conference in York next week Wednesday, exactly six days from today, the nineteenth of this month. I assured the department that we can have this on the Secretary of State's desk by noon tomorrow. I do realise the day is exceptionally hot, but I need you, please, to make a concentrated effort to have this done for me today and you can finish telling me about this special fan of yours some other time."

"OK, Mr Austin, I shall turn to it straight away: and I will take you up on the offer to listen to my story at some other time. It is important to me," Bianca replied enthusiastically, as she moved towards a row of filing cabinets in another corner of her shared office space and without any of her usual loquacity.

She did, however, wonder why the putting together of these statistics would be of such importance to Mr Austin.

Indeed, what Mr Austin did not share with Bianca, or for that much with anyone else because he was sworn to secrecy by the anonymous informer, was that the availability of these statistics could result in Mr Austin being invited as a special guest on the platform with the Secretary of State at the York Conference and, most importantly, was a pre-cursor to a knighthood coming his way, in particular for the work he was doing at Dixon Pen Comprehensive School.

This was being viewed at high levels as a contribution towards making our society, indeed, the world, a fairer and more equitable, and just place for everyone.

Mr Austin felt that after all these years of hard slog in the educational jungle, now that he was nearing retirement, it would be a magnificent accolade with which to retire. To hear His Majesty the King proclaiming to him on a day at his palace, his ornamental sword resting lightly on his alternate shoulder—'Arise, Sir Allan Austin'—would be a golden cap on his life's endeavours.

He was determined to do all he could to make this the ultimate reality, especially now that he knows that the work which he and his team have been doing at Dixon Pen was pivotal to his dream being realised.

Mr Allan Austin, a medium-built figure of an Afro-Caribbean man with greyish curly hair, an almost white beard, and protruding gut, had been the headteacher of Dixon Pen Comprehensive School for over a dozen years. The school, which was in the poorest part of Edgbaston, Birmingham, had two entrances directly from the popular main City Road which provides a radiation of bus routes to almost every part of Birmingham.

The main school itself was housed in a large Victorian building which had enjoyed the benefit of some modern renovation under the leadership of its present headteacher. It had very large playing fields which separate the main buildings from a more modern building on the far side of the fields. This more modern building was once a secondary modern school but was later absorbed by amalgamation to become part of the existing Dixon Pen Comprehensive.

This Headship was, in fact, the second for Mr Austin. His debut in school leadership was in Western Yorkshire where he became hardened and toughened and learned to survive all things mucky and resentful. In his domestic life, things had always been even shakier and over the years, he had counted three wives, two in divorce and the last in death some nine years ago, and five children, all of whom, bar the last, seventeen-year-old daughter, Doreen, were grown up and had flown the domestic nest.

A man of vision, stern leadership, and discipline; a clear insight into curriculum development for multiracial equity and community school development, he had pulled back this (fifteen hundred 11to 18-year-old pupils) multiracial school with its 60 or so teaching and auxiliary staffing from decline to be the prestigious bright star that it was at present.

In Mr Austin's younger days, he had developed a great love for the game of Cricket, a propensity for both amateur and professional boxing and international travelling. Presently, though, at age sixty-one, his only extra-curricular activities were fenced around home gardening, playing chess, and being one of His Majesty's very popular local Justice of the Peace on the Birmingham Bench.

The task of getting the statistical analysis and breakdown done for the Secretary of State now allocated, Mr Austin, then set off for his own office.

Hopefully, putting the statistics together will not take Bianca more than a couple of hours so that by the end of the day, I can be checking them through. Mr Austin thought as he continued in the direction of his office. Immediately, he turned the corner leading to the foot of the stairs which lead to his office, he observed Frankie Watson going in the opposite direction, and yet the change of lessons and end of morning break bell had sounded for almost five minutes.

"Frankie, why are you not in lesson? You are almost five minutes late, so far," the headteacher asked looking pointedly at his watch.

"Sir, it's because I had to show a man where Miss Edgewater's office is. It's her brother coming to surprise her, he said. Sorry sir!" Frankie said as he sped off in the direction of his mathematics class.

Frankie Watson was a member of the school's fifth formers. He was a tall young lad with red curly hair, freckled face with dimpled cheeks. He had a reputation for seeking out ways to be helpful to his class, his teachers, his school, and others, even at the expense of his lessons, especially if the lesson was mathematics. Sometimes, though, the tasks find him, such as the time when a parent of the school had a wheel puncture and sought his assistance in changing the tyre to the spare.

On that occasion, Frankie assumed total responsibility and performed the given task most enthusiastically and efficiently even though it was at some minutes cost to his lesson. Today must have been one of those times. Frankie's school reports tend to reflect a very likeable character with flaws that could also be counted as positives. In some of these school reports, Frankie's teachers refer to this young man as very helpful but capable of losing his temper very easily.

Whilst his school attendance was without blemish, Frankie's punctuality was often questionable. It seems that his hobby of identifying specified makes of cars and recording their registration numbers for a regular competition often interferes with his call to the lesson.

Mr Austin, now in the enviable solitude of his spacious office, was able to catch up on some of the day's correspondence without interruptions. He was also expecting Bianca—Mrs Burney—to deliver on the Secretary of State's request sometime before the school's bell at four o'clock signifies the end of the school day.

Bianca Burney, (Alias: Smith), second in charge of the school's admin office, was the longest-serving administrative officer at Dixon Pen Comprehensive. She had been on the school's admin list since over seventeen years ago when the school, then a Boys' Grammar School, became amalgamated with its sister Girls' Grammar School from the same site and two other close-by secondary schools to make the fifteen hundred strong 11to18-year-old pupils Dixon Pen Comprehensive.

Bianca Smith, as she then was, came from one of the secondary schools as did several other auxiliary staff, teachers, and pupils from all the schools in the amalgam under headteacher, Mrs Ann Mitchell who was later succeeded by the current headteacher Mr Austin in open competition. Bianca became Mrs Burney when, a year ago, she married Carlos Burney at the local registry office.

The school's management bent over backward to facilitate Bianca's wedding as it was all done on a school day and during school hours and some of the school personnel had bridesmaid and witnessing roles to play. The headteacher personally wanted to be part of the occasion.

However, the great day coincided, day and time, with the regular monthly meeting of Birmingham Secondary headteachers and it was Allan Austin's turn to chair that august body. Because of this, Mr Austin had regretfully asked to be excused and sincerely offered his best wishes to the soon-to-be-married couple.

The occasion was a splendid one: It was a warm and sunny May Day. The picturesque school gardens where the couple chose for their wedding photos were still showing off the roses, the crocuses, the daffodils, and the tulips at their most attractive best.

The wedding album was now suitably catered for the newly married couple and their guest moved to the Majestic Inn located just across the other side of City Road for their splendid wedding reception which will provide memories for the couple long into the years ahead.

The bride was stunningly beautiful. Her characteristically long flowing black hair hung deliberately loosely across her shoulders, contrasted nicely with her immaculate white gown, white gloves and white stylish shoes. Bianca's physique tends to be a little on the stout side but ever so shapely. This was not dissimilar to her husband's frame and he, on that special day, was dressed in a hand-tailored black suit, black bowtie, black shoes, and folded white handkerchief in his left breast pocket.

He was scrumptious. They were both decorated with the same matching creamy white roses that formed the bride's posy, she on her dress and he on his lapel. It was believed that both Bianca and Carlos were of Irish descent though they were educated and have worked and lived all their adult lives in the city of Birmingham.

Also, in attendance on that wonderful and blissful day was Gaston Burney, Carlos Burney's twenty-five-year-old son from an earlier marriage that ended in divorce. This young man was the spitting image of his father. They both have blond hair and blue eyes. Truly, only age sets them apart. Similarly, Helen Smith, Bianca's twenty-three-year-old daughter from an earlier relationship made a graceful appearance. She had legs that would turn the eyes of any man.

Just like her mother, she had long free-flowed jet-black hair that reminds you of some of the cutest film stars then and now. Going with her beautiful hair and stunning legs, she had a shapely presence that people write home about. In total, she was a cut above the ordinary in terms of beauty.

But for these two and a number of friends, the couple had no other relatives present either at the marriage ceremony or at the afterward celebratory activities. Those gathered as witnesses and participants in the celebration had mainly flattering and positive good wishes for the couple's future which made the thirty-eight-year-old bride and her sixty-six-year-old bridegroom hilariously happy and hopeful for their new life ahead.

Mr Austin looked anxiously at his watch, as he wondered what was happening with Bianca and the project for the Secretary of State. As if by telepathy, there was a knock on his office door a full ten minutes before the school bell signalled the end of the school day. First, he glanced furtively at a monitor which hangs conspicuously among the artwork, some professionally done, and others by pupils of the school, which adorns the walls of his huge and spacious office.

The identity of the caller, thus determined, the headteacher pressed his remote buzzer which released the security lock on the door. Standing there was Bianca holding a folder in her left hand and her adorable fan in the other as if she wanted to remind the headteacher of his commitment to listen to what she had to say about the origin of her fan.

Beckoning with arms gesticulation both invitingly and enquiringly, Mr Austin said, "Come on in, Bianca. How did you get on?"

"I think it is all here," she replied as she handed the folder to the headteacher.

Her talkative urges got the better of her and, even before Mr Austin could open the folder, Bianca remarked.

"I see you have reorganised your office. I did ask Elaine to tell you that I would come up and help you with your reorganisation whenever you contemplated it. Did she tell you?"

Neither the headteacher nor Bianca noticed Mrs Edgewater entering through the still open door to the headteacher's office.

"No, Bianca. I didn't get around to telling him because everything has been so hectic these last few days. However, I got the caretaker to assist me in moving the furniture around in accordance with the head's wishes so you can cease looking for ways to undermine me. Why are you here, anyway, have you finished the letter to the parents about the school concert which I asked you to do earlier today?"

"I will do the letter tomorrow, but I had to do something which was considered most urgent for the head. It is that that I have completed and brought up for the head to check."

"But you didn't tell me you were doing something for the head. You all know that it is the department's policy that I should know what task all six of us are always working on. How else can I efficiently manage the resources and make the team as effective as is desirable?"

The headteacher, hearing this not-so-friendly conversation between his two most senior admin members, thought he detected a dagger that was aimed not so much at Bianca but at him. He felt it was time to diplomatically intervene and prevent an unnecessary conflict that was clearly in the making.

"Elaine, please go easy on Bianca. It is entirely my fault. Because you were already working on an important project for the governors when this extremely urgent matter came up, I thought I would not burden you further; and so, went directly to Bianca with a request to get it done. It was my intention to drop by your office to let you know that I had done this. I am very sorry for over-looking this—not so much over-looking, more like forgetting. At the grand old age of

61, I am to be forgiven for forgetting the odd thing of importance," Mr Austin said, intending his last sentence to be a pacifying jocular note.

"Talking about forgetting to drop by to see you, I understand that your brother came to give you a surprise visit today. I didn't know you had a brother: how many of you are there for your parents?"

The headteacher's jocular intervention did much to bring back some pleasantry, as was evidenced by the broad smile on Elaine's face as she quizzically responded to the head's question about her brother's surprise visit.

"Sir, my parents have three of us: and all three of us are girls. We have no brothers, so, I could not have had a surprise visit today by my non-existent brother," Elaine chuckled.

The puzzled Mr Austin, visibly annoyed that he had been taken for a ride by Frankie Watson earlier that day at the change of lesson, quickly and quietly explained to the two ladies that he got this information from Frankie Watson whom he had challenged this afternoon at lesson change over for being late for his math lesson.

"Frankie," he explained, "told me that the reason he was almost five minutes late for his math lesson at change over this afternoon, was that he was showing this stranger who claims to be Mrs Edgewater's brother, to her office. He said the stranger said he was paying his sister a surprise visit. If Frankie thinks he has conned me off his case that easily, then he has another thing coming. Elaine, please arrange for Frankie to be sent to my office first thing tomorrow morning."

"I don't know if we are talking about the same student," said Elaine, "but there are some coincidences here. The reason I am here to see you, Allan, concerns this boy called Frankie who has walked out of his math lesson after being extremely abusive and rude to the teacher, Mr Brooks.

"Apparently, he told Mr Brooks that he didn't want to be taught by a nigger. We put out a search party trying to find this Frankie, but he cannot be found. Mr Brooks contacted the reception office whilst I was there expressing deep concern for Frankie's safety and whereabouts. I told Mr Brooks that I would be seeing you about the matter and I would speak with him later."

The silence which fell over these three officers was deafening. The headteacher will be shattered by this one massive blow from Frankie. Mr Ivan Brooks was an Afro-Caribbean teacher of mathematics whose prospects, at Dixon Pen and beyond, were pretty well assured.

A nicer and more caring teacher would be hard to find. Some of this teacher's caring attitude was discernible from the report that he delivered to reception. Despite the racial abuse he had just received from a fifteen-year-old student, he was most concerned about the boy's safety and his whereabouts.

Dixon Pen Comprehensive was shortly to be held up as a beacon exemplar of good educational practices for sound race relations in multicultural Britain. Significantly, this was a school where parents have a greater say in their children's educational development than you would find anywhere else in this city and beyond.

The headteacher and his colleagues firmly believe that you cannot truly have equity in education unless the school's focus was pupils and parents centred.

How could this Frankie Watson response to Mr Brooks square with the philosophy, values, and open practices of a school led by me and my team? Mr Austin pondered.

Clearly, we as a school have a lot of work to do and we shall begin with Frankie Watson tomorrow. Mr Austin thoughtfully reflected.

"Elaine, please contact Frankie's parents and alert them about what happened with Mr Brooks today and that Frankie unilaterally removed himself from the protection of the school's premises. Let the parents also know that I will need to see Frankie first thing tomorrow and that their presence would be of immense worth to me."

Mr Austin then turned to Bianca who had, miraculously and with great wonder to the others, remained quiet fanning away with her brightly multiple-coloured fan throughout both incidences involving Frankie.

"Bianca, we still have these statistics to go through so that I can understand what is there before I ask Elaine to fax it to the Department of Education for the attention of the Secretary of State in the morning."

"OK, sir, whenever you are ready."

Mrs Elaine Edgewater then excused herself and left the other two together to conclude their urgent business.

It didn't take the headteacher very long to grasp the layout and breakdown of the school's population statistics as Bianca had presented them. He planned to take them home and go through them once more before taking them back for Elaine's attention in the morning.

"I thank you very much, Bianca, you have made me proud. This is sterling work. The bell is gone, so no doubt you wish to leave for home. Do you still have someone giving you a lift home?"

"I still have my lift, but I asked him to come a little later tonight as I wasn't sure that I was going to complete these statistics on time. As it is, I have a little time to spare."

"Oh great, so you can tell me about that fan which seems to hold so much ecstasy for you these days. It is not often that you see a mature woman in such rapturous delight over a functional instrument such as a fan, beautiful though it is."

This was a signal to Bianca to do what she truly excels in doing, talking.

"It is a present from Jamaica, see the colours, they are the colours of the Jamaican flag," she said holding up the fan against the background light of the headteacher's office.

"It was given to me by a very special person who I would like you to meet someday. This person has visited this glorious and colourful island on many occasions and brought this back, especially for me on the last visit. These days I am feeling so special, happy, and hopeful about everything. There is so much that I wanted to say and do but maybe the time is not yet right.

"I get not just comfort from this fan; it is also a link to my joys and expectations. I better stop going on about my fan at this point because my lift should be arriving any time now and I am sure you must be going home soon, so I better go downstairs and get my things together."

"Before you go, Bianca, I want to say that I hope I didn't create a problem between you and Elaine earlier. It sounded like she was very upset with you or us about something. Is there normally friction between you?"

"No, not at all, other than a little strangeness soon after her appointment, we are mostly friendly. Two days ago, at lunch, the girls and I were admiring that beautiful ring which she wore on her left hand. She was so proud of it. She wears it instead of her wedding band. Apparently, it is a special kind of white gold with a ruby, opal, and diamond set. It seems unique and expensive.

"The girls asked her why she wears such an expensive piece of jewellery all the time. Would it not be safer to insure it and wear it on special occasions? Her response was that anywhere that ring goes she must be there too. Elaine has always been friendly and helpful. The girls and I thought that we may have been a little unfair, maybe a little jealous in the early days of her appointment.

"So, today took me by surprise and really shut me up for a while. Truly, some people thought that she was the boss and the only black in the team would lead to difficulties; but, as I said, after the early days, things flowed very smoothly. Maybe, I should just put today down as a bad day for her. Things will get back to normal tomorrow."

"OK, I will take your word for it, and I must not be so casual with school policies in the future," the headteacher declared.

Sometimes, Mr Austin displays a somewhat nervous disposition about the institution of the school's values and equal opportunities policies, especially at present. He had always wondered whether appointing a black chief administration officer to manage a department of five other admin staff, all white, would reinforce the equal opportunity policy or introduce unhelpful conflicts in the school.

The admin department consisted of a complete team of six—all-white—until two years ago when the chief admin officer, Mrs Barron, retired leaving just her deputy, Bianca Smith, assistant admin officers, Sheila Robinson, Mary Anderson, Phyllis Brown, and Torah Small. The vacancy was immediately advertised and fielded ten candidates, two Afro-Caribbean ladies, and eight Caucasians. The short-listing process whittled down the list to four candidates.

One of these four was the only internal candidate, Miss Bianca Smith, who was the deputy to the outgoing chief admin officer, and three external candidates which included one of the Afro-Caribbean candidates, Elaine Edgewater who was also the youngest of the bunch, and two of the Caucasian candidates. And if Mrs Edgewater was appointed, it was observed that she would also be the youngest member of her team.

To listen to Bianca's talk of friendly and helpful relations was music to the headteacher's ears. So far, he had no regrets that the interviewing panel insisted on the criteria of meritocracy and proven skills as opposed to perceived conflict ahead. The systems and structures he and his team have put in place were working even if there was the occasional Frankie Watson.

"We will see each other in the morning, Bianca," Mr Austin said as he closed his office door behind Bianca's departure.

As Mr Austin exited the parking lot and the school gate, his white BMW motor car heading north towards Sutton Cold Field and his home, he began thinking, once more, about what the Frankie Watson's incident that emerged today really means for the school's policy and race relations in the school and beyond. Surely, the school didn't seem to have made a sufficient dent in entrenched attitudes as far as pupils were concerned: especially those who joined the school later than year seven.

Much work needed to be done pastorally, and much stronger messages need to be sent via the planned curriculum too. Although the headteacher didn't want to be seen as too reactionary, he resolved that both the curriculum and pastoral deputies, Mrs Jones, and Mr Graham respectively, should have an urgent meeting with him, sooner rather than later, so that the school can strategize against 'Frankieism' whilst it was still young and before a fashion sets in among the copycats.

As far as staff development was concerned, his efforts and those of his team seem to have been rooted well, as, in his mind, he reflected on Mr Ivan Brooks' attitude under stress and the report from Bianca of good relations. The story about how a unique and seemingly most valuable ring that seems to be inseparable from Mrs Edgewater's left hand, illustrates good relations among her, her boss, and other colleagues was quite impressive and made Mr Austin hopefully optimistic, as he retired his car in the garage at his home in Lavender Mews.

Daniel, the domestic helper who had been with Mr Austin, since his last wife died, had prepared a most welcoming meal; his favourite Italian meal, Lasagna Verdi al Forno. Whilst he waited for Daniel to set the table and give him the green light to commence eating, he took a further reassuring glance at the documents prepared for him by Bianca earlier that day simply to re-confirm his satisfaction and its readiness for Elaine to fax on to the Department of Education for the attention of the Secretary of State tomorrow morning. This done, he was ready to dine.

Once he consumed his meal with a glass or two of the connoisseur's best red wine, the headteacher headed for the showers and then to bed. Tomorrow will be a demanding day; he needed to be thoroughly refreshed to deal with it. Talk about understatement, this was some under-thought without comparison.

Chapter 2

The next day was not a day for fans of any type—electrical or beautifully hand-made ones such as those owned by Bianca. For this time of year, it was exceptionally cold and windy. Gloves, overcoats, and scarves were in order.

Mr Austin peered through his bedroom window the moment he got out of bed. The scene outside was not welcoming but he had a school to run no matter what. Besides, the documents for the Secretary of State were still in his possession and he needed Elaine to get them to the Department of Education by noon today. Then there was the Frankie Watson's issue which made a serious dent to the exemplary race-relations practice for which the school was known.

The start of dealing with this matter was scheduled for this morning. He had asked to see Frankie, preferably with his parents, for two main reasons, first thing this morning; and as this matter had much wider implications for the entire school and beyond, a subsequent meeting with his deputies was of the highest importance.

These were the early morning thoughts that preoccupied the mind of the headteacher as he made his way to his bathroom facilities. As always, he had enough time to navigate his morning chars, have a good breakfast start to the day, and then face the morning traffic build-up for the journey to Dixon Pen. He bade Daniel goodbye after saying that he enjoyed his breakfast and off he went.

On his arrival at school this morning, not many car parking slots were yet taken. This fact supported the message both the dashboard clock and his wristwatch were telling him: that he was earlier than usual. On his way into the building, he met the school's caretaker, Mrs Jackson, who greeted him very reverently as was her wont.

The odd boy or girl was already milling about and others slowly drifting in. Except for a few who were diligently committed, teachers tended to arrive nearer the nine o'clock point for arrival. In just a few more minutes, the place had become magically alive for another day's educational input.

On his way up to his office, he called into reception. All the admin staff, bar Bianca whose lift had not yet arrived, had already arrived, and got all set up for the day.

"Good morning, Sheila, good morning, Mary, good morning, Phyllis, and good morning, Torah. All set for the day?" He greeted them warmly.

They reciprocated his greetings and Torah announced that she was making some coffee and asked if he would like her to bring him up some to which he replied positively. Mary, also, volunteered the useful fact that Elaine was with them earlier and had just left for her office.

As he was about to leave to continue his way to his office, he met Bianca rushing in apologetically to the other girls for being a wee bit late because her lift got slightly delayed in the morning traffic. The head and Bianca exchanged greetings and he was then on his way. He had to pass by his PA's office on the way to his, so he would drop off the documents and check on the arrangements for Frankie and his parents.

He knocked on Elaine's office door but there was no reply, and her door was locked. He knew Elaine was about because the rest of her team had already advised him.

"Oh, she is probably checking with Mr Brooks for an update and will, no doubt, reappear shortly." He thought.

He didn't have to wait long for Elaine because his diligent PA was already displaying her usual conscientiousness on the seat just outside his office in anticipation of his arrival.

"Good morning, Elaine."

"Good morning, Allan."

They both said to each other, demonstrating their first names and friendly professionalism.

"I thought I would better see you quite early to give you an update on Mr Brooks' position on what happened yesterday as you might wish to share that with Frankie's parents when you have your meeting this morning. I have arranged for their arrival at ten o'clock, oh, I also jumped the gun a little and invited Mr Graham in his pastoral deputy head capacity to your meeting.

"Also, it seems like the whole thing started because Frankie got to Mr Brooks' math class after morning break almost ten minutes late and Mr Brooks demanded an explanation. Frankie blamed you for detaining him, but Mr Brooks would not accept that excuse and the whole thing escalated into where we are now."

"Thank you, Elaine, come in," he said as he opened his office door.

"That is eminently sensible. It is my intention, anyway, to involve both deputies in this matter. That you have already engaged Kelvin is a very useful start."

Just at this point, Torah entered the room carrying a small tray with some chocolate biscuits and a single cup of coffee.

"Mary sent you the biscuits." Torah said to Mr Austin.

Noting the presence of her line manager, she continued: "Had I known you were up here, I would have brought yours up too. I think Phyllis or Sheila is taking yours over to your office for you," Torah remarked before turning to leave the head's office.

"OK, please tell them thanks. I will be down shortly. The coffee will still be warm," Elaine remarked, thankfully.

Torah, now out of the room, so Elaine returned to the conversation with the headteacher.

"Do you want me to get hold of Mrs Jones now?"

"No, no, that won't be necessary, I will brief Patsy afterward. What did you learn from Mr Brooks?"

"Mr Brooks is an amazing man. He holds no grudges. His main concern was that the boy was safe. Once I was able to inform him that Frankie got home safely, he just wanted to move on."

The headteacher became momentarily silent whilst he pondered to himself that this was more reason why we as a school must fix this and not have a repetition of this kind of behaviour. We cannot always rely on the good nature of individuals.

He snapped out of his thoughts, looked anxiously at the old grandfather's antique clock in the far corner of his office, and then confirmed its truthfulness by looking quickly at the watch on his left hand.

"Elaine, the nine o'clock bell is imminent and as I am leading assembly this morning, I'd better let you have these papers to send on to the Department of Education."

He rested his briefcase on the edge of his huge mahogany desk, flicked it open and removed the documents, checked once more that it was all there and that he didn't unwittingly leave anything at home before handing the folder to

Elaine which she took with a courteous smile and left the room for her office on the ground floor bound for a rendezvous with the fax machine.

The nine o'clock school bell sounded almost simultaneously with Elaine's departure and the headteacher immediately unhooked his gold-trimmed academic gown from the handcraft wooden stand where it was always perched. He wears this garment only when he leads school assemblies. In his own words, "This is the only bit of old-fashioned indulgence I maintain."

The assembly will be held in the north hall which was much larger than the south hall which was normally used for smaller gatherings. The north hall accommodates the entire school with considerable ease and today the entire school will meet.

Normally, the headteacher would have had his address to the assembly preplanned. Today, he will improvise. It was an early opportunity for reinforcement of the school's values and to send a message of disapprobation to 'would-be' copycats in view of yesterday's open breach of school policy by one individual in the presence of an entire class of thirty individuals.

As is normally the case, the pastoral heads of years, with the aid of form teachers would have organised the pupils in their regular positions in the north hall in readiness to receive the headteacher. Selected teachers will have settled the scene with verses read from the Bible and the Quorum, at least. one well-chosen hymn.

At the sight of the head, the hall became a deafening hush as Mr Austin took to the mobile rostrum which was strategically positioned in the hall to give the headteacher a commanding view of all under his leadership.

"Good morning, Dixonians. I need you to listen to me more keenly than you have ever listened to me before. Approximately twelve summers ago, I joined this family, you, your parents, and our team of staff. I pledged then to stand by you through thick or thin. To date, it has been mostly thickness.

"Something, however, happened in this school yesterday which amounted to one member of this family picking at the thin scab of racism which should be further away from us as the furthest planet beyond. I personally found this to be fundamentally disturbing. No doubt, news about this has already spread because I have heard it. This must not become fashionable in any sense.

"We should never belittle ourselves by inflicting insults on others. What is the point of throwing insults, if the insulted only pity you and become fearful for your welfare? This way you achieve nothing but lose a measurable amount of your dignity, and your respect, and impugn your character. This school wants every one of us to be the personification of 'bouquets of humanity' in dealing with others, whether we are here in our school home or anywhere else representing the school abroad.

"We must all be strong, tolerant, and reach out for a just society for all people. Strong people do not pull other people down. We lift them up instead if need be. We must all do right by our fellow men. And remember, the time to do right is always now.

"Our greatest strength is in the power of our example, not the other way around: not the example of our power, verbal or otherwise. From this day onwards, we need to see those powerful examples of love and respect for all mankind in full display in our school and beyond its bounds.

"Whatever you are, be a good one. And remember, it is not your age but the age of your ideas and practices that counts. Let us be mature when dealing with our peers and our teachers and our parents, in short, all mankind.

"On issues of racial bigotry, there can be no accommodation at Dixon Pen Comprehensive. And please don't exhibit behaviour that challenges me; for if you do, you should know this: it will be a cold day in hell before I compromise on such matters. The higher you build your impenetrable barriers to the values that this school holds dear, the taller I shall become. The firmer is your resistance, the more muscular will be my resolve.

"I bid you a most productive day in your classes this morning and for the remainder of the day…good morning once more Dixon Pen and thank you, my colleagues."

This said, the headteacher departed the hall, his countenance as serious as it was ever seen as he headed in the direction of his office. The orderly dispersal was now left to heads of years and form teachers. The bell signalling the start of the first lesson of the day would go soon and so subject teachers would move quickly to their classrooms in readiness to receive their classes.

As pupils moved to their different classes at different geographical locations throughout the school, there was a hum that signified a seriousness of purpose, and that the head's message was well taken and should be acted upon accordingly.

Even the teachers and other staff dotted strategically throughout the hall as the head spoke could be seen nodding their heads in the voluntary agreement.

On his way out of the hall, Mr Austin was met by his PA, Mrs Edgewater, who gently reminded him that his ten o'clock appointment was nearing. She also pointed out that, in fact, Frankie and Mr and Mrs Watson were already waiting in the reception area.

Mr Austin casually glanced at his watch and remarked that there were still fifteen minutes before the meeting, so, he asked Mrs Edgewater to alert Mr Graham and to pick the visitors up at ten o'clock as arranged.

Mr Austin went back directly to his office and un-robed in readiness for his visitors. He shifted a chair here and a chair there to accommodate the anticipated number of people. At the stroke of ten, there was a silent knock on his office door.

The head shouted, "Come on in!"

Mrs Edgewater, escorting all three visitors, entered the room on command.

Mr Watson, as was his son, was tall with reddish curly hair. His bulky frame ensures an enviable and commanding presence. Frankie's freckles and dimples are clearly owned by his shorter, shapelier mother who clearly takes some pride in her appearance.

Mr Graham, a stoutish but elegant figure who was not far behind, joined them shortly afterward.

On occasions like this, the head would have normally requested some minute-taking support from the administrative team, but today he proposes to rely on Mr Graham's note-taking skills to get by, so, Mrs Edgewater was politely excused, and the meeting commenced.

Formal introductions out of the way, the headteacher turned directly and immediately to Frankie and asked.

"Frankie, why are we here"?

Unhesitatingly, Frankie began to explain.

"Sir, I messed up badly yesterday, sir, and lost my temper because sir didn't want to listen to what I was telling him. I tried several times, but he didn't want to hear. Because I am not very good at math, he called me dumb, and the class started to laugh at me. This made me mad and that is why I called him, what I called him, and walked out of the class."

Coincidentally, both Mr Austin and Mr Graham, upon hearing Frankie utter the term "messed up", began thinking, quite independently, that all was not lost. Being able to identify your error was half the job done.

"What was it you were trying to tell Mr Brooks?" The headteacher followed up.

"Because I was late for his lesson, sir wanted to know why I was late. I explained over and over that you had already dealt with me and that I had already told you why I was late because of showing that man where his sister's office was but sir didn't believe me."

"But how much of all that is true, Frankie, and how much is fictional?" Mr Austin asked.

"All of it is true, sir. You remember stopping me and asking me why I was late yesterday, don't you, sir? And didn't I tell you that the man wanted me to show him Mrs Edgewater's office because he hadn't seen his sister for a long time, and he was going to give her a surprise visit?"

"Yes, you did tell me all of that. But did you pull the wool over my eyes with the story about this strange man? The strange man part of your story doesn't really exist. You just made up that to get me off your case didn't you, Frankie?"

"It is true, sir, honest to God. Please ask Miss. She will tell you."

"Well, that's just it, Frankie. You see, I asked Mrs Edgewater about this yesterday, and she didn't know anything about it. What's more she hasn't got a brother, never had. What do you say, now, Frankie?"

Frankie began to cry.

"She is lying, lying, just to get me into more trouble," he emphasised.

At this point, Mrs Watson drew closer to her son. She put her arm around him as she wiped his tears with a tissue. This was of no avail. Frankie became exceedingly angry and got up, casting off his mother's arm and was heading for the door when Mr Watson held him back in a firm restraint.

"Come on, son, show some character here. We must get to the bottom of this. Losing your temper gets us nowhere."

At this point, Mr Graham tactfully intervened. He wanted to explore the benefit of what he perceived to be locked up in Frankie's initial 'messed up' comment. The headteacher, too, felt that staying on the 'strange man' issue any longer and at this time wasn't going to be helpful.

"Back to Mr Brooks, Frankie, we noted that you considered that you "messed up". Please tell your parents, the headteacher, and me why you think you 'messed up' and what you think will be the best way forward."

"I messed up, sir because I broke the school's policy very badly. The teachers have tried so hard to teach us respect and to value each other as we want to be valued. I don't think I would ever do that again, ever. I think I need some help with my anger control, and I want to apologise to sir in front of the class very soon, sir."

"I appreciate your good sense, Frankie, and I for one will be making the school's Psychological service available to you for assistance with your anger control and I will be reaching out to Mr Brooks to see how and when we can avail you the opportunity to make your apology," Mr Graham said with an obvious sigh of relief.

The headteacher felt that this was a suitable point at which to terminate the meeting. He invited Mr Graham to take Frankie outside so that he could have a private word with Frankie's parents.

Mr Graham enquired of Frankie whether he had come prepared for school. Frankie answered positively and so they left the room, Mr Graham bidding Mr and Mrs Watson goodbye and thanking them most profusely for attending and for being so cooperatively helpful and understanding.

Now that the headteacher was alone with the Watsons, he made it known that he wasn't satisfied with the 'strange man' aspect of their son's story, but that he felt that it wasn't going to be very productive to pursue it any further today.

On that point, he would communicate with the parents sometime in the not-too-distant future as these warrants further investigation when the time was right. He also felt that the measures suggested by Frankie himself, for sorting out the main issue, would put us all back on the road in good time.

He too thanked the Watsons for coming and for being supportive in trying to find solutions to our problems and volunteered to escort them to their car in the school's reserved parking lot. This he did. Then he headed toward Mr Graham's office for a review of the meeting.

As Mr Graham's office was in the opposite direction to that of Elaine's, he decided that he would call her from Mr Graham's office to get some verification that the documents for the Department of Education for the Secretary of State's urgent attention have been sent as planned. He needed that assurance because this was going to be very big for Dixon Pen when the Secretary of State addresses the York Conference next week with all the local, national, and international media present. There must be no slip-ups: certainly not from this side of the fence.

Mr Graham was in his office. In fact, he had just concluded a telephone conversation with his fellow deputy colleague, Mrs Patsy Jones, about this morning's meeting with the Watsons when Mr Austin arrived. Before he opened the review with Mr Graham, he rang reception and asked to be put through to his PA from Mr Graham's office.

"Elaine, how did it go with the papers for the Secretary of State? Have they gone?"

Elaine's response was inaudible but must have been positive because Mr Austin's countenance brightened with a supporting smile. He was placing very much on this.

The men then reviewed the morning's conflicting but, nevertheless, satisfactory outcome from the meeting with the Watsons. They agreed on what was now necessary for reinforcing school policies using both pastoral and curriculum techniques. Mr Austin was most happy to learn from Mr Graham that Patsy Jones, his curriculum deputy, had enthusiastically signed on to the way forward during her earlier telephone conversation with Mr Graham.

It was almost midday and Mr Austin reminded Mr Graham that he had a working lunch with Mr Sampson (C.E.O.), the director of education for the city of Birmingham. The director was eager to learn more about why one of his schools was being earmarked for big things.

This luncheon will provide the headteacher with the opportunity to bring the director fully up to date. According to the director, some politicians from both parties had picked up rumoured snippets and wanted to know what it was all about.

It was just gone two o'clock in the afternoon when the headteacher returned to his office following directly on from the luncheon meeting with the chief education officer. It was time to catch up on the day's issues and correspondence. He was certain that his PA and admin office personnel would be, by now, metaphorically pulling their hair out in frustration because they cannot get hold of him. At least, he had missed no diary appointments, which was a thing not to do as far as Elaine was concerned.

He was right. His desk was piled high with documents requiring his signature, and a long list of calls to be returned and he noted that there were several members of the teaching staff who had booked slots into his diary for the end of school that day and over the following days.

He first prioritised his call list and settled himself around his awesome desk to get started when: "Blast it!" He exclaimed.

The fire alarm had sounded.

In such circumstances, the pre-ordained school policy must be followed precisely. At the yonder fence—furthest away from the school buildings—of the large playfield, there are designated areas permanently marked out for each specific year group, year 7 (11-year-olds) graduating to year six (lower and upper groups).

In the event of a fire alarm whether for a practice drill, or a real or false alarm, pupils should be guided orderly and quickly by staff to their designated areas. The head of year and form tutors associated with a particular year will join them. Specifically, certain named staff have special duties which are activated at once.

It was the school's caretaker's responsibility to summon the fire department, check and account for members of the caretaking team; the heads of years together with form tutors to check off and account for the children in their year according to the class registers for that day; deputy headteachers check and account for all teaching staff and the administration team will redistribute class registers to all form tutors; the chief administration officer to check and account for all admin staff.

That very well accounts for everyone. The checkers must report any discrepancies directly to the headteacher on completion of their checks. No one shall depart his or her designated area without the say-so of the headteacher or the deputy headteacher, who, in turn, relies on the all-clear signal from the fire department. On school fire-drills days, of course, the fire department's role will not apply for obvious reasons. The headteacher alone shall act in such circumstances.

Whilst the school was being assembled in the appropriate areas, the increasingly louder and blaring sirens of the fire vehicles approaching the area of the school could be heard from miles away.

The system, despite its apparent complexity, worked like clockwork and had never failed in the past.

Remarkably, this time, there was a sole failure.

Every sector of the school reported favourably to the headteacher, bar one. Just the smallest department, the administrative department's head did not check in. The headteacher's tick-board quickly revealed that he did not hear from Mrs Edgewater, the Chief Administrative Officer. Because of the size of the department, a quick visual revealed that all members of that team were present at bar one, who should have reported to the headteacher. If this was noticed by anyone else, that was not known to the headteacher.

"Maybe, she is still inside checking or returned to fetch something she forgot: no, nonsense, anything like that would be a blatant breach of the rules and Mrs Edgewater doesn't break rules. She is a stickler for rules and policy compliance."

These were the kind of thoughts going through the mind of the headteacher. They were momentarily suspended as he saw the fire department representative approaching him.

"Mr Austin, I believe?" The fire department representative queried as he approached the headteacher.

"Oh yes, I am," the thoughtfully and anxiously waiting headteacher replied.

"Sir, everything is fine. We have inspected thoroughly and there is absolutely no sign of a fire anywhere. We also carried out a smoke test and the results were negative, as we expected. We seem to be having a great many of these pranks from schools, lately. I hope this is not the case here. You have the all-clear to return the school to order, sir."

The fire representative instantly obtained the signature of the headteacher and departed.

Mrs Edgewater's failure to report was now a troubling enigma for the headteacher but he was not ready to raise the alarm. He wanted to get to the bottom of this as quickly as possible with the minimum of fuss.

To enable him to prosecute his inquiries quickly, he summoned his deputy, Mrs Patsy Jones, and to her, he delegated the task of returning to the school rooms for what will now be the last period of the school day.

"Patsy, the fire department has given the all-clear. It is safe to return the school. There is no fire anywhere, but it seems they suspect that it might be a pupil-prank. We will have to get the caretaking team to check out the different points to see if any of the fire glasses has been broken—can I leave these to you?"

"Yes, sir, it will be done," Mrs Jones answered as she moved into action.

Still puzzled about the whereabouts of Mrs Edgewater, Mr Austin nevertheless watched with silent amazement and admiration how quickly and orderly the school was returned to normality.

The headteacher knocked on Mrs Edgewater's office door, as was his plan, but there was no reply. Elaine was not at her desk, he thought, and so gently eased opened the office door.

She was at her desk alright: that is exactly where she was but sprawled out dead: dead as a Dodo; her left arm dangling off her blood-stained desk. Her throat adroitly severed; her lifeless eyes staring at the headteacher as if pleading; there was blood everywhere; together, the whole gruesome picture presented a scene of bloody carnage rarely seen.

The headteacher's first impulse was to panic and raise the alarm, but the spirit of the old and hardened pro just as quickly trumped that idea and reason stepped in. Mr Austin had seen blood before. As a young teacher in London, he had separated many fights between pupils and twice had to rush pupils to the nearby hospital because they had been stabbed. When he worked at a school in Worcestershire, he witnessed one of his colleagues being shot by a gun-toting fifteen-year-old from a neighbouring school.

With experiences like those, you do become hardened. Yet, they were nothing compared with his current situation. Nevertheless, they would instinctively serve to condition his response now. All his responsibilities and obligations confronted him at once as he calmly exited Elaine's office.

The police, fifteen hundred pupils and their parent's expectations, the other fifty-nine members of his staff, the chairman of the school's Board of Governors, and the local education office are all now mentally competing for a position on his priority ladder of action.

One wrong move or neglect and a jungle of failures would sink him in the publicity that was now inevitable. Normally, in times of crisis, the headteacher would have his full team of administrative staff to handle his directions. All he would have had to do was to instruct his chief administrative officer, who doubles as his personal assistant, accordingly and she would then direct the others of her team as she determined. But she wasn't going to direct anyone right now.

He will have to manage it all by himself this time. The hour of the day became very important. If only he could minimise the size of the crowd that will gather when the news breaks. The strategy would be to get fifteen hundred scholars on their way home without raising the alarm. This would not be easy because the school day still had twenty minutes to the end. Four o'clock was the end of the school day and it was just gone three-forty and counting down.

Even when the time passed, there would still be teachers about the place for a variety of reasons, auxiliary staff reporting for cleaning purposes and caretaking, stragglers, homework clubs, and several extra-curricular activities which characterised a thriving school. Once they saw the police vehicles and personnel their curiosity will get the better of them and control of the situation will be lost.

With all these thoughts milling around in his troubled head, the headteacher reached for his master key which was hooked to his waist at most times. He discreetly used it to lock Elaine's office door whilst fully conscious that he may have blood from the floor on his shoes and his fingerprints would be all over her doorknobs.

The crime scene thus temporarily secured, Mr Austin went quietly but directly to the relative privacy of his office from where he would break the news to the police, the chairman of the governors, and the education office in that order. Once he had hung the 'No disturbance' notice on the outside of his office door, he called down to the school's reception office to ensure that he would not be, in any way, disturbed by telephone or pedestrian callers.

Time was moving on and, in the circumstances, he would let normality prevail as far as the emptying of the school was concerned. Trying to cancel after-school activities would only arouse suspicions and inquisitive inquiries.

Mr Austin knew the chief constable of the West Midland Constabulary Force exceedingly well. They played the odd game of golf in the past and belonged to the same Rotary Club in West Yorkshire. As fate would have it, their individual career paths had brought them together once more, this time to the West Midlands.

The headteacher wanted the minimum of publicity and thought that, rather than contacting directly the Harbourne Police Station, which was the station for Edgbaston, he would prevail upon Alton Brown, the chief constable, to assign the right personnel to this sensitive matter in the light of the headteacher's immediate concerns.

"There will be no siren; there would be the minimum number of police vehicles and personnel coming to the school as soon as possible," the chief told the headteacher.

By the time the headteacher had accomplished the tasks of making those calls and had been promised prompt visits from all three departments, it was four o'clock and the automatic release of pupils and staff would begin.

The headteacher, from the view of his office window which strategically allows him to see the main entrances to, and exits from, the school as well as a clear view of the main road and popular bus stops on opposite sides of the road, was able to see numerous pupils hastily scrambling out of the school gates and rushing to the bus stops whilst others footed it in opposite directions.

Similarly, those teachers with no after-school commitments, those with prior appointments, and those with an urgent need for the domestic sanctity of their homes could be seen pointing their cars in all directions: some headed for the bus stops like the pupils whilst others simply walked away out of sight. Even the loquacious Bianca shuffled away aimlessly, this evening in a different car.

Her usual lift had arrived somewhat early, this day because he was using a borrowed car and its return was time linked. They were all oblivious to the unbelievable event of the day.

How will they respond when they turn on their radios, access their chosen social media, and switch on their televisions a few hours from now? They will be shocked, flabbergasted and dumbfounded to know that they were all present when it all happened.

At the dot of ten minutes past the hour of four, Mr Austin observed the surreptitious entry of a strange car coming through the main school gate. The car was unmarked. The driver pulled into one of the now numerous available parking slots and immediately reached for some communication instrument and began talking. Before he was finished talking, the Chairman of Governor was seen arriving and immediately behind him was a representative from the education office.

Their vehicles are very recognisable to the school's personnel. The guy in the strange, unmarked car turned out to be a forerunner for the police. He clearly was there to do some reconnoitring before the team descended shortly afterward.

Just as the police teams were arriving—marked cars from opposite directions of the main road—the headteacher heard a knock on his door. He opened it to see the Chairman of Governors, Mr Oscar Wilde, standing there together with the education officer, Mr Baldwin Sing.

"Ah, gentlemen, you are just in time to join me in receiving the police. They have just arrived. Let's go down."

And down, they went only to see a massive rush of people rushing through the doors of the school, demanding answers to their curiosity thirst.

The village grapevine had already sprung into quick action—going on a wildfire mission. The marked cars and uniformed police officers did not escape notice. Many pupils were still milling around, and it seems that they used their cell phones to spread the excitement which attracted even some of those who had already left for home.

Adults from the immediate vicinity of the school and from neighbouring ones were heading into the car park in burning curiosity. The dedicated teachers that stayed behind for clubs, homework endeavours, detentions, and similar arrangements, all abandoned their activities and filled the reception areas, the halls, and corridors in a massive curiosity quest.

Only a few minutes ago when Mr Wilde and Mr Sing arrived there was none of this crowd and still, they know nothing except the imagined conspiracy theories which seem to have dominated the entire Birmingham geography by now. What will it be like when reality becomes known?

From the earlier conversation with the headteacher, the chief constable had already ascertained an almost perfect layout of the school and of the crime scene. Using their means, this information was already communicated to the trained officers on the scene so much so that the headteacher, the governor, and the education officer who, by this time were totally lost in the throng of things were not even needed to direct the officers.

They already knew the location of the deceased and were now doing what only they could do so well—controlling the crowd and securing the crime scene.

With absolute efficiency and with a minimum of time, the police officers had managed to empty the school buildings of all individuals except the most senior personnel of the school, the headteacher and his invited visitors among them, and those several individuals whose badges and lapel tags identified them as bona fide members of the press and other forms of the media.

Outside, the crowd had become extremely boisterous. It had grown exponentially so much that it was spilling over into the street and seriously interrupting the flow of the evening rush hour traffic. The power and the effects of social media are sombrely illustrated. The officers within were compelled to summon additional help for the purpose of regulating the external melee before an accident became inevitable.

A lull in the external fury gave the signal for progressive action on the inside. The headteacher was now asked to cause the door to his PA's office to open. The headteacher had, earlier, locked that door using his master key; but, instead of re-opening the door, he motioned to Mrs Jackson, the most senior of the caretakers. He didn't think, hardened as he was, he could possibly take in that gut-wrenching scene again.

Mrs Jackson timorously moved towards the door which had 'Chief Administration Officer' very clearly emboldened on it. She reached for her replica of the headteacher's master key, inserted it into the lock, and with a quick twist she was able to push the door open.

Her instant scream was ear piercingly frightening. She fainted immediately and fell directly into the arms of the police officer who had followed very closely behind her. The team of police officers had their own first aid paraphernalia, medic, and counsellor always on the ready for action in such cases as now.

It became immediately necessary to take remedial action on the caretaker who was quickly rushed to a close-by classroom greatly in need of reviving attention. Just as well the officers are so equipped because, under the present circumstances, the school was in no position to activate any of its own provision.

Amid all this, the men and women behind the cameras were clicking and flashing away; and, even with no story to tell, began contacting their news departments with their pictures and speculative made-up and half-baked stories. This was supposedly all parts and parcel of a free press and free speech as perceived in British democracy.

They will print their stories; they will broadcast them, and the world will take its lead from this pool of misinformation until sometime in the future the truth will prevail if allowed to be corrected. It was only a pity that falsehood was so difficult to correct because of the thing about false impressions. Until such revelation becomes possible, lives could be wrecked, schools could be closed, projects could become stifled, and reputations become irrevocably tarnished.

The headteacher's mind was now totally preoccupied with several things but foremost among them were these two which stood out with the greatest emphasis. Firstly, who could have committed such a ghastly deed? Secondly, how will Dixon Pen survive all of this?

The second of these was inextricably linked to what was expected to happen at the Secretary of State's conference in York next week.

For the police, the issue was, who 'murdered' Mrs Edgewater and why. The answers to these questions will enable them to bring the perpetrator—whomsoever it might be—to justice in accordance with the law of the land as soon as possible.

For this purpose, Chief Inspector Harding, the officer in charge of what was now a homicide at Dixon Pen, indicated that he wished to start asking questions of key people. Preliminarily, he wished to go in conference with the headteacher, the chairman of the governors, and a representative of the director of education.

To this end, Mr Austin, Mr Wilde, and Mr Sing moved to a close-by conference room whilst everyone else was asked to go home until further notice.

Chapter 3

Meanwhile, the news that a murder had been committed at Dixon Pen Comprehensive School in Edgbaston, Birmingham, dominated every television and radio news broadcast. Some news flash had spectacular Headlines that the principal of the school and the chairman of the governors have been detained for questioning.

Others splashed gruesome and sensational pictures of the deceased sprawled out across her desk in a pool of blood just as she was seen when first discovered. Others, still, concentrated on showing different pictorial angles of the school. There was no shortage of speculative stories attached to these pictures.

The images and stories popped up on people's phones; in their inboxes; everywhere, as social media was set alight. The news would have been too late for the evening papers but great splashes in tomorrow's tabloids can be gambled on. The nation was informed and will be informed whether it wanted to or not. Yet, one member of Dixon Pen, the deputy to the murdered woman, remained totally oblivious to the news of the moment.

Bianca Burney, the loquacious know-all, knew absolutely nothing of what was going on. This was because she was deeply caught up in a war of her own at her home. Her 67-year-old husband, Carlos Burney, of a year ago, had noticed her being dropped off that evening by some stranger. Her usual lift to and from school, on some occasions, was done by his son, Gaston, who drove a white E-Type Jaguar.

This day, Carlos noticed a green Toyota Celica driving into the driveway of their home. From the window of a friendly neighbour from across the street, Carlos was sure that he saw his wife in a close passionate embrace with the driver of this strange vehicle before emerging from the car which wasted no time before reversing and speeding off in the opposite direction from which they had come along Passion Street.

All hell broke loose when Carlos opened the door immediately after she had entered and shut it behind her.

"Where are you coming from, honey? You are not usually out this time of the evening?" Bianca responded with sheer surprise.

"Don't you honey me? I saw you kissing that character as you got out of his Celica. How come you didn't bus it, as you normally do, if Gaston wasn't able to give you a lift tonight? What the hell is going on?" Her angry husband indignantly responded.

Bianca knew she was in trouble and that she must suffer the consequences of these glancing blows. She thought back to her first clandestine adulterous meeting with Gaston and how she was almost caught by Carlos. She was lucky that time. This time, it seems she was good and truly caught and in such a way that she was impotent to do anything about it. She was thinking that, well, you cannot be lucky all the time.

She could seek to contradict her now clearly extremely jealous husband by convincing him that it was Gaston who dropped her home, in fact, and have him call Gaston to substantiate it. But how would she, indeed, how would they, explain that display of sexual passion that factually took place in the car tonight? She reasoned that if she took the bruises, it might blow over eventually.

The alternative of seeking Gaston's verification, she further reasoned, would give the whole thing away for her, and for Gaston. She remembered very clearly what Gaston once said to her.

"Sweetheart, my dad should never know anything about our affair. I don't want to be disinherited and I am certainly not ready for eviction."

So, she decided on the former and so it was that for the entire evening, the fracas was nasty, accusative, and bitter and she had no option other than to suffer it in relative silence. Carlos accused her of abusing him because of his age. He said that she was in this marriage for what she could get out of it and that she had no love for him.

It was difficult for Bianca to respond to any of all this largely because of guilt. She got to think that Carlos was right and what was more, she knew it. She fell out of love with him within a few days of marrying him. The love began to fade the very day of her nuptial and when she met Gaston for the first time, she recalled.

Even if she hadn't been able to be honest with her husband, she had already admitted to herself that her marriage was merely a sham for a source of convenience, companionship, and security. Her other great desire in life was hot and frequent sex. Gaston provided all of that. Her husband wasn't up to much of that.

At first, sex was all that she needed from Gaston as that was the only thing preventing her life from reflecting absolute completeness, but as time passed, she became more and more emotionally attached to Gaston Burney the stallion of a man. At the present time, and even despite the love triangle, she felt quite sure that she had fallen deeply in love with her husband's son.

When Gaston started to court her with flowers and gifts she recalled, she honestly thought that this was clear evidence that her love and desires were being reciprocated. She was thinking right now about Gaston's recent return from the Caribbean, he brought her back what he described as a rather special gift.

This was a hand-made fan in the bright colours of the Jamaican flag. She grew so attached to that fan that it was a fair bet that it will feature in every conversation that she will ever have with anyone.

The younger twenty-five-year-old Burney who had become her world does provoke every sexual nerve in her entire being. His six-foot frame, attractive and shapely with a pronounced 'six-pack' and his blue eyes contrasting with his neatly kempt shoulder-length blond hair, she found to be irresistible.

This was raw sex personified, she thought. Her wedding day activities and celebrations had done nothing to erase the mental images of her and this muscular beast of a man in bed enjoying hot sex sooner or later, preferably sooner.

Before the wedding day was done, Bianca had had every reason to be exuberant: the exuberance opportunely disguised as that of a woman who had only hours ago said, "I do."

She was recalling how as she strolled gaily among the quests at her wedding, she had ensured that her route took her in the direction of where Gaston was seated and engaged in light-hearted conversation with Helen Smith—Bianca's 23-year-old daughter from an earlier relationship. As she neared them, she clearly noticed that Gaston looked up and very definitely gave her a suggestive wink and a smile before continuing his conversation with her daughter, Helen.

It was that day that she discovered that Gaston still had a home with his dad. This was a facility that was not always used but there are occasions when he was and will be at home. The night of the wedding was one of them.

It occurred to her that this hunk of a man had roots, outside his father's home, both nationally and internationally. These thoughts, which in other circumstances would have been caused for rejection, proved only to make Gaston more intensively attractive in the foolish and sexually blindfolded eyes of Bianca, she openly admitted.

Bianca was recalling how it was not long before she cashed in on the promise behind that indicative wink that she had from her stepson on her wedding day. The next day, after their post-wedding breakfast for three, a call had come from Helen informing Carlos and Bianca that, as a present, she and some friends would be around by midday to prepare a grand supper for them, and if Gaston was at home, he, too, was included, Helen and her two friends have worked the hotel scenes for many years and have prepared a diner or two in their time.

After the post-wedding breakfast, Gaston had told the newly married couple that he was popping out to see a friend but would be back soon because he certainly didn't want to miss out on the grand supper.

Mrs Burney was remembering how she had gazed wistfully as he left for his mission unknown; but deep down, she had only cared that he should, very soon, return as he pledged.

She remembered that Gaston was true to his word on that occasion and was back some thirty minutes before the planned supper was served.

All six guests had then sat ceremoniously around the six-seating dining table which Carlos's mother had passed down the family line to him once upon a time. She recalled that the meal was sumptuous and more tasty and delicious because of Gaston's presence.

Once seated, the newly married couple was toasted with glasses of one of the best Williams & Humbert Dry Sack Feno Sherry which represented the first of a four courses meal.

This was closely followed by small plates of diced chilled melon from the local country garden or a soup concoction specialty of Helen's team for the second course. The third and most substantial course was Trout a. la Crème served on a bed of rice and two vegetables with a choice of white wines (red optional) which any authentic connoisseur would proudly recommend.

The follow-on dessert was chocolate soufflé or Italian ice cream served with fresh strawberries. Everyone had the option of closing his or her postprandial account with some of the finest Taylor Fladgate 40-year-old tawny port and/or Rémy Martin XO brandy.

That grand supper experience had remained indelibly stamped in Bianca's memory as one of her most joyous and jolly for as far back as she can recall if for no other reason the alcohol consumption had loosened and freed everyone's inhibitions and heightened related confidence. Even with her daughter present and her husband's participating presence, Bianca had felt comfortable openly flirting and trading winks with Gaston Burney.

Amidst the frivolous party spirit at the time, Gaston Burney had casually reached for his cell phone and looked it over for a few minutes. He had then, just as casually, shouted to Helen.

"Hey Helen, it looks like some people have been trying to get hold of me, but my phone might not be working, I didn't hear it ring. Can you test it for me? This is my number—06804 627 598—just call it and let me see if it rings."

Helen immediately obliged. Gaston's phone had nothing wrong with it as it rang out loudly.

"Oh, well maybe it was all the noise we are making why I didn't hear it ring."

She was remembering how he then rose from his seat and went to the toilet and returned soon after to continue partying.

It wasn't too long after Gaston had returned that Jo and Jacky (for those are the names of Helen's two friends) announced that it was time they packed up as they had to go to work early the next morning. Helen had acquiesced with that sentiment reluctantly.

But Bianca was still very jolly as though she could have gone on all night, but the older Mr Burney was showing signs of needing to get some sleep and said so.

"Before you go off dad, do you have anything for a Headache about the place? I seem to be having a kick-back from all this drinking. I am going to need something to take up with me shortly," Gaston had asked of his dad.

"I will have a look, son: I should have some Solpadine somewhere. If I find any, I will ask Bianca to take some up for you in a few minutes."

That said, the older Mr Burney had bid the young ladies goodnight after expressing his warm gratitude for the splendid and grand splash they had presented. He then had retired to his bedroom leaving Bianca to see off the girls who had, by then, brought back some semblance of order to the dining room and the kitchen.

Bianca, too, was profuse in her gratitude to the young ladies for their skills, companionship, and thoughtfulness in coming up with the ideas for the meal and all that went with it. She remembers how she had thanked them from the bottom of her heart and hugged each of them very sincerely before they left for their several homes. Gaston, who was standing immediately behind Bianca, also added his gratitude for the supper event.

Bianca remembered gently closing the door behind the girls and turning around only to find herself only inches away from the tall and imposing younger Mr Burney. He was so close to her that she could feel his warm breath registering a definite interest simultaneously on the base of her neck and the entrance to her cleavage which she had intentionally opened to reveal her low-cut bra which was the home of her pair of temptations. It was not done by the older Mr Burney and Gaston was certain of that fact.

In the dimness of the hallway, Gaston pulled his new mother-in-law to him in a close and passionate embrace. His lips searched for hers and found them before wandering off to her already exposed nipples. His right hand had wasted no time at all. He had met no resistance.

Theirs was a very large four-bedroom house. From the roadway, you drive onto a driveway with a double garage door facing it. You enter through a front door into a vestibule or small hall. This then opens into a much larger hall which conveniently divides the ground floor of the house into two distinct units. To the right, at the far end, the couple's two-bedroom self-contained marital suite is located.

To the left were their open-planned kitchen, dining room, and bathroom facilities. On the first floor which overlooks some beautifully landscaped gardens, and which was accessed by a carpeted stairway leading up from the left side of the house, are the other two bedrooms diagonally opposite each other on either side of the landing at the top of the stairs.

The larger of these two rooms on the left, the ideal luxurious bachelor pad, was used by Gaston when he was at home. The other on the right was rarely used and was identified by the occupants of the home as a guest room.

Gaston, now armed with oozing sexual confidence, had whispered to Bianca that she should go fetch those Solpadine that his dad promised earlier.

"Is your head still hurting?" Bianca had sympathetically inquired, her eyes melting with desire.

"No, it never was," Gaston had answered.

"Then why did you request the painkillers?"

"It gives you an excuse to come to me, doesn't it?"

"And how did you know he would ask me to take them up to you?"

"I know my dad; he shuns having to climb those stairs. Before you came to join the family, he often expressed some worry that I might one day become ill up there, and he would have difficulties reaching me to give any attention I might need. He adores his only son, you see," Gaston commented with a wry smile which complimented his wooing lips and eyes at the time.

That remark had brought Bianca to the realisation that two can play this game. She was not the only schemer even if she was the only dreamer.

"OK, I will take them up for you."

Her sexual hunger clearly dictated her compliance.

With that assurance, Gaston had moved quickly up the stairs to put any last-minute touches to his bachelor's domain and to himself and to wait in anxious expectation for his father's new wife—his stepmother since one single day ago.

The older Mr Burney was already in slumber land. Bianca had heard familiar snoring sounds as she approached their marital den. She had entered very quietly so as not to wake her husband at such an inconvenient time. That also meant that she would have had to search for the painkillers even though they were not needed, never were needed. She took the point that Gaston had made that the painkillers should be seen as an excuse for being upstairs should one be needed.

Carlos had had a very tiring day, so this was to her advantage. He should sleep soundly long enough for her to get the painkillers to Gaston and collect something for herself. She was just thinking that she didn't really know where Carlos kept his Solpadine when she spotted them on a side table next to her side of the bed.

Carlos had not forgotten his son's needs and had placed them prominently for his wife to see them and hopefully take them up to Gaston so he could get some relief. The reader will pardon the pun.

Bianca had then gone to her in-suite bathroom and did some preparation. She was now in a slip-on slip-off dressing gown loosened at the front to reveal her tantalizingly sexy small pieces. She had headed back to her bedside and got into it, shuffled a bit before she got back out of the bed. None of that had disturbed her husband's sleep. He was soundly asleep when she departed the room shutting the door gently behind her.

Gaston, from his slightly cracked open bedroom door could hear the thud of feet ascending stealthily. His anticipation translated and determined that just three more thuds and she would be there. She was.

He had opened the door wide for her and nakedly received her into his outstretched arms. His lips found hers. Her slip-off dressing gown and small pieces found spots on the floor where they were thrown. The light had remained dimmed just as they were left adjusted in preparation by the tenant of the den whilst Mrs and Mr Burney, Bianca, and Gaston, realised the benefits of their project.

Soon, their respective relief releases would silence the groans of ecstasy and the screams generated from man's pleasurable indulgence in the call of his basic instinct; and maybe sleep would visit upon them.

Sleep urges had come knocking but were never invited in for Gaston had wondered whether Bianca's last scream before she was calmed was loud enough to carry to his father's bedroom.

"Hush!" He said to Bianca as she moved to entice him further.

They both listened and were convinced that there was a faint cough coming from downstairs. Bianca had only had time to reach for her flimsy dressing gown and made a dash for the stairs leading down to the kitchen areas whilst still in the act of covering her nakedness. Her small pieces were left behind where they had fallen.

She had tipped down the padded stairs as quickly as she could just in time to hear Carlos call out for her.

"Sweetheart!" He shouted once more.

"I am out here, honey. I felt a bit queasy and needed a cup of something warm to shake me up."

Bianca had just switched on the kettle when Carlos, in his pyjamas, entered the kitchen.

"Oh, there you are. When I didn't see you in bed, I wondered for a moment whether you were still on the doorstep chatting with the girls. Did you give Gaston the Solpadine? I left them on the side table?"

"Yes, I gave them to him before he went off to bed. We would know in the morning if they brought him any relief."

That awful pun appeared again.

Bianca was in a state of confusion because she wasn't sure of how long Carlos was up looking for her. He had Gaston on his mind because he asked about his health.

She had hoped that Carlos didn't come any closer to her because she imagined that she might still be tainted with his son's odour. In her favour, she thought, were the facts that the hall lights were left on, the stairs light was off and the side of the bed she shares with Carlos was ruffled. She was not altogether certain of the situation, however, even as she played along.

"I decided on a cup of coffee, sweetheart, shall I make you one too?"

"No, no I just want you back in bed. Hurry up and let's get back to bed."

"OK, honey, I will rejoin you in bed very shortly, you go on till I get there. Just as soon as I finish my drink, I will be with you."

Bianca had read the signs. Her husband was feeling amorous and wanted his wife. She was now deep in thoughts about how she was going to handle the situation. She could not disappoint her loving husband on just the second night after their wedding.

She reflected that in all her life she never had two men sleeping with her in the same week; not the same month; not even the same year much less the same night. Bianca knew what she had to do; but she needed to clean up and be refreshed. The outcome then would become a bit of history for her.

Because she never really wanted a drink, and with Carlos back in bed, she aborted the coffee making and hurried to her bathroom where she cleaned up and refreshed herself so that she could engage in Act 2 without giving away her infidelity.

Her husband, too, like did his son a couple of hours before, was waiting, and waiting: no pyjamas now, for his newlywed wife. And it happened in some way. And then they slept.

All of this came flooding back to Bianca with vivid clarity as she suffered the thunderous onslaught that was engulfing her at the present time. And yet, she dared not call for help from Gaston who means so much to her. She was silently praying that Gaston doesn't come home immediately or that tonight becomes one of those many nights that he doesn't come home at all. She just doesn't want him to witness the open rows she was having with his father.

Even though it had been inconvenient, indefinite, and secretive, Bianca had enjoyed the relationship with her stepson if only for the sexual content that she cannot get from her lawful husband.

It was now well past the time that she and Carlos would have turned into a bed. In less contentious times they would have had their nightcaps and gone to bed where they would indulge in small talks, gossip, reviews, and forward planning until sleep took control.

Still, Carlos was relentless in condemning her treacherous behaviour and she saw no signs of him ever stopping. Maybe she ought to try to do something to calm things down. After all, it was her behaviour and that of the man she truly loves that have brought all this on her.

"Honey, let's stop all this nonsense and come to bed. It must be so very tiring for you. Have you taken your medication?" Bianca enticingly offered as she sat on their bed in a pacifying attempt.

"I don't wish to share a bed with you anymore. Who would want to share a bed with a whoreson dog?" Her husband remonstrated.

This was far too much for Bianca to take. She knows that she was adulterous, but she was not a woman of the night. Carlos had gone too far. The idea of sharing his bed was no longer just disdainful to him but had now become a reciprocated sentiment for her too.

"OK, I will go to sleep in the guest room so that we are distant apart if that is what you want," Bianca angrily responded.

Their compartment in the house brags a second bedroom but Bianca was ignoring that fact so that she can be as far as possible from her husband's abusive fury right that minute.

"I don't care where you go as long as you get the hell out of my bed," Carlos shouted vehemently and pointed at the door.

Bianca, now too insulted; too broken and too ashamed to retaliate, quietly removed herself from their joint quarters and headed reluctantly towards the stairs at the opposite end of the house. At the foot of the stairs, she momentarily paused as she reflected that this was the route, she had taken on her many clandestine rendezvous with her lover.

These stairs lead directly to the guest room. She couldn't help thinking that this time, going up them will be different in purpose…different from the many previous nights she climbed and descended these stairs surreptitiously.

She knew, for sure, that it would be different because only an hour before, she had received a WhatsApp message sent to her phone by Gaston. The message briefly told her that:

"I won't be home, tonight, baby. I am at the airport. My flight leaves in exactly five minutes. I will be away for a few days on business. Not pleasure," he facetiously assured her.

It was a sweet and bitter moment for her when she had read that message. She was extremely glad that the Lord had answered her prayers not to let Gaston come home tonight because she not only wanted to protect him from the tumultuous disorder which characterised their home that evening and extended into the front part of the night, but she could not have taken the risk of their closely guarded secret being revealed.

However, it was a massive jolt to her heart and soul to learn in this coldest of ways that her man will be out of her reach and confidence; and so indefinitely at a time when she needs him to be near her, even if in secret. Gaston was in the habit of leaving her for long periods without notice like he did a few days after the grand super following her marriage to Carlos.

That time he disappeared for over a week without knowing whether he was abroad of in the United Kingdom. But Bianca missed only the sexual aspects of things in those early days. Now, however, she was emotionally attached to her lover and so his disappearance means a great deal more to her.

This time there were no nervous steps in tipped-toed fashion; no sexual expectation as she ascended the stairs for her debut in the unfamiliar guest room which was located so near to her lover's den. And yet they will be so far apart.

Removing herself from the scene of contention seemed to have helped the situation. The swearing and ranting sounds coming from down the stairs were lessening; the intervals between outbursts grew longer and longer still, until, it seemed to her, Carlos had fallen asleep. He would not come after her even if he was awake and had the inclination because he abhors the climbing of these stairs, she remembered gratefully.

Gaston had told her. This fact gave her the confidence to retire to bed in a strange room: her head whirling with romantic projects and wishes that she knew would not be realised. Instead, she switched to hope, the hope of a different kind: that the passing of the night would calm her husband down so that they could resume some semblance of civility without the filthy insults and demeaning raucous she had been enduring since she got home from school that day.

Fortunately, their closest neighbours were some distance away and could not possibly have learned all these things about her from her husband's rants.

She fell asleep with little struggle and slept soundly throughout the rest of the night until the clock was approaching five o'clock in the morning.

Chapter 4

Without getting out of bed, Bianca found herself totally preoccupied with two main thoughts. Firstly, what was Carlos going to be like this morning? Was he going to be sufficiently calmed down to allow for some civilised discourse?
As she could not provide answers to any of these rhetorical questions, her mind drifted off to Gaston, his whereabouts and what he might be up to at that very moment. She concluded in her own mind that these were idle thoughts that would provide no answers.

She got out of bed and went to the room door, paused, and listened before quietly cracking open the door. Everywhere and everything was still and quiet as a graveyard. She was just yards away from that other door with which she had greater familiarity. But he was not there. Then a thought came suddenly to her. Was the text message just a hoax?

Did he come home after all? She moved quietly across to Gaston's room door. She tried turning the knob and, to her consternation, the door was not locked as it always was when Gaston was away. Perhaps, he did intend to be back because he didn't secure his den. Maybe whatever it is, it took him suddenly and he had to leave in a hurry.

Bianca could not resist the temptation, so she opened the door and eased herself in as she was accustomed. That 20 x 16 inches framed picture of Gaston when he was 13 years old and his dad that always adorns the wall just above the head of his bed was slightly leaned. Dutifully, Bianca went over to straighten the picture and made a discovery that maybe should not have happened. That picture was not just a decorative feature.

It effectively hides a secret compartment built into the wall. The last time it was visited, it seemed Gaston forgot to lock it. He must have been in a hurry because the tiny key was still in the tiny door. The picture frame was not neatly placed back as it always had been though it seems like there was a clumsy attempt to do so. Added to these facts, his room door was not locked.

Bianca opened the tiny door to reveal two passports. Her very quick glance revealed that one of these was a Swedish document; the other clearly showed European Union and United Kingdom of Great Britain and Northern Ireland embossed on it. Just beyond these documents, was a tiny brochure with a single sheet of paper within it? She did not have much time to examine these things because Carlos was known to be an early riser.

Instead, she quickly returned to the guest room and to her handbag from which she took her mobile telephone and returned to Gaston's room. She carefully took pictures of everything she found in the hidden safe and replaced them in their exact positions as she found them.

Once more, she vacated Gaston's room taking care to pull the door shut as it was. She thought that she would have considerably more time today or on Sunday to make sense of her find. It did, however, make her wonder what passport Gaston used to fly out to wherever last night?

By the time it was six o'clock that morning, Bianca detected the first sign of movement downstairs. The shower was on, and Carlos was humming as he always does when he was in the shower. She thought that given that she normally makes breakfast on the weekends, she should get the breakfast show on the road.

She would prepare something extra delicious for Carlos. It was often said that the way to a man's heart was through his stomach. Could this be a way to his forgiveness too? There was no harm in trying.

Carlos was a great lover of smoked salmon and fried eggs. She can manage that for herself too even though it would not be her first choice, but this morning was for Carlos. She was determined to reconcile with him.

Meanwhile, Carlos, too, was giving independent thought to their marital situation. He was hurt and somewhat bitter but did his jealousy lead him over the top? What would he do at his age were Bianca to split from him?

He recalled some of the difficulties that he had to endure when his first marriage ended when Gaston was just ten years old, and he became a single dad. Then, he could not forgive his wife, June, for disserting him for another younger man. June ensured that he would always hate her. Their marriage vows were for better or worse, but she never remembered that.

Their marriage was good, sound, and loving for almost all the fifteen years it lasted. In the fifth year, the marriage was wonderfully productive at last. A healthy eight and a half pounds baby boy—christened Gaston Burney—arrived on the scene and their marriage was complete. But things changed drastically when a year before he was forced to divorce June, who was ten years his junior at the time, he became seriously ill.

The medical diagnosis was that he was afflicted with the dreaded prostate cancer. Although he acted quickly and employed the best medical services that money could buy, and although he clearly survived the operation to remove his prostate, his sexual prowess was severely diminished. The worst part of the blow was that he can no longer have children even if with the aid of Cialis and other measures such as Viagra, he can still manage some sexual activities.

His deficiency in this department seemed to have been a savage blow to the sexually robust, June Burney. It was then that she began to deceive him and eventually deserted him. Perhaps, he might have continued struggling with that marriage till this day had June not used his sexual weakness as a rod with which to beat him at every quarrelsome opportunity.

She taunted him with it mercilessly until his hatred for her became irrevocably entrenched. The situation eventually ended in a very bitter and nasty divorce with him getting custody of Gaston. He was once a very wealthy Structural Engineer but all that changed drastically when June took him to the cleaners through the divorce court. He was no longer a wealthy man. He was not broken, just very comfortable as things were today.

For some thirteen years or so he refused to have anything to do with any other woman. He dreaded them. He was, therefore, forced to bring up a young boy all on his own. He believes that, although he couldn't give Gaston all the guidance he needed, he did well to turn out this lad who was still very much a part of his life. Since his late teens, the boy had drifted away from his control and seemed to have meshed with the company of his own choosing.

Gaston had never brought home any of these characters that have become such an integral part of his adult life. He was just left to wonder who they were and what their occupations might be. He was particularly worried that Gaston seems never to be interested in a steady job. He gave up full-time studies when he was age nineteen and since then seems to have become an international traveller.

Often, he had received telephone calls at odd hours from across different time zones from Gaston simply to check how he was and to tell him that he was OK.

Of course, he realised that Gaston would flee the nest someday and it was probably that realisation that persuaded him to tie the knot once more. That knot was now threatening to come loose and, it would seem, for similar reasons to his first marriage.

This would be so unfair because he had gone to a great deal of precaution trouble to explain every aspect of his health, sexual and otherwise to Bianca before they became married, he didn't think he could survive all that hell once more so maybe he should try and find common ground for patching this contentious dilemma with Bianca.

As Carlos was reflecting on his past life and on what the future could be, Bianca was busy preparing their breakfast. She too was pondering ways to embrace and enhance peace. She thought that, perhaps, she should try apologising and making a pledge not to see that "character" ever again. She knew that she would be lying but she dared not be truthful.

An element of Machiavellianism—whatever means necessary—to muster some peace and civility, was needed right now. The truth not only had serious implications for their marriage, but it also had drastic implications for the relationship between Carlos and his son and for the relationship between her and Gaston. She would therefore go for the alternative truth.

"Darling, how was your night? I hope you didn't neglect your medication. You need to stay well. I have made you your favourite breakfast; please join me whilst it is still warm," Bianca addressed her husband.

On the dining table was a collection of cereals, some cold milk, an array of jams, marmalade, honey, butter, and margarine. The toaster was at the ready and the tea-pot spout was also at the ready.

Carlos joined his wife as per her request but remained silent throughout. Carlos showed some interest in some cold cereal, and a slice of brown toast covered only with marmalade. Next, he then turned to a serving of smoked salmon and fried eggs and poured himself a cup of tea. And still not a single word was shared with Bianca.

Not to be defeated, Bianca thought she would break the silence herself.

"Honey, I thought long and hard all night about our situation. I agree with you that it is my entire fault. I confess that I should never have allowed this 'character', Charles, to take me home yesterday. When Gaston didn't show up, I headed for the bus stop as I always do when I have no lift, and, as it turned out, Charles came by and offered me a lift before my bus came.

"I really should have refused the lift. The ride home was uneventful until we got here, and he became amorous. For one reckless moment, I gave in to his advances and that was what you saw. And look at where it got us. Honey, I have been extremely foolish and weak. I am very sorry for everything, and I sincerely ask for your forgiveness. It simply will not happen, ever again."

During Bianca's soliloquy, Carlos remained in thoughtful silence throughout.

For all the previous evening, right through until now, there had been no television, no radio, and no use of the phone. For this reason, this household had been starved of all information about what had happened at Dixon Pen and the implications for everyone.

Bianca had just one more trick up her metaphorical sleeve. It was breakfast time and Carlos absolutely adores the anchor, Miranda, on the BBC's breakfast show. She reaches for the TV remote and switches it on in search of the breakfast show.

The shock was too huge to comprehend. They became numbed, stunned, confused, and flabbergasted in sheer disbelief. She was suddenly dumb. He was already dumb all morning. Now they reached out for each other and clutched each other tightly: not believing their own eyes.

On their own television screen, in their own home, almost on their own breakfast table, there beneath their very eyes, was Bianca's boss sprawled out across her desk in a pool of drying blood. Her lifeless eyes stared at them, and her left arm extended across the desk as if pleadingly seeking help.

The bloody and gruesome murder scene from last night news was now being repeated and will be repeated over and over throughout the day for today's viewers. Scenes like these were usually prefixed by a warning to viewers, especially children; but it was possible to miss such warnings if you didn't turn on your television in a timely fashion.

It was so terribly frightening for the aging Carlos, it seemed he fainted; but before Bianca could summon the ambulance, he screamed out as if coming out of some dreadful nightmare of a dream. The accompanying news report was loaded with three words in particular: Dixon Pen and murder. No one would be able to escape the notion that the great school, Dixon Pen, was inextricably linked to a gruesome murder.

The fact that the headteacher and chairman of the governors were being questioned by police appeared several times in several sub-texts in the report. According to the report, everyone that was linked to the school was under suspicion, and the police have already identified key people that were of interest to them.

It would be reasonable to assume that if the police had already identified key individuals who were of interest to them in this case, it would have been because of their preliminary interviews with the headteacher, the chairman of the governors, and the education officer on the evening of the murder.

Although Chief Inspector Harding had indicated that he only wanted a preliminary meeting with the headteacher, Mr Wilde, and Mr Sing, these last two being the chairman of the governors and the education officer respectively, he and his colleague Detective Corporal Brown who was also at the preliminary meeting might have unearthed important indicators about this homicide.

In that meeting, the officers had quickly ascertained that the chairman of the governors' role in connection with the school was largely directive and administrative from afar. The chairman had no day-to-day relationship with anyone at the school beyond the headteacher. This was even more so in the case of the education officer.

The police officers had, therefore, taken their contact details and told both distant officers of the school that they could leave but should remain accessible. Once Mr Wilde and Mr Sing had left, Chief Inspector Harding and Detective Corporal Brown focused their attention on the school's chief executive officer—the headteacher.

The chief inspector then formally introduced his colleague Detective Corporal Brown as the officer who will work most closely with him on the case over the coming days and for as long as it will take to solve it.

Once the fundamental details pertaining to name and address, age, and similar matters were noted, the headteacher asks of the two officers:

"Am I being considered a suspect in this case?"

"Sir, right now, everyone in this school is a possible suspect. It will be our job to eliminate the innocent ones."

The headteacher was quite used to referred to as 'Sir'. By dint of his profession, it was automatic, especially from pupils. This time, however, and coming from the chief inspector, it sounded eerily different and somewhat sinister.

The chief inspector then got right down to the interrogation of the headteacher.

"Mr Austin, please tell us about the deceased? Who is she? What is her role in the school? And how long had she been working here"?

"The late Mrs Elaine Edgewater was our Chief Administrative Officer leading a team of five other ladies besides her. She doubled as my personal assistant (PA). The records will show that she joined us just about two years ago when the previous chief, Mrs Barron, retired and her job was nationally advertised. Mrs Edgewater was one of many applicants, including one internal candidate, who competed for the vacant post," the headteacher thoughtfully replied.

"headteacher, did I understand you to be saying that she successfully competed for her job against an internal candidate? How did that work out for departmental relationship?" the detective corporal interjected.

"Oh, very well, indeed; initially, there were those who thought there might be some problems, not only because Mrs Edgewater is black and would be leading a team of all white ladies who have been in the school for a very long time, but also because she was also the youngest at age twenty-eight. In fact, such fears were totally unwarranted.

"Come to think of it, over the two years or so since Elaine joined our school team, there was never a hint of friction, that I observed, among the members of that team until yesterday evening when Elaine was demonstrably annoyed with her deputy, Bianca Burney in my presence. And even that instance was largely my fault. It arose out of a situation that I, admittedly, had handled somewhat clumsily," Mr Austin carefully explained and pointedly emphasised that there was no relationship problem in the school's administrative department.

The detective corporal probed further:

"Who was the internal candidate against whom Mrs Edgewater competed?"

"That was Bianca Burney who admitted to me that at first when Elaine was appointed, there was, maybe, a little bit of jealousy among the girls, but that emotion did not last very long. They soon found a common interest in getting along with their new boss. One thing that engaged their common curiosity was the beautiful and apparently hugely expensive ring which Elaine wore at all times and from which she was inseparable," Mr Austin replied as he watched the police officers make, what seemed to him, very copious notes.

The chief inspector then intervened. He was interested in:

"Sir, I do appreciate that at the present hour, you are without clerical support, so may I give you notice that on Monday? I will be arranging to collect the files on the deceased and that of Mrs Burney. As a matter of fact, we shall want to speak directly with her once we have seen her file."

The headteacher nodded to indicate that he understood the request and was willing to ensure compliance.

The detective corporal interjected once more:

"Does the school have a policy for dealing with visitors to the school, and do you keep a record of such visitors?"

"Yes, we do: all visitors, including parents, must report to reception on arrival. The signs that are on the gates clearly state this. At the reception, their names and purposes must be recorded and subject to the nature of their business, they will have an escort to and from parts and persons of the school if considered appropriate," the headteacher confidently replied.

"Did you have any visitors to the school today, headteacher?" the chief inspector followed up with a query.

"I cannot answer that question beyond personal speculation as I was off the premises for about a couple of hours. I had a working lunch with the director of education earlier today. However, what I can say factually is this; I met with one of my pupils, Frankie Watson, together with his parents, Mr, and Mrs Watson at ten o'clock this morning. They should have an entry in our visitors' records. The records should also speak for the other parts of the day," this was Mr Austin's attempt at accuracy for a reply.

"May I ask the nature of your meeting with Frankie and Mr and Mrs Watson, headteacher?" The chief inspector calmly enquired.

"Yes. It was a disciplinary matter."

(At which point the headteacher momentarily paused as though something quite horrible had suddenly occurred to him before continuing his reply).

"You see, Frankie Watson was very abusive to one of his teachers yesterday because the teacher would not accept his lame excuse for why he, Frankie, was late for his math lesson," Mr Austin continued his reply.

The headteacher's ominous pause had not escaped the trained professionalism of the astute detective.

"Sir, please expand. What was the excuse that was being rejected by the teacher in question?" The detective further probed.

Then there was that hesitancy again before the headteacher gave the further details that the detective corporal had just requested.

"Frankie was trying to convince Mr Brooks, his math teacher, that he was assisting a stranger and that this delayed him. Frankie claimed that Mr Brooks should have accepted his explanation since I had already dealt with him pertaining to that matter."

"Had you, headteacher?"

"Hardly," the headteacher replied. "When I encountered the boy and realised that he should be in a classroom somewhere, I remonstrated with him whilst he was hurrying on the move to the lesson for which he was approximately five minutes late by this time. It was whilst he was on the move that he echoed the story about assisting some unknown stranger who caused him to be late. This too, was part of the reason for having the meeting with Frankie's parents this morning."

The chief inspector then asked that the school's visitors' records should also be on the list of documents that he wishes to collect on Monday for examination. He also asked how old Frankie Watson was. On learning that Frankie was only fifteen years old, the inspector told the headteacher that he, too, wanted to talk with Frankie in the presence of his parents on a date to be arranged through the school.

The inspector then coldly asked: "Do you have a mobile phone headteacher?"

"Yes, I do. Is that important?" Mr Austin enquired.

"I cannot be sure until we have had a look at it, sir. We would like you to take leave of your mobile phone, sir, to allow for a forensic examination. We do realise how important that instrument might be in the very busy life of a school principal and for that very reason, we will ask that the forensic department should attach absolute priority to it, sir. In no time we will have the phone back to you, sir."

With this assurance, the chief inspector indicated that they would wind up the meeting but left open the possibility that they might want to see him again and or other staff and pupils as the case might dictate. He informed the headteacher that whilst they were having the meeting with him, the deceased would have been removed to the police morgue and that the fingerprint specialists would have thoroughly dusted down the crime scene to see what prints and other evidence they could find.

The principal was now free to operate school as normally though he should expect to be bothered by the police from time to time until the case was brought to a proper conclusion. He also warned that the media will have a continued interest in his school and individuals associated with the school after today.

The head and his team will need to have a strategy for dealing with them. The officers then escorted Mr Austin to his car and bade him good night as they left for beyond the school.

Mrs Mavis Jackson—the school's caretaker, who had fully recovered from her early frightening shock was now able to oversee her team in safeguarding the school for the night. They will also have some cleaning of a different kind to do.

Chapter 5

Bianca, still in shock to learn of her boss's brutal murder in this way, began wondering whether she was counted among the police already identified key individuals who were of interest to them. She could not see how she could be useful to the police and so became dismissive of that idea and allowed her mind to wander off in many directions, mainly about her lover, Gaston.

Bianca's train of thoughts suddenly broke because she heard a WhatsApp message, one of many that had been coming in all morning, come to her mobile phone. She immediately turned to Carlos to ascertain that he was OK. He acknowledged her query and answered that he was good if somewhat still dazed from the shock of the moment.

Bianca felt inwardly pleased that she was back in communication with her husband even if it was at a time when the world seems to have been turned upside down for everyone. His companionship was so vital at the present time. He needs her too, especially given that his beloved son was not around. This thought led Bianca to think of how helpful it would have been if Gaston was here now to lend her some support and be with his father.

Just then, she remembered that she had taken some photographs of the contents found in the secret compartment in Gaston's room. The multiple passports angle was of major interest to her. She had to admit that she was feeling suspicious; or was it unfounded jealousy? Perhaps, if she could excuse herself by making use of the bathroom this would provide her with a private opportunity to learn about the contents of her find.

Maybe she would gain some valuable insight into what Gaston gets up to on his many sojourns. It would also allow her to quickly flick through some of those numerous messages that have been coming to her phone throughout the course of the morning.

Bianca excused herself and left Carlos still catching up on the many different stories about the events at Dixon Pen and the related activities of the police whilst she went to the bathroom. Once secluded, Bianca reached for her mobile phone. She found her gallery icon easily and tapped on it. The pictures which she had taken of Gaston's hidden treasure were now located among some of the many forwarded photos and videos that friends, relatives, and colleagues have been sending her since the Dixon Pen matters broke.

Bianca checked firstly for the pictures of the passports. She needed to know if the Swedish passport belonged to Gaston: and for that matter, was the British one also his. She found them.

The magnifying facility on modern mobile phones was of great value in these circumstances, though Bianca. She blew up the image pages on both passports. There was no mistaking those sexy come-to-bed blue eyes and the shiny blond hair. This was Gaston, alright. The British one bore his name, at least the name she knows him to go by Gaston Burney.

However, on the Swedish passport, the name was different. On this document, Gaston was Jason Musgrave. Bianca was now wondering who the hell he was travelling with on his present jaunt and what country he was representing when she noticed something familiar. She magnified the picture on the front of the brochure. She was sure that she had seen that ring before, but her memory wasn't exactly being faithful to her. Still, she will keep thinking.

Bianca then turned to the information on the receipt. This document was issued in Jamaica at an in-bond store in Ocho Rios. The store was SATISFACTION IN-BOND, Main Street, Ocho Rios, St. Ann, Jamaica. The document was fully supported with telephone numbers, fax numbers, and the business' e-mail and website details. It was dated five years ago—the third of July 2016.

The document was issued as a genuine receipt for the purchase of a white golden ring with a ruby, opal, and diamond cluster with the related brochure and two ornamental Jamaican hand-made straw fans. The total sum paid was J$3m in cash. Written on the receipt was the purchaser's Jamaican passport number: A1238760. The holder of this passport was Robert Reid.

Bianca was no clearer about what all this was about. In fact, she was far more confused.

Maybe, she was taking too long a time in the bathroom whilst her husband was alone watching the many versions of the Dixon Pen's murder and the detective work going on. She did not want to spoil what looked like a mending relationship. She quickly flipped over to her messages.

There were about forty of them. The first one was from Helen, her daughter. The second was from Sheila Robinson, her work colleague. She decided that she would stretch the time further to check out just these two. Later she would go through them all.

Both messages carried photos of Mrs Bridgewater from different angles sprawled across her desk. These were the kinds of pictures that were doing the rounds. The other messages on Bianca's phone were likely to be more of the same, she thought, so viewing them was not going to be all that urgent.

In their different ways, both Helen and Sheila were drawing her attention to Elaine's left arm hanging from the table on which she died. Bianca had on several occasions talked with Helen about her boss's attachment to her special ring.

Helen was now indicating in her message that Elaine might have forgotten her ring at home yesterday. Sheila's message on the other hand wondered whether the killer robbed her of her precious ring.

And suddenly, the penny dropped. Bianca now remembers where she had seen that ring pictured on the front page of the brochure which she discovered in Gaston's secret compartment. That ring was identical to the ring that Elaine was never without. There could not have been two of those rings. It was unique.

Bianca, now in stupefying confusion emerged from the bathroom and quietly went to rejoin her husband with an 'are you OK stroke' along his shoulders and down his back.

Bianca grew hungry for news beyond the various media outlets. She needed to talk with someone who had her current concerns in common either on the phone or in person. She telephoned her daughter, Helen, to ask her to come around even though she was not really part of Dixon Pen and therefore wouldn't know of too many related gossips. She was, however, mobile, and that would be useful for getting around because, right now, public transport would not be ideal.

Bianca was thinking that maybe she should go to visit a work colleague and Helen could take her on such a visit. She decided to ring Helen. After two attempts, she was unsuccessful and as there wasn't a definite message to leave in her voice mail, Bianca rang off. She seemed to remember that Helen sometimes worked on a Saturday. Hotel work was by its very nature erratic and uncertain, so its workers have to be prepared for flexible timing and hours.

Bianca contemplated her next move but almost all her ideas seemed to be frustrated by the absence of private transportation and her wish not to leave Carlos alone for too long a period.

It was a sensitive time; misinformed jealousy might still be lurking, Carlos' mealtimes, his medication and his companionship needs following the shock, all combined to make it almost impossible to leave the home; so, Bianca decided that she would try and speak with Mr Austin on the phone, instead. Speaking to management, she thought would be a far better and more reliable route to the truthfulness of the present situation.

She flicked through her mobile contacts and located Mr Austin's mobile number and rang it without any hesitation. There was no clear reason why she wasn't getting through to the headteacher. The number wasn't ringing. She tried several times but still had no luck. Bianca gave up on calling the head's mobile number. It could be out of action for a verity of reasons.

Indeed, the headteacher, himself, might have switched off his phone because of the amount of traffic that would be directed to his phone on account of the present circumstances. On the other hand, she thought, he, being a public official, both as a Justice of the Peace and as headteacher of a large and important school, it would be irresponsible for him to make himself incommunicado.

It would be bordering on a disciplinary offence—what with the education office, the governors, the department of education, and people in need of Her Majesty's Justice of the Peace services. She concluded that the headteacher did not turn his mobile phone off; some other reason must be operative to explain the loss of the service. She would try calling him on his home fixed line instead.

Bianca then remembered that only two members of the school's staff, besides the deputy headteachers, had access to the headteacher's home fixed line. She had no access to the deputies so she would need to ask one of those two if she could have access to the headteacher's fixed line number. One of the two people who had that number was Elaine Bridgewater and she certainly wasn't going to be able to give it to her.

The other person with that number was the senior caretaker, Mrs Mavis Jackson. Her number was one of the numbers that Bianca had among her mobile phone contacts and so she promptly rang Mrs Jackson. After some hesitation, Mrs Jackson deemed it urgent enough to disclose the headteacher's fixed line number to Bianca.

Bianca then used this number to telephone Mr Austin. Daniel Johnson, the domestic helper answered the phone.

"Good morning, please allow me to speak with Mr Austin; my name is Bianca Burney, a member of his administrative team at the school," Bianca declared.

"Oh, Mrs Burney, Mr Austin is not at home presently. He is attending an identification parade in the next Borough, you know, in his capacity as a Justice of the Peace. I am expecting him back home later this afternoon. Can I take a message for him?" The domestic helper enquired.

"Please, just inform him that I called and will call again later. By the way, is his mobile phone working? I could call him on that?" Bianca interjected enquiringly.

"You are not going to get Mr Austin on his mobile phone because it has been unavailable since Friday evening. Hopefully, it will be back in action soon. I happen to know that Mr Austin feels totally lost without it. I will tell him that you called. What is the name again?" Daniel Johnson asked.

"It is Bianca Burney," Bianca helpfully replied.

"Bianca, Bianca Burney. Are you the Deputy Administration Officer at Dixon Pen?" Daniel Johnson asked.

"I sure am," Bianca wonderingly replied.

"Mr Austin will be glad you called. He was expressing a desire to be in touch with you before school on Monday, but as you can imagine, with all this bad news, everything has been upside down for the poor man recently. I will tell him that you called and promised to call back later," the housekeeper assured Bianca.

"OK, I will try around five o'clock. Thank you oh…?" Bianca stammered to recall the name of the person with whom she was conversing.

"Daniel it is, Daniel Johnson," Daniel assured Bianca before hanging up the telephone.

Bianca began wondering why Mr Austin wanted to be in touch with her. She was also wondering who Daniel Johnson was and what was her relationship with Mr Austin?

On the very stroke of five, Bianca dialled Mr Austin's home number just as she had promised. This time, it was the unmistakable voice of Mr Austin at the other end.

"Oh, Bianca, it is so good of you to call back, I need to have an important discussion with you and preferably before school is back in session on Monday. I know that you couldn't possibly have missed all the news about this terrible thing and, I am sure, like me, you regret the terrible loss of Elaine, especially in such a terrible way," Mr Austin greeted Bianca both mournfully and excitedly at the same time.

"Oh, yes, sir, the whole thing is maddening and evil. I am dreading what the school environment and atmosphere will be like on Monday and beyond—oh, the media, the parents, staff, and pupils, all their curiosity will need to be satisfied. The pressure on management is going to be enormous," Bianca predicted with some sadness.

"Bianca, you are hitting the nail on the head. These are some of those issues I need to discuss with you. Can you join me here at my home for a working lunch tomorrow, Sunday?" Mr Austin followed up in agreement.

"Yes sir, I have nothing else planned so I will be there for lunch time tomorrow as you suggest," She said in reply.

"What will you do for transport? Is your usual lift available or shall I send a taxi for you? This will be down to school expenses?" Mr Austin offered.

"I will appreciate the taxi being sent as I have no other ride besides the buses, and they can be so unreliable at times."

"That will be done, Bianca. I will have a taxi to pick you up at your home for eleven-thirty a.m. tomorrow. That will enable you to get here just after noon."

Mr Austin and Bianca then exchanged addresses on the telephone and bade each other goodbye until their working lunch the next day.

It was now after dinner on the Saturday before Bianca's meeting with the headteacher the next day. She was now having a postprandial relaxation chatter, with her husband Carlos, during which she would tell him about the arrangements for meeting with her headteacher the following day and, at the same time, to enjoy the usual to and from exchanges with Carlos before their nightcap cup of Ovaltine drink to send them off to bed, when their front doorbell rang.

They both wondered loudly as to who could be calling on them so late in the evening and without prior notice.

Bianca moved to answer the doorbell. It was a mixture of joy and sadness to see her daughter Helen standing there on the doorstep. Bianca was always happy to see her daughter. But this time, Helen had pains written all over her face.

"Come on in, my daughter, come on in!" She commanded Helen.

"You are not looking so good, are you OK?"

"Yes, mother dear, I am good. I was in the area and thought I would drop by to give you an invitation personally. On Wednesday, this coming Wednesday, the nineteenth of May, I would like you to join me for supper.

"I am afraid that the invitation is for you only because there is something that is very important and very serious that I want to share with you, mother, and I wouldn't feel comfortable sharing it with you in Carlos' presence. I would pick you up straight from school. I am giving you all this notice so you can prepare Carlos for it and decide on his care that day. Obviously, I will get you back home at a decent hour on Wednesday," Helen implored.

"I will ensure that I manage that. It is clearly a matter of importance. You are wearing it on your face. Super is on Wednesday. I was just about to make Carlos and myself a cup of Ovaltine, would you like one too?" Bianca enquired of Helen.

"Oh, yes mum, I could do with a drink. I haven't had one all day and it will give me the opportunity to have a little natter with Carlos before he goes off to bed and then I shall be on my way."

"Carlos, look who is here: it is Helen. She was just passing through the area and decided to pay us a surprise call. She is going to join us for Ovaltine, and then she must be gone."

Helen greeted Carlos warmly. The warmth was reciprocated, and they chatted whilst Bianca made their drink. The drinks were over and Helen was soon gone. Now Bianca and Carlos can retire to the same bed tonight when Bianca can let Carlos into the picture about her luncheon tomorrow with the headteacher and her date with Helen for Wednesday after school.

Carlos and Bianca had just united in bed when the phone on the bedside table on Carlos' side of the bed rang. The dial pad showed that the call was coming in from Switzerland. Carlos hesitated before lifting the receiver because he didn't know anyone from that geographical location.

Then it suddenly occurred to him that it might be Gaston from whom he heard absolutely nothing since he called for and took Bianca to school last Friday morning. With some very mild encouragement from Bianca, Carlos lifted the telephone receiver and answered hello. It was, in fact, Gaston on the phone.

"Gaston, my son, where on earth are you?" Gaston told him the truth.

"I am in Switzerland, Geneva at the present time. In two days, I will be meeting friends in Zurich and then in Bern before flying back to the UK."

Before Carlos could intervene with his usual admonishment about his son roaming the world and having no job, Gaston hurriedly continued.

"Dad, what kind of news are you having on your side, anything interesting? There is a dearth of British news over here right now."

"Our city is on scorching fire at present. There has been a gruesome murder at your mother-in-law's school—Dixon Pen and the media is running wild with speculation. It is even thought that the headteacher might be involved. The police are grilling him and apparently will be interviewing other suspects from the school and beyond in the course of time," Carlos told his son.

"Will the police be talking to Bianca, too?" Gaston enquired further.

"They are saying everyone is a suspect so that is a possibility, we just don't know yet. We will just have to play it by ear, my son," Carlos added.

"Give my love to Bianca and tell her that I wish you both well and hopefully see you both as soon as I can get a flight back to the UK. COVID-19 has impacted flight arrangements everywhere; one just must work with the system which is always subject to changes," Gaston said as he was trying to terminate the telephone conversation.

But his dad was not to be fobbed off so easily.

"Gaston, it is high time that you settled down in a responsible job so you can start a family with a sensible and respectable young lady. How are you affording your present lifestyle?"

"Dad, let us just say that I thank you for these good looks which I inherited from you. Purse strings are opened because of it. I will be fine, take good care and hopefully see you soon," Gaston then hangs up the phone at his end of the line before his dad's anger explodes.

Bianca became very troubled by Carlos' last piece of advice to his son. "…start a family with a sensible and respectable young lady."

These were very painful words. She thought to herself that she was not 'young' and she also had reservations about whether she could be considered 'sensible and respectable' in the present circumstances.

Clearly, Carlos would not approve of her as a suitable choice for his son. She quickly abandoned that hurtful thought and suggested to Carlos that they should go to sleep. Tomorrow could be a very busy and most interesting day.

Chapter 6

It was now Sunday, and the rare May sun was peeping through the Burney's bedroom windows. The sweet songs of carefree wildlife coming from her colourful gardens were much in audible evidence. Bianca romantically thought that it would be so wonderful to just lie here all day listening to the euphony of sounds from the birds and having flashbacks to her time as a child in the Irish countryside where she grew up.

She could only allow that luxury for a few more minutes before she would have to leave the comfort of her bed and the warmth of her husband next to her— her husband who hours ago she almost lost. Those few more minutes took her back many years to the many school holidays which as a young pure and innocent virginal lass, she had so much enjoyed.

Her parents were often glad to lose her for the school holidays and so would gladly dispatch her on the long trek to Dublin in southern Ireland by train to her aunt and uncle and their extended family, especially for the long summer breaks. She had usually found the train journeys particularly enchanting and adventurous.

As the train rumbled its way through the strikingly beautiful and romantic countryside, Bianca recalled how the journeys would take the passengers past grazing animals, miles and miles of wind-bent grasses and luscious cultivation: cultivated and uncultivated green vegetation of varying sizes.

On the journey, mostly intermittently, she could still recall the many flights of birds fluttering their wings vigorously as they soared into the evening skies to evade the rumbling and approaching train.

Further down the track, she could see coveys of partridges, swifts, goldcrests, and wrens adorning the blue skies in picturesque formations; whilst the blackbirds and the goldfinches maintained a visible presence in hovering buoyancy just above the green shoots of the several varieties of trees that lined the train's path.

These past sentimental reflections were, however, soon become domesticated by the reality of the day's urgent agenda, and, so, Bianca eased herself gently out of the bed. It was now six a.m. and Carlos was, surprisingly, still soundly asleep.

He was normally awake before her. Perhaps, it was Carlos' sleep deficiency of the previous night combined with Bianca's anxiety about the day ahead that produced this unusual result.

Bianca knew that she not only had to prepare breakfast for her husband but in her preparation, she had to make allowance for the fact that she would not be at home for most of the daylight time and Carlos would be home alone. She, herself, must be ready and waiting for the arrival of her taxi at eleven-thirty a.m.

Exactly on the dot of eleven-thirty a.m., the doorbell on the Burney's front porch sounded. It was the taxi that was commissioned by Mr Austin as he had promised. Bianca was ready to take that trip to the headteacher's home for an important working lunch.

Bianca hugged and kissed her husband goodbye and then walked the short distance to where the car was waiting. She got aboard and the journey was set in progress.

On the journey northwards to the posh suburbs of Sutton Cold Field and the home of her headteacher, Bianca quietly thought that this was going to be a first. In the more than a little over twelve years that Mr Austin had been headteacher of Dixon Pen, she was never invited to his home. She doesn't know what to expect. WAs his home large or small? What kind of comfort and luxury did he enjoy or otherwise?

She had heard on the grapevine that his wife had died a few years before he won the headship for Dixon Pen but, beyond that, she knew nothing more about his family situation. She didn't know whether he had children; and if so, where are they? Does he live with a common-law wife?

Who was the female that answered the phone when she first called the headteacher's land line yesterday? She sounded extremely knowledgeable and informed. Could she be the mistress of the home at which she was now destined to arrive in just a few more minutes? As this was going to be a working lunch, it might be just Mr Austin and she; but who will be preparing lunch?

On this last thought of Bianca, the taxi driver turned his vehicle into Lavender Mews and pulled up outside number ten as he echoed just four words: "This is it, Madam."

"Is this the home of Mr Austin?" Bianca asked herself rhetorically as she alighted from the taxi.

"Thank you most kindly," Bianca said whilst reaching for her purse.

"Oh, no madam, there is no cost to you, the full cost of your trip is already taken care of and so will be your return trip when we are told to come and collect you later today," the taxi driver assured Bianca.

The taxi driver then turned his vehicle around and headed back in the direction from whence he had come.

The front door of number ten Lavender Mews opened to receive Bianca a full nine seconds before she could ascend the full flight of three steps of decorative stones that led to the opened door.

Standing in the expansive doorway was a woman of some class hinting very strongly of conservatism with a small 'C'. Her hair was neatly combed in a coiffure. She was elegantly dressed in a powder blue morning suit and matching shoes with modest heal. She wore necklaces, earrings, and bangles of similar styles and expensive taste. She had rings—one on each hand but none on the traditional ring finger of her left hand. She seemed immaculate in appearance.

Bianca's quickest summation was that this was no maid. She might not be a married woman but in this home, she was a woman with considerable authority.

"Hello, Mrs Burney, I believe?" Daniel Johnson queried with a strong degree of certainty as she welcomed Bianca into the reception hall of the headteacher's home.

Bianca, sporting one of her most infectious smiles, nodded to confirm her identity as she stepped inside the magnificent hall of some awe.

"Please wait here whilst I let Mr Austin know that you have arrived. I am playing hostess today so if you would like a drink of any sort before, during lunch or after, do, please let me know and I will make it available at any time throughout your stay."

Daniel, having laid out her hospitality intent, set off to find Mr Austin in what seemed like a maze of a house. She was gone for only two minutes but that was sufficient time for Bianca to take in the scene. Two things, in particular, immediately caught Bianca's attention.

Firstly, there was that beautiful oak antique desk in the right-hand corner of the reception hall. It clearly doubles as a conference table and a dining table for working lunches as it will do now. The dining table function was much in evidence because the table was laid for two people and two note pads with pencils lay to the right-hand side of the intended diners. This was confirmation of what Bianca had already imagined that the luncheon was just for two people—the headteacher and herself.

But of much greater and perplexing interest to Bianca was the framed picture that adorns the centre table in the headteacher's reception room. Bianca was dumbstruck as she steered in disbelief at the young man—beefy, muscular, and tall with blue eyes and shoulder-length blond hair. Why delay the truth, this was Gaston Burney gazing lovingly into the gorgeous eyes of a mixed-race beauty of some years his junior with his left arm lovingly around her divinely shaped waistline.

She, too, steered upwards lustfully and admiringly into those stunning blue eyes of Gaston Burney. She had the same kind of expression on her young and beautiful face as Bianca imagined had been written all over her face when she first met Gaston on the same day she married his father, Carlos Burney.

Bianca remained standing by the centre table frozen in shock as Daniel re-entered the reception hall to announce that Mr Austin was now aware of her presence and would be down shortly to join her.

"May I please ask who this couple is?" Bianca, still in shock, asked Daniel.

"Oh, I don't know the young man, but I believe his name is Jason. She is Doreen, Mr Austin's youngest and last child. They were recently engaged to be married soon after the end of her studies—he is Swedish but speaks perfect English, I understand.

"At least, so she has told her father; Doreen is such a wonderful, responsible, and ambitious young lady. I have known her since she was three years old. I have missed her ever so much since she went to pursue her study in Sweden," Daniel fondly explained.

Just then, they were joined by Mr Austin who had overheard the tail-end of Daniel's explanation and tried to fill in the gaps.

"She is presently in the final year of a pre-university course for the prestigious University of Umea, a highly rated bastion of education in the coldest part of northern Sweden. Apparently, it is one of the best places to study medicine which is Doreen's steadfast ambition. My last piece of advice to her and by extension to him too, was not to let romance get in the way of her medical pursuit.

"However, she has assured me that this young man whom I have yet to meet is very steady sober character who is gainfully employed in one of Stockholm's

Scientific Laboratory. He is about 400 miles by road approximately six hours ride, so they won't be spending much time together until they are married and can be together at some geographical location as they will then choose," Mr Austin explained with some proud fatherly visionary interest before suggesting to Bianca that it was time for lunch and some urgent business.

This was the signal to Miss Johnson to mobilise on the luncheon arrangements during his meeting with Mrs Burney.

Mr Austin, leading the way, Bianca followed, if just a little unenthusiastically, under circumstances known only to her. Ringing in her ears was the statement from the headteacher that he had yet to meet his son-in-law to be. It was that remark that forcefully reminded Bianca that the headteacher had never met Gaston and, therefore, was not aware of his identity or of his connection to her.

Indeed, on account of previous commitments, Mr Austin was not able to attend her wedding to Carlos when and where Gaston was a prominent guest. The headteacher had later met Carlos at a school concert where Carlos was her special guest. However, although whenever Gaston was around, he would give her rides to and from the school, the two men had still never met.

Mr Austin and Bianca then took their places at the big oak table ready for the promised business.

Bianca was wondering how it was that she was going to get her mind back from where it had gone and back ready for what she was at this house for in the first place. She could also smell some sweet aroma coming from somewhere in the house. Inviting though the aroma seemed, Bianca doubted whether she could enjoy a meal given that the discovery she had made had done negative things to her already small appetite even under normal circumstances.

Mr Austin then reached for his notebook which revealed an agenda.

"Bianca," he began, "I am lost without Elaine. In times such as now, she would have been a tower of strength. Ironically, it is the very tower that is absolutely lost. I will grieve that loss for many long years. How could anyone be so cruel, so brutal, I will never understand? Had you seen what I saw with my own eyes, you probably would have lost all trust in humankind forever.

"You probably have read that or heard that it was I who discovered the body. Mrs Mavis Jackson, our senior caretaker as you know, also witnessed what I saw when she was asked to open Elaine's office door for the police and the shock of what she saw made her pass out, requiring some trained professional attention.

Fortunately, the police were well prepared and equipped and were able to render immediate assistance which ensured her full recovery before the night was over.

"Elaine was the only designated reporter who did not report to me, in accordance with school policy, following that false fire alarm at the school last Friday. Frankly, I selfishly kept that fact to myself until I could personally discover the real reason for that unusual failure.

"I didn't want to raise the alarm publicly as I didn't want to turn on the pressure from those who might have thought that a black headteacher was shielding a black administration officer, and head's PA, who had failed to perform in a way which could have endangered life. Admittedly, I was extremely annoyed but given that it was so much unlike her, I determined that I would investigate the matter for myself, and any necessary action could follow appropriately.

"It was that that made me go to Elaine's office when and where I discovered that horrendous slaughter euphemistically being termed a murder on all the media outlets presently. Having discovered what I did, I realised that it was vital that the announcement of it be in an atmosphere of the minimum crowd or else the school would have lost all control of the situation. Here too, I had to remain silent until most of the school—staff, and pupils—had left for home before I could raise the alarm by reporting to important others and those who must know.

"Even then, the word-of-mouth grapevine, the smartphones, and social media were so quickly effective, it was absolute chaos in minutes by the time the police were on the scene. Because they were trained for this kind of thing, they quickly took control of the situation and managed it the best they could. The police saw fit to grill me extensively on the same night and have left open the possibility that they might see me again. They have also identified key others, which includes you, that they want to interview."

Bianca was most alarmed to hear that the cops had investigative interest in her and immediately interjected a searching question.

"Why on earth would the police want to see me? Are they thinking that I might have something to do with the murder?"

To this question, Mr Austin answered that:

"The cops had stated that everyone having any connection with the school is a potential suspect. In your case, their interest was aroused because you, being an internal candidate, had unsuccessfully competed with Elaine for the post that she held up to the time of her death. There is no need for any alarm: the police are only doing their job and they, like us and other professions have rules, systems, and guidance to follow."

Bianca did not seem all that satisfied with the headteacher's defensive comment about the police plans but decided to go along with the headteacher's lead, especially with the other burden she was inwardly carrying weighing her down. Right then, she was thinking that the end of this working lunch cannot come too soon so that she can be on her way home when and where she can be alone with her thoughts.

The headteacher then continued:

"There are also a number of documents that they will be seeking from the school tomorrow morning, and this is where I want to begin our discussion today."

"Item one on my agenda," he said, "is to explain to you what Elaine's job description was."

Bianca had seen this job description in written form before when she unsuccessfully competed for that very job now vacated by Elaine in such unfortunate circumstances. However, a refresher course was always very useful, she thought as Miss Johnson entered the room carrying a tray with steaming soup, and freshly made bread rolls with a choice of tiny butter or margarine frozen blocks.

Bianca, whilst indulging in the first course of the lunch, listened intently as the headteacher methodically went through Elaine's job description, pausing intermittently only to part-take of his served course of lunch. He was very careful to emphasise those areas that are most vital to the management of the school of which he was the head.

Bianca found the outline of the job description most interesting despite the internal pains she was silently enduring. As she listened to the headteacher's explanation, she realised that the job was far more demanding than she had previously imagined: and yet, Elaine had made it look so easy and manageable.

Bianca considered that posthumous congratulations and appreciation were due to Elaine for the examples she had set the team and to her as she listened more to Mr Austin, she developed a feeling that protecting the headteacher from targeting forces was a major aspect of the job but would not be easy for the holder of the post whenever it was filled.

Bianca started to wonder about how soon the headteacher would set in motion the apparatus to replace Elaine. Right at that moment, she didn't think she would be considered suitable and so she wouldn't even think along that line.

At that moment, Miss Johnson re-entered the meeting room to collect the used soup bowls and cutlery. She also announced that the second course was on the way.

Mr Austin was at that point winding up on agenda item one. He suggested that they take a short pause to enjoy Miss Johnson's second course of Snappers cooked in butter and lemon sauce served with a choice of vegetables; there was a reserved dish of macaroni oven-baked pie, just in case Bianca was not a fish eater. As it turned out, Bianca was an avid lover of fish meals. Mr Austin, it seems, will be having macaroni oven-baked pie for dinner later, Bianca mused.

The second course was now over, and Mr Austin decided to continue with his previously prepared agenda.

"Before moving on, Bianca are there any comments, questions, or observations you want to make in relation to the outline of the job description and the recent events that have brought us here today?"

"Yes sir, I am here wondering what has happened to Elaine's corpse and if you are going to fill her post immediately? I am asking these questions because if the school is to function efficiently, we are going to need more hands in the administration department to cover what will be undoubtedly greater pressures on the school following all that has happened over the last few days," Bianca responded thoughtfully.

Mr Austin at once began to answer Bianca's first question about Elaine's corpse to the best of his knowledge.

"Elaine's corpse, it is my understanding, is still under the control of the police and might well be with them for a great deal longer for evidential and forensic purposes. Not until the police have exhausted those areas of investigation are they likely to hand over the body to Elaine's next of kin for burial."

Bianca then followed up with something which, on the previous day, was brought to attention by at least two individuals who had seen the pictures of Elaine's corpse that had gone viral since last Friday night and were still in circulation.

"Does that mean that they—the police—were also responsible for the deceased valuables? I am asking about this because it was brought to my attention by two people who know of Elaine's attachment to her famous ring that the pictures that the media of all types were circulating show no sign of Elaine's beloved ring.

"It is something that Elaine would not have removed from the finger on her left hand where it had found a home. It was a magnificent ring deemed to be almost unique and exceedingly expensive. Since the ring did not appear to be on the corpse, I am wondering whether the police removed it from her hand for safe keeping and will eventually hand it back to Elaine's next of kin too"?

"Your question about the missing ring: I must plead ignorance about such matters. I wasn't even aware that the ring was missing from Elaine's hand. I tend to agree with you that it is strange, if that is the case, because, from all that I had heard about Elaine and that ring, they were inseparable. I will make a note to prosecute some timely inquiries and will share with you what I find," Mr Austin commented with some assurance to Bianca.

"As to whether I will immediately fill the vacancy which has been so suddenly and brutally trusted upon us, I can tell you that that will take some time because, it being a substantive post, I must follow all the education authority's protocols and procedures to make it happen.

"The post will have to be advertised both nationally and locally in the right media outlets and then followed through from there. What I can do immediately, however, is to appoint an Acting Chief Administrative Officer who will act until such a time as the substantive post is filled. This brings me nicely to the next point on the agenda," the headteacher remarked.

Miss Johnson returned with the final course of the working luncheon. She showed up with a choice of tea or coffee and there were supporting biscuits and a collection of cheeses. Both the headteacher and Bianca selected their choices and whilst they consumed them, the meeting continued.

"Mrs Burney, forgive the formality. I want to offer you, here and now, the position of Acting Chief Administrative Officer and in extension the personal assistant to the headteacher at Dixon Pen School with effect from tomorrow's date. You already know what the post involves. Would you be prepared to accept that position and associated remuneration and condition of service?

"That would also involve someone from the existing team acting up in your current position and it would further mean a temporary appointment at clerk level to the team; all of which I am prepared to act upon with immediate effect. And before you answer, here are two carrots worth considering; 1. Experience has taught us that nine times out of ten the person acting in a position eventually aspires to the substantive post'.

"2. The Acting Chief Administrative Officer will commence the job working from a completely new office which, on my prior instruction, has been identified and refurbished in anticipation of this appointment and eventually the appointment of the substantive post holder. The office once used by Elaine has now been evacuated and has become a storeroom for cleaning equipment and other similar caretaking usages," Mr Austin was most forthright in his offer.

This offer amounted to yet another shock for Bianca. It was never part of her wildest dream that she would come away from this meeting with a promotion. This was a weird world she reflected. Since last Friday evening, everything had been going wrong for her and all of them have taken her by shocking surprise. This was the first of these many 'shocks' that don't bring pain in its stance.

There was a great deal of work involved but the pay was much better too. Above all, it will be a form of anaesthetics to help her to survive all the other unknowns that were piling up in her life presently. This was the kind of reasoning which preoccupied Bianca's thoughts as she found some stimulated appetite for more biscuits and cheeses consumption.

She determined that her answer to this totally unexpected offer must be a resounding and enthusiastic, "Yes".

Turning to the headteacher of Dixon Pen, Bianca was brief and to the point.

"Mr Austin, Sir, I do accept your kind offer and I am ready to serve immediately."

"Acting Administrative Officer, Bianca Burney, these are your first assignments. 1. Tomorrow morning, the police will arrive to collect from your department the following documents:

a. The complete file for Mrs Elaine Bridgewater
b. The complete file for the then Deputy Administrative Officer
1. Morning assembly for all pupils will be as usual in the North Hall but:
2. Please advise ALL staff (teaching and non-teaching) of an impromptu staff meeting at four fifteen o'clock tomorrow afternoon at the end of the school day.
3. Please remember to search the Education Guardian Newspaper on Tuesday for any entry about Wednesday's Secretary of State's Educational Conference in York.

4. Also, kindly advised the parents of Frankie Watson that the police will want to interview their son Frankie in their presence on a date to be arranged with them through the school. They should be given the choice regarding the place where the interview will take place: at their home, at the school, or at the Harbourne Police Station. Once you have arranged that date and related details, you will kindly convey this information to Chief Inspector Harding—the officer in charge of the homicide at Dixon Pen or Detective Corporal Brown—working with and for Chief Inspector Harding. Both were based at Harbourne Constabulary Station.
5. In tomorrow's edition of School News under the headteacher's column, kindly report your appointment and my intentions regarding the post you were relinquishing and the clerk to be temporarily appointed.
6. I will meet with my Cabinet of Senior Staff at ten o'clock soon after the morning assembly.
7. Finally, and to bring this meeting to a close, you should know that I do not want to see or entertain any visitors or media representatives at any point throughout the day. I will accept all calls or visits from the police, officials from the education office, the department of education, and the governors of the school."

"Mrs Burney, my good friend, Bianca, I do appreciate you giving up your valuable time on a Sunday to progress our school which has suffered such a macabre blow and so suddenly. But we must survive and move the school forward regardless. Thank you greatly for your time and I will see you tomorrow. I believe Miss Johnson has already summoned your car which is now waiting to take you back home," Mr Austin said smilingly as he closed the meeting.

Bianca reciprocated the headteacher's smile, rose from her seat, thanked him profusely for the events of the day, applauded Miss Johnson for such a delicious lunch as she quietly closed her notebook and slid it securely into her handbag, bade both people of the house goodbye and then turned to head for the front door and her waiting taxi.

She could not resist the urge to take one more glance at the centre table and remarked intentionally loudly: that Jason Musgrave was a very handsome man.

Neither Mr Austin nor Miss Johnson could remember telling her what Jason's surname was, but they thought to themselves, quite independently, that it was not significant and, so, let it drop whilst Bianca went down the three flights of decorated stone steps, admiring them as she descended. She got into her taxi and waved goodbye as the taxi roared off southwards for Mrs Burney's residence. She had missions to accomplish, Bianca contemplated.

On the journey home, Bianca found that the excitement of having been promoted to the top job in her department, albeit in an acting capacity, overshadowed the many and varied other issues that were currently vying for her attention.

Nevertheless, some of these other issues did manage to parade themselves at the forefront of her thoughts, if only fleetingly, during what seemed to be a much shorter journey than the outgoing one.

Bianca reflected on many things in turn. First and foremost, how will the other girls react to her? Will the relationships remain the same? The team had an excellent relationship with Elaine after all; would she be able to replicate that? Would there be room for improvement?

Which of the girls did she think would be most suitable to succeed her as Deputy Administrative Officer? They were all excellent and hard-working. She knows that the headteacher will be expecting her to influence his choice on an equal opportunity basis. Much of this, she thought, would be resolved once she had had an opportunity to speak with the girls individually.

Bianca's thought moved smoothly to the odd instruction that she was just given by the headteacher to hand over her own file history to the police in the morning on the first day of her new job. She could not figure out why the police should be so interested in her, except that, as Mr Austin said, they were only doing their job as required by their training and policy requirements.

Oh well, she thought as she dismissed the idea as not serious and not deserving of any further attention. She will hand over the file as instructed and so be it. She was no murderer and thus had nothing to fear.

The previous thought thus vacated, and the room was made for Bianca to ruminate on Gaston Burney posing as Jason Musgrave the Swedish national. This young man who was currently gallivanting in Switzerland that she so carelessly allowed herself to fall in love with was turning out to be a skunk of an individual. During the working luncheon with the headteacher, she had surreptitiously had a peep at the pictures which she had taken of the contents of Gaston's secret compartment.

She did this to quickly refresh her memory of the name on the Swedish passport. Jason Musgrave it was. No cruel coincidence here; just cruel reality.

She resolved with absolute determination to find the other jigsaw pieces if it was the last thing she would do.

And to think that his father holds him in such high esteem, so much so that he was encouraging him to "…start a family with a sensible and respectable young lady."

One could metaphorically feel the weight of the loaded sarcasm buried disdainfully in the recesses of Bianca's mind as she reluctantly jumped to a tamer thought.

In three days', time, she will be enjoying dinner with her daughter who wishes to discuss important matters with her alone. She was not sure what could be so important. She was not given the slightest hint. It will be good, however, to get a recess from the kitchen that night and be with her only kin.

She won't entirely escape the chores of the domestic kitchen on Wednesday since it will be incumbent upon her to make alternative preparations to accommodate Carlos who will be left alone on that date.

Really, she thought, her domestic life was a complicated mess right now. There was so much that she knew but it was impossible to share some of this with Carlos without opening a bottomless ditch in which to fall. Perhaps it might be best to say nothing to Carlos.

Gaston's absence brought it home fully how alone she was. Yet, she had no right to blame anything on Gaston's absence. His companionship was never part of the unspoken deal. Hot sex it was and by gosh, she had a lot of that.

This sex in abundance thing caused Bianca then to reluctantly turn her thoughts to something that she had been neglecting for some 17 days now largely because she wasn't totally convinced that a woman so close to her fortieth birthday—thirty-eight years of age—wouldn't find it difficult to conceive. Her menses should have been with her some seventeen days ago but so far there had been absolutely no sign.

It could be all these stressful issues and times that were combining to frustrate her regularity, but she now thinks that it might be prudent to pick up a pregnancy test kit from the round-the-clock chemist five minutes up the top of her road as soon as the taxi drops her at her door.

As if by coincidence, the driver of the taxi turned his vehicle into Passion Street and pulled up at the driveway to number fifty.

Bianca expressed her appreciation to her journey chauffeur and as he drove off, she looked at her watch. It had just gone five o'clock in the afternoon. She strolled the short distance to the chemist and purchased a couple of pregnancy test kits which she briskly took back to the privacy and domesticity of her home where she could read and understand the instructions on the test kit before application.

Carlos was in the living room still catching up on the Sunday papers. All of them still featured the recent murder at Dixon Pen as their main story. Because his wife, Bianca, had returned, it seemed a good idea to abandon the papers for a while and spend some time catching up on her stories of the day.

"Hello," Carlos said on seeing his wife enter.

"Hi honey, I am home. How was your day without your wonderful wife?" Bianca announced and queried facetiously.

She continued before Carlos could reply.

"Have you had your evening meal yet? Did you enjoy your lunch?"

Carlos was glad for an opening to give his replies to all three questions, "I am not so sure that a 'wonderful wife', as you put it, would have left her lonely husband languishing all day on a Sunday. Our Roman Catholic principles alone would dictate that we should be taking communion together at our nearest place of worship. We shouldn't really let our values slip away from us; you know. And yes, I did enjoy my lunch and I had my evening dinner.

"Thanks for the thoughtful preparation: you are such a good cook, or shall I say chef par excellence? And how was your day? Was it productive? Have you learned anything more about the murder of your boss? Did Mr Austin say why his mobile phone was out of order?" Carlos was not to be outdone, he showed that he could string questions together too.

"Carlos, you know that I completely forgot to enquire of Mr Austin about his mobile phone and he didn't mention it once; so, I am none the wiser there. The same is true about the murder. No one seemed to know anything that could be helpful, not even the headteacher. The police have sworn to be relentless in their investigation, though. They even want to interview me; what for, I don't know, but Mr Austin seems to think it is just part of the job and that I should see it that way and cooperate fully.

"They are, in fact, coming to the school tomorrow to collect my file history and, apparently, plan to interview me later. Now they are going to be so disappointed to find that I cannot help them. Anyhow, my day was very good. In fact, it was extremely productive. You are looking at the Acting Chief Administrative Officer for Dixon Pen School.

"I will begin this role with effect from tomorrow with a forty percent pay rise and a new office. The headteacher is committed to appointing me an Acting Deputy and increase—rather make-up—the department's staffing by one temporary clerk until he fills the substantive post permanently."

Bianca dared not mention anything about Carlos' Swedish son—Jason Musgrave. She wisely thought that that might be opening a can of worms and, so, she ended her account of her day's experience at this point.

Carlos was very pleasantly surprised that his wife had gained promotion to the top job because of the recent awful development at the school. He fondly embraced and profusely congratulated his wife and wished her well for the road ahead.

Bianca proudly acknowledged the showers of congratulatory remarks being heaped upon her by her husband and then enquired further:

"Did you manage to go for a walk today, honey?"

"Yes, I popped out for about thirty minutes brisk walk soon after you left. The morning air was still fresh and stimulating. I got back home to settle down with the Sunday Times seeming complete account of the Dixon Pen murder: but for all the tea in China, I cannot find what I did with that paper. All the other ones are here but it was the only one that seemed to have some reasoned speculations about the murder.

"There was also what seemed like a speculative story about an unsolved murder in the not-too-distant past and its possible connection to the Dixon Pen's murder, which I wanted to read. The paper has just disappeared, and I am sure that I didn't take it away with me.

"I know that you did not take it with you because it was after you left that I noticed it among the pile of Sunday papers the paper boy had delivered. Maybe I can get another copy tomorrow if they are not completely sold out. On occasions, I can remember seeing old copies on their shelves up to four days after publication. Maybe I will be lucky," Carlos said in hopeful anticipation.

"How odd," Bianca remarked, "where could it have gone? You didn't bin it, did you?"

"No sweetheart, the bins are still here with all their contents. Let us just put it down to growing old and senility."

Bianca thought it strange and excused herself saying that she had wanted to go to the bathroom for the past several hours but resisted because she was more comfortable using her own toilet facility.

This was a façade for learning about and applying the instructions for testing her pregnancy status.

Bianca was gone for just over twenty minutes when she re-emerged looking somewhat dejected. She was pregnant: pregnant without a doubt. How cruel could the circumstances of her life be, she asked herself rhetorically. And only moments ago, Carlos had reminded her of their Roman Catholic leanings.

Carlos was very puzzled about mislaying his newspaper but somehow Bianca was not puzzled. She had already arrived at the firm belief that whilst Carlos was out walking, they had had a visitor and that that visitor was none other than one Gaston Burney who had called his dad from Switzerland only last night.

Bianca had read somewhere that modern technology allows people to make conference calls and the participants may be anywhere in the world. If Gaston had got a contact to dial his father in a conference call including Gaston himself, the location of his friend would register on Carlos' bedside phone showing the caller to be in Switzerland.

As soon as Carlos answered, the contact dialler would have been previously primed to remain silent whilst Gaston would speak as though he was the initial caller. Bianca had been coming across so many examples of intrigue that have Gaston teetering on the edges if not at the very heart lately; she had become grossly suspicious of everything that features Gaston.

One way to verify her current suspicion and belief, she thought, was to find a reason to access Gaston's room at the top of the stairs.

"Honey, have you got anything for the washing machine? I need to do some washing tonight. I must also fetch the sheets from the spare room after sleeping on them on Friday night. I will just go and fetch them. I will be back in a few minutes," Bianca said as she headed towards the stairs and ascended them.

She quickly entered the spare room, pulled off the sheets and dropped them on the landing, and headed straight for Gaston's room. The door was still not secured as it normally used to be when Gaston disappeared for long periods. Bianca quickly entered the room and went directly to the secret compartment quite expecting that the passports and other documentation would no longer be there.

She was spot-on: they were all gone but in their place was a bundle of money with a foreign language of a sort written on the notes. The outstanding word on the notes was "Kronor". These notes were in units of 100 and 500. It looked like there were thousands of them. There was no time to count them. She closed the secret compartment leaving everything intact, exited the room and closed it back as she found it, gathered up the sheets, and descended the stairs.

Bianca now had clothes to put into the wash before it was supper time and the usual routine before joining her husband in bed for what was now bound to be a restless night…of all the night.

It was Monday: the first day of school since the horrible murder and it was Bianca's first day in the top job as Acting Chief Administrative Officer. She had no idea how her team had got words about her promotion, but they had. If she had any doubt about a positive reaction from the team, it suddenly vanished. Although she had made it her number one priority to get to school earlier than usual, the other four members of her team had clearly outmatched her in this time operation.

As Bianca entered through the front doors, there they were, all four of them, holding out a placard that they had quite clearly hastily put together.

It read: "Congratulation to our new boss, Bianca—the team will stay strong and determined. You have our support because we know you have our backs."

This was enough to melt away all the background issues which were eating away at the Acting Chief Administrative Officer.

Hovering in the background, were the headteacher and his two deputies observing all that touching welcome and congratulatory scene that engulfed Bianca on her arrival?

Bianca warmly acknowledged the efforts of her colleagues and the presence of the senior personnel of the school and then said to her team, "Come on in, we have much to do."

Early as Bianca was, on her arrival, she couldn't help but notice that the media and their technical apparatus were many and strategically dotted about in the close vicinity of the school. She had thought to herself that that was as far they would come.

At the school assembly for all pupils, the headteacher was careful to stress the need for pupils not to lose sight of their purpose in school. Whilst it was true that this was a most unusual time, this would pass and when that happens, we will still be here in search of our purposes in life. Pupils, he said, should avoid speaking to the media and inquisitive others because they have no useful knowledge of what happened and therefore, they should not offer up themselves to be the subject of miss-quotations and conspiracy theories.

The headteacher pleaded with his teacher colleagues, who were present at the pupils' assembly, to get on with their classes as normal and insist on that being so by everyone. He announced the fact that he would have more to say at the staff meeting that was called for the end of the school today. The heads of years and form teachers were then left to settle the school for teaching as was normal. So far, the pupil responses have been tremendous: it was as though nothing unusual had happened at the school recently.

At the head's meeting with his Cabinet of senior staff, the Cabinet was one in their resolve to take the school past this difficult period. They were aware that the police operation must go on despite the stress of normality. Thus, there was a fixed resolve to give quiet but total cooperation to them.

Some major worries were flagged as needing particular attention in view of recent events: these are future pupil intake and the school's high-profile policy on equal opportunity and anti-racism. Before breaking up, the Cabinet resolved further that staff should be given the opportunity at the staff meeting at the end of today to report on anything which was considered out of the ordinary.

Throughout the day, the headteacher had to deal with several calls, mainly seeking updated information, from official offices and the governors of the school. He was never bothered in the least by any member of the media fraternity. His recently appointed Acting PA seemed to be doing a great job, it seemed to him.

At the end of the school day, the school personnel undertook their normal dismissal arrangements; and whilst that was happening and the staff began gathering for the staff meeting, the head took up his usual vista from the windows of his secluded office. Nothing out of the ordinary was happening.

Pupils were scrambling in their various directions, the buses on both sides of the roads were filling up and a few hyper-cautious parents took the precaution to collect their children, mostly the younger ones, from the school gates. Subject to what he will shortly hear at the staff meeting, this first day back, after the most gruesome of events in the history of the school, seems to have gone well without a hitch.

At the staff meeting, the headteacher formally thanked the staff for their, what looks like almost one hundred percent, attendance. He needed to get a few domestic details out of the way before getting down to the crux of the matter for this gathering.

The headteacher then informed the staff in confirmation about his appointment to replace Elaine Bridgewater and the chain of staffing adjustments that had emerged because of it. He also put the staff into the picture as to his intention to deal with that staffing chain and new office space provision.

Of course, all of this you will read in the very next edition of School News. He then turned to why they had gathered.

The head continued to say that, given what had happened here, he expects to have many sporadic visits from the police in the days and weeks ahead. He would expect all staff to be fully cooperative if they were identified by the police as people who might be able to assist them.

"Of course, if you are the murdering culprit, you might not want to follow my advice so enthusiastically," the headteacher said as, for the first time, he interjected a bit of well-taken humour.

"Beyond this, I can confirm that it was I who discovered the body because I was seeking out Mrs Edgewater for an explanation for why she didn't show up to report following the fire alarm as she was supposed to in accordance with the policy of the school. Because of this, their fingerprinting experts would have found my fingerprints all over her office doors.

"I wonder what they will be making of that. And yes, I have had a thorough going over by the police on the very night of that very brutal event. It is also true that the police have taken the view that everyone associated with the school and possibly others, is a potential suspect until they eliminate them during the time. It is for this reason that I seek your fullest cooperation should you be called upon."

Mr Austin then told his staff that if any of them wants to report any unusual development throughout the course of today, he will be glad to hear of it with a view to ensuring the normality of the school going forward.

Only some of the heads of years had anything to report.

There was a noticeable increase in the number of parents of children from years one, two, and three who, as a matter of precaution, decided to collect their children from the school gate today. The effect of this was to cause a degree of congestion in traffic which we are not normally accustomed to having at that time of day.

The only other report came from the newly appointed Acting Chief Administrative Officer. She reported that she and her team had great difficulties preventing the media people from invading the school but, except for a few minor scuffles, they accomplished that task successfully and they surely will be on their guard tomorrow and thereafter until this whole thing was all over.

Mrs Burney also confirmed that the police, as we were forewarned, did turn up at reception to collect some documentation which included her own file of the deceased and visitors to the school records. Finally, following instructions from Mr Austin, she had dutifully arranged for Frankie Watson of year five, in the presence of his parents, to be interviewed by Detective Corporal Brown for a week today, Monday the twenty-fourth of May in the afternoon.

The parties have voluntarily agreed that the interview will be done at our local police station in Harbourne. Head of the year, form teacher, and subject teachers please take note. Frankie should not be penalised in any way for his absence from school that afternoon.

No one else had a report to make and so the meeting allowed for a question-and-answer session. Since all the questions were about what was being reported in the various forms of media, the answers were mainly speculative; we don't know where they got that from, or flat-out condemnation as fabricated lies designed to sell newspapers and improve viewers' ratings.

The headteacher then brought the meeting to a close, by openly stating that he didn't think that there was a murderer at large in the school and so he hoped that his full team would continue to discharge their duties professionally and, indeed, fearlessly. On this note and a signal from the headteacher, the staff began to disperse, heading for their various homes. Tomorrow will be another day.

Mr Austin arrived home at Lavender Mews to find Detective Corporal Brown waiting patiently in his car for his homecoming.

As the headteacher slowly drove his white BMW motor car towards its garage facility, the detective rolled his window down to reveal his presence to the headteacher. They nodded a friendly jester to each other as the headteacher continued to drive his car into the garage.

Once he had accomplished this regular activity, he then returned to the detective who, by this, was waiting for him at the foot of the stone steps which lead to the front entrance of the headteacher's home.

"Good evening, headteacher. I did call the school but was told by your caretaker, Mrs Mavis Jackson, that I had just missed you; so, I figured that you would be on your way home. When I arrived and realised that I got here before you, I thought you might have gone elsewhere before coming home.

"I was just about to postpone my call to tomorrow when I saw your car approaching. I do appreciate that you would have had a very tiresome day but, as promised, we made it a priority to get your mobile phone back to you as early as possible and so I am very pleased to tell you that its return is part of my business at this time," the detective apologetically explained to the headteacher.

"Part, Detective Corporal, part?" The headteacher emphatically enquired.

"Yes, sir, I just need to ask you a few questions about some of the contents we found on your phone, it shouldn't take very long. I hope you don't mind, sir."

The headteacher was beginning to feel quite angry about this intrusion into his private life in connection with matters about which he knows nothing, but he quickly recalled the kind of advice he had been giving his colleagues about cooperating with the police.

"Detective Brown, I am very tired and somewhat hungry, but I suppose I could give you about twenty minutes or so. Would you like to come in?" Mr Austin said as he reluctantly extended an invitation to the detective to enter his home and as if he had any choice in the matter.

"Thank you, sir; it definitely won't take that long. Ten or fifteen minutes at the most, sir, and I shall be gone leaving you in peace, sir."

Up the three flights of steps they went, and the headteacher opened the front door and escorted his guest inside. They took seats in the reception hall—the same hall where the headteacher held his working lunch with Bianca the day before. As they sat down, Miss Johnson, the domestic helper entered to greet the headteacher and was surprised to see that he had brought home a guest without giving her some warning.

"Detective Brown, this is Miss Johnson. Miss Johnson, this is Detective Corporal Brown. He wants about fifteen minutes of my time and then I will be ready for dinner. Please leave us alone undisturbed for that period," Mr Austin advised her.

No sooner than Miss Johnson gracefully withdrew, the detective turned to the headteacher and remarked as he pointed to the framed picture of the headteacher's daughter, and her fiancé seated on the centre table in the reception hall:

"Sir, it is this picture that I want to ask you about. We have gone through your phone very thoroughly and could find nothing, absolutely nothing of interest. We did, however, notice this very same picture in the gallery of your phone and the chief inspector thought it prudent just to ascertain who the couple might be.

"That is why, sir, I told you it would not take us very long. Then, as if to save us even more time, the time that would be needed to open your phone gallery, the very same photo is already presented here. For the records, sir, will you please tell me who they are and how they came to be sending you the picture which I now notice has a central place in your home."

At this point, he handed back the headteacher's mobile phone to him, "Very simply, Detective Brown, do assure the chief inspector that the picture is showing my youngest daughter, Doreen, and her Swedish finance, Jason. They had just become engaged and had that picture taken. They proudly sent the picture by WhatsApp to my phone that is why you found it where you did.

"I so love that picture that I took my phone to the photo laboratory where they were able to download and enlarge it to create what is now the centre of attraction it seems. Only yesterday, I had a luncheon in this room and the picture was the conversation piece for my guest," Mr Austin assured the detective.

"And please, sir, may I ask who that guest was?" The detective probed further.

"Oh, that was Mrs Burney, Bianca Burney, and our current Acting Chief Administrative Officer since yesterday's luncheon," Mr Austin's very quickly and directly responded.

"Are your daughter and her fiancé staying with you now, sir"? Detective Brown asked.

"Oh no, not at all: Doreen is in the pre-university year at the University of Umea, northern Sweden, with plans to read medicine. Her fiancé is a Swedish national living and working in Sweden. They plan to be married as soon as Doreen finishes her medical degree," The headteacher thus expanded on his earlier information.

"That is very interesting! See, it didn't take us that long," The detective commented whilst looking at his watch as if to confirm his earlier assurance.

On that note, he rose to his feet, grasped, and shook the outstretched hand of the headteacher, and departed leaving the headteacher to get on with his domestic arrangements.

Two crowned Heads will lie uneasy tonight.

At the meeting with his Cabinet of senior staff earlier in the day, it did not escape the headteacher's notice that one of the two matters that most likely would be adversely affected by the recent unfortunate event would be 'the school's high-profile policy on equal opportunity and anti-racism'. Because he was committed to absolute secrecy, the head was only able to agree with this view at a shallow level: he could not fully share how true that vision was.

Tonight, he continues to wonder what effect all this was going to have on the York Conference at which Dixon Pen was due to figure high on the agenda? What will the spinoff be for his anticipated glorious retirement? Wass this going to tarnish his chances of a knighthood? If these things were adversely affected, it would be so grossly unfair both to him and his school. He was not a murderer and had no connection to one, so would, therefore, find it very hard to accept.

In these circumstances, it would be far better for the murderer if he or she wasn't born at all because, if the cops did not get him or her first, he, the headteacher, would surely make it his business to hunt him or her down, even to the Gates of Hell. This prospect of a knighthood would be so fitting and could come at an opportune time to lend kudos and prestige in the time vicinity of his daughter's marriage to her Swedish fiancé—who could wish for a better grand finale?

Before sleeping off for the night, two other matters appeared in the thoughts of the headteacher but only fleetingly. Firstly, he had not forgotten the fact that he had yet to resolve the outstanding issue of a stranger keeping Frankie from getting to his math lesson on time. He had promised Frankie's parents, Mr and Mrs Watson, that he would communicate further with them as soon as he had that matter clarified.

The headmaster was not totally convinced that Frankie was being truthful. After all, this young man hates math lessons and would do almost anything to help him evade them. When speaking to the Chief Inspector and Detective Corporal Brown on the night of the murder and impromptu interview, the headteacher remembered twice hesitating at points in the interview when he had to refer to Frankie's reported stranger.

He remembers now that those hesitancies had to do with it occurring to him that he had a murderer on his hand and a pupil had reported a stranger in the school the day before. The head vaguely wondered to himself whether there might be a connection, but he also remembered personally checking the

'Visitor's to the School Record' on the day in question but there was no such entry.

In any case, the headteacher had thought the alleged visitor was not on the day of the murder. It was said to be the day before. Frankie, in the presence of his parents, will now be interviewed by the police. The headteacher wasn't sure why but maybe the fact that he had mentioned a stranger in the school looking for his sister, Elaine Edgewater, was pertinent as far as the police were concerned.

If that was the case, then it would bring closure to this outstanding matter to his parents' satisfaction, and he could thereby drop the matter too. Everyone should know the outcome of Frankie's interview very soon in any case.

Secondly, the headteacher distinctly remembered asking his PA to search tomorrow's Tuesday Education Guardian News Paper for any reference or report concerning the forthcoming York conference and she knows that he was definitely very interested in that conference, even if she didn't know the full extent of his interest.

He could therefore go to sleep knowing that even if circumstances should present diversions to prevent him from personally seeking out the Education Guardian; he had a reliable backup in his PA.

Meanwhile, over at Burney's' house, Bianca was in a quandary. During the school day, the complexity and multifarious demands of her job successfully keep her mind well shielded from the pressures of the many extraneous issues threatening to sink her. Away from the job, however, they all come rushing back to her with renewed venom.

It was extremely difficult for her not to be able to share some of these matters, beyond school matters, with Carlos. And yet, in time, he will get to know about them whether he or she wants him to know. It was just a matter of time before it will be all out into the open. For example, how will she ever be able to explain to Carlos that he was to become a father?

Carlos had been medically informed that he was no longer able to have children following his prostate operation. Gaston, the true father to be of her developing foetus, was nowhere available to her to discuss the matter with him at such a crucial time. She had these three choices facing her. In no order, they were these.

1. She could consider taking the easiest way out of her predicament by having an abortion at the relevant time. The practicalities could be made private

and convenient if timed for the approaching school summer holiday but that was as far as she was prepared to take that because that was absolutely forbidden by her religious tenets. Her conscience would be a forever burden on her already overloaded mind.

2. Bianca contemplated telling Carlos that a divine miracle had happened and caused him to father a child. At almost sixty-eight years of age coupled with his known medical record, it would be an extremely difficult one to sell. Carlos was already suspicious of her unfaithfulness. He had only recently gone into a tirade about some unknown 'character' he witnessed ravaging her with her consent in his car. Almost certainly he would see this baby as the product of all these clandestine sessions which I was, supposedly, having with this character. Almost certainly, such an attempt would signal the end of their marriage. This option, too, sees Bianca putting a line through it as extremely unworkable.

3. The third option was to come clean and be totally honest about the entire thing going back to just the first day after her marriage. Never mind how shameful it would seem for a woman to shamelessly sleep with her husband's 'Romeo' son just one day after she married his father and just the second day, she had known this Romeo, the resounding blow landing upon a father and son relationship would be unpredictable in its outcome. It would probably be fatal for Carlos to know that his wife and dearest son have for so long been deceiving him in his ignorance. This would mean blood on her hands so must, also, be a definite no. The futility of undertaking this analysis seems to be so stark that Bianca simply abandoned it and moved on to other equally challenging matters.

So much depends on finding out what was going on with Gaston, she thought. What was he up to? Does he know that the girl he was allegedly courting in Sweden had links back to her? Obviously, he did not; otherwise, he would not have taken the risk of sending his photograph to the headteacher of the school where his mother-in-law, who doubles as his concubine, works.

On the other hand, he might not be aware that his photo had been sent to his prospective father-in-law. More worrying was this Swedish connection, if Gaston was to, sometime in the future, marry the headteacher's daughter, he would be doing so fraudulently—impersonating someone else for the purpose of a nuptial arrangement.

What was in it for Gaston that would make him go to such an extent of deception? Bianca had no way of answering any of these questions which she was addressing herself. The only thing that was clear was that the whole inexplicable thing was one hell of a mess with serious implications for her, Gaston, his father, Doreen, Mr Austin, and maybe a great many others.

By way of mentally signing off for the night, Bianca turned to any urgent business that she had lined up for tomorrow. There were not many: just one: one very important one. On her way to school tomorrow, she will call a newspaper agency and pick up a copy of the Tuesday Education Guardian Newspaper. She knows this task to be very important because her boss had told her so.

The head had given her the special responsibility to chart the school in terms of its ethnicity breakdown and that was linked to some conference which was scheduled to happen in Yorkshire—The York Conference—she believes it was entitled, and the Secretary of State for Education himself, the Right Honourable Dean Hutchinson, MP, was scheduled to chair it with a lot of big names from the business and political worlds were expected to be in attendance on Wednesday of this week.

Such an important conference was bound to be featured in the Education Guardian's last edition before the conference, hence Mr Austin's special interest in tomorrow's edition of that paper.

The thought that finally sent Bianca into a deep slumber for the night was of her daughter, Helen, wanting to entertain her on Wednesday. Helen was a wonderful girl. She was Bianca's only child who was now twenty-three years of age. She had the misfortune of being brought up by a single parent after her mother and daddy drifted apart soon after she was born.

Consequently, she had grown to be the love of her mother's life. Bianca will do anything for her daughter. She only must ask. This Wednesday was going to be a soothing tonic for Bianca, who had a very good relationship with her daughter in that they do talk very openly and honestly with each other.

Helen had expressed a wish to talk privately with her about something which was very important but maybe she too could use the opportunity to lighten her load by sharing some of the things that were causing her deep worries and sleepless nights at present. She might even get some good and workable advice from her lovely daughter and soul mate, she thought, as she snoozed away.

Chapter 7

"Wow, Mr Austin isn't going to like this!" She skimmed the pages of the Education Guardian for the second time to ensure that she missed nothing of importance.

On her way to work, Bianca had bought a copy of this morning's edition of the paper as planned. The only thing she could find that was of relevance to her search was a snippet of news that was tucked away on page three. It read:

"The Secretary of State for Education, the Right Honourable Mr Dean Hutchinson, MP, wishes to advise readers and all interested parties, that the education conference on ethnicity scheduled for Wednesday 19th May 2021 at York, had been cancelled."

That was it. There was absolutely nothing more.

It said "cancelled," not postponed.

Bianca picked up the Guardian News Paper, exited her new office and closed the door behind her and set off for the headteacher's office. She knocked on the door but there was no response. She was just about to knock again when the door to the headteacher's office began opening. Standing in the open door was the legitimate tenant of that office space; his countenance had a glum painted all over it.

"I know what you are here to tell me," he spoke, "On my way in I managed to pick up a copy of the paper and I found what you are holding in your hand right now," he continued.

Without expanding very much he murmured that this was the first real causality of that brutal murder. Bianca heard this. She said she was very sorry and departed to continue her day.

Meanwhile, back at Police Headquarters, the murdered victim's file was proving to be very revealing. With the aid of records from the social services department, the police have managed to piece together some facts about Mrs

Elaine Bridgewater who was linked to the National Insurance number: YA 66 10 53 B and which had been active and in the service at Dixon Pen until recently.

It was beginning to look as though Mrs Elaine Bridgewater did not die at the hands of a murderer. She was dead, alright but not by murder. She died of natural causes if you were to rely on the official autopsy report of fifteen years ago. She left behind thirteen-year-old identical twin girls, Gloria, and Madge. At the young age of forty when she passed away peacefully in her sleep; she had, even at that age, outlived two husbands.

John Upton, father of the identical twin girls was her first husband. He was killed in a motor car racing accident three years after they were married. The twins were just two years old. Some years later when the twins were five years old, Elaine, their mother remarried to Parker Bridgewater.

Even though Mr Bridgewater wasn't much of a father to the girls, he did try to keep them on a straight and narrow moral path until his own passing because of cancer when the girls were ten years old. Sadly, the girls also lost their mother, she too from cancer, by the time they had reached their teens.

Another oddity, the police found, was that the holder of the National Insurance number in question was a much older person than the murdered victim who was just twenty-eight at the time of her murder. Who then was the murdered imposter? The police were very much thinking that if they find the answer to this question, they should be well on their way to solving this crime.

Another matter of concern to the police was what became of the identical twins? Forgetting the pun, this could mean a twin tract investigation for the police department.

Somewhere else at Police Headquarters, the file of Bianca Burney was proving to be equally interesting but for different reasons. There was absolutely nothing in this lady's file that was of relevance to issues at the school. She had been around for many years and seems to have applied for the top job at least twice and each time she was unsuccessful.

On the second attempt, she lost to a black woman who was ten years her junior and for the last two years, she had had to take orders from her. These two facts, without more, by themselves, provide a credible motive for murder. The situation changes, however, when it was realised that, so far, Mrs Bianca Burney was the only person in the entire school that had benefited from the death of Elaine Bridgewater.

On the third day following the suspected murder, Mrs Burney finds herself sitting in the chair of the top job, albeit in an acting position.

On the strength of this third piece of fact, the police decided that Bianca Burney should be formally interviewed. This will be relayed to her as soon as possible, said Detective Corporal Brown who was a party to this decision.

On Wednesday morning bright and early Detective Corporal Brown was at the school to break some news to the headteacher as well as to inform Bianca Burney of the police's decision to conduct a formal interview with her and to agree on the time and place.

Mr Austin found it extremely difficult to understand and accept that for two long years he worked with and managed a PA and Chief Administrative Officer who was essentially an imposter. The detective wanted to know some more about the process through which she was appointed to the post two years ago. For example, did she hold a similar post before?

There were no notes on her file to answer that question. The headteacher immediately summoned his curriculum deputy, Mrs Patsy Jones who, together with the head and an education officer who is no longer with the education authority, was the third person on three persons interviewing panel that appointed Mrs Edgewater.

"Two out of three-panel members from two years ago, that is not bad. In fact, it is quite good," the detective corporal commented.

Once Mrs Jones had arrived, the headteacher then repeated the question which was of concern to the detective for her benefit.

"My recall is that she had no experience of ever working in schools before and she told us that straight away. I remembered thinking how forthright and honest she was with this important fact. Some other candidates might have tried to deceive the panel by omission.

"I think, in compensation, she had a high-powered executive reference which testified to her brilliance in performance as a personal assistant not to just one person but to all of three the top directors of a Board of Directors. If I remember rightly that reference also hailed her as an extremely quick learner and a compulsive workaholic. All three of us were exceptionally impressed with that reference, you might recall," Mrs Jones recalled.

"And in very quick time, the veracity of that reference was fully borne out in all its aspects. It truly amazed me how quickly she had grasped the job and how efficient and reliable she was. It is not uncommon to receive highfalutin references with the sole purpose of getting rid of dud staff. This was not one of those," the headteacher remarked.

"Was that reference put on her file?" Detective Brown asked.

"That would be normal procedure, detective," the headteacher answered.

"We did not find any references for her on her file, could anyone has removed it or them if there was more than one?" The detective probed further.

"It is distinctly possible that it could have been removed. However, who could have done that? All staff files were under the physical and confidential control of the deceased. She had access to her own file, obviously, and could, therefore, have removed it. But why would she: it was a flattering reference; the kind of thing any normal person would have wanted to proudly keep?" A thought contributed to the discussion by the headteacher.

"Was she a local candidate? The Board of Directors for whom she was working at the time, was based where? and what was the company's name?" The detective searchingly followed up.

"Ah, all those details would have been revealed on the notepaper on which her reference was written. I have seen and read so many references for this job; it is extremely difficult to recall accurately such essential details without the advantage of being able to consult relevant documentation. I am almost certain, however, that she was a Plymouth girl. Plymouth has come up often enough in many conversations she had with me," the headteacher thus supplemented his previous recall.

"Finally, can either of you enlighten me about the management of candidates', indeed, employees', National Insurance numbers?" the detective asked the headteacher and his deputy to bring closure to the impromptu interview.

This was an interview that he silently evaluated as being extremely helpful. In fact, it was exactly what he expected to hear if, as it seems, he was secondarily investigating the activities of an imposter: activities that may well have contributed to her death which was his primary concern.

"All matters to do with taxation, the Inland Revenue, and the National Insurance office fall squarely in the lap of the education authority. We, as a school, would simply advise the authority of any appointments we make, and they would take it from there. Why is that significant, detective?" Mr Austin counter-queried in his reply.

"Yes, it is very significant because I can share with you; that the deceased was employed on a National Insurance number that was never allocated to her. It might seem like an extraneous matter, but it could help in locating the murderer," the detective said as he rose to his feet, politely terminating the conversation with the headteacher and his deputy and asked to be directed to Mrs Burney's office.

Mrs Jones volunteered to escort him, on her way down, to the office in question.

As though she was anticipating his arrival, Mrs Burney welcomed Detective Corporal Brown into her new office most warmly.

"I have come to return your file, Mrs Burney. Our investigators can find no further use for it. We thought it was best under the circumstances to bring it back to the school at once. However, it was also thought that it would be prudent to have on records that we have spoken with you personally about the unfortunate events that took place in this school last Friday if you do not mind?" Detective Brown explained to the Acting Chief Administrative office with some directness.

"I can't say that I am not puzzled that anyone would want to talk to me about the recent events if, for no other reason, my ignorance of all that has happened is completely profound. Still, if you can extract anything from the totality of my ignorance, then, I am willing to cooperate with your investigation. When and where shall it be, Detective Brown?" Mrs Burney opined in reluctant surrender knowing full well that this was a pre-ordained inevitability.

"We could have this done here at the school if you could find us a private enough room, or your home could possibly work with us and, of course, we have specialised provision at the station. Any day in the next week, morning or afternoon would be good for us: the choice is going to be yours." This was the detective's response.

"Detective Corporal Brown let's get this over as quickly as possible. I will opt for next Monday the twenty-fourth of this month in the afternoon. I shall report to the station in Harbourne at two o'clock if that is OK with you. I can say with absolute certainty that my boss will accommodate that arrangement," Bianca said as she agreed with her choices.

"Good, our team will be very pleased to hear that we can get two interviews over in one afternoon. You will recall that, through you, we had arranged to see Frankie Watson and his parents also on Monday the twenty-fourth of May at the station. This is going to be most convenient for everyone," the detective exclaimed.

Bianca opted for the choice she did.

a. because she wants to minimise the number of visits to the school from the police because their presence tends to keep alive the curiosity of staff, pupils, parents strangers, and the media—all of which make the job for herself and her team considerable harder.

b. she chose not to have the police at her home because she didn't want to start any neighbourly gossips and certainly did not want this whole sordid affair to get any closer to her husband, Carlos and, if perchance he is at home, Gaston Burney as pissed off as she is feeling about the latter at the present moment.

The two officers of different sorts shook hands professionally and nodded to each other signalling that their minds had met regarding the arrangements just outlined and the detective was off on his way. It will be at least another week before he or his representative will be back at Dixon Pen Compressive School.

On his way home from school, the headteacher could focus on nothing else, at least not for long, beyond the loss that he and Dixon Pen Comprehensive School have clearly just suffered because of some atrocious action on the part of a brutal killer. The most painful part of all this is that he is unable to share the extent of his pain. What was more, he had no way of telling how far the blow had penetrated.

Is it total or could there be a recovery with time? He resolved that he would give it a few days to blow over and then he will contact his informant who swore him to secrecy to see if he can learn anything about the current thinking in high quarters. Maybe he will learn something that will allow him to quantify the depth of the blow and to gather whether there was anything that he can do to ameliorate the situation.

Or will he learn that all was totally lost? In other words, and directly to the point, was 'Sir' Allen Austin a lost dream or likely to be realised in the future, near or far? He needs to know something: it was driving him crazy in ways that cannot be imagined.

For a moment, he allowed a thought to creep in about his former PA and Chief Administrative Officer. Why would she impersonate anyone? What did she have to gain by doing this? Had this got anything to do with her ultimate slaughter?

The system had failed almost everyone including Elaine Bridgewater in not detecting the false use of another person's National Insurance number for over a period of two years, surely? Maybe we will have some answers soon, he thought as he pulled into his garage at Lavender Mews in Sutton Cold Field.

At four o'clock precisely, Helen Smith pulled into the visitors' car park at Dixon Pen. She was punctual as was her wont. She didn't want to keep her darling mother waiting.

On the way home to Kings Heath, for that was where Helen lives, the slow-moving evening rush hour traffic was the sole conversation piece. A normally twenty-minute journey was, on account of the traffic, stretched to almost one hour.

It was an understatement to say that mother and daughter had, at times, become miserable and frustrated with, what seemed at times, like standstill traffic. Nothing of substance was injected into the conversation by either party until they arrived at Helen's home.

Helen had prepared a most delicious dinner. The dinner table was already spread and set for two people before they got indoors. Once Helen had served up the previously prepared meal, they both sat down to enjoy what seemed like a sumptuous banquet. It was then that the conversation in earnest truly began. The loquacious Mrs Burney set the ball rolling with a detailed update on the scandal at Dixon Pen.

Helen came to know all about who was interviewed by the police, who was next in line, and that her own mother was scheduled for the coming Monday where and why. She received a good lecture on how her mother came to be promoted within two days of the ghastly murder at the school.

"Mother, darling, you came to listen to my concerns, but it seems like you have hijacked the evening. There is so much more that I would like to know about all those things you were talking about but that would mean postponing tonight's arrangements for another time," Helen timely intervened.

"Oh no, we must not do that. Tonight, is your night. I am sorry that I went on and on about all those other things. They can wait for another time, really. I know you arranged this evening because you have 'important' matters which you want to discuss with me, so I will shut up, continue enjoying this wonderful meal, and give the floor to you," Bianca said as she handed the talking reins to her beloved daughter.

"Did you want to call Carlos and check whether he is OK?" Helen asked her mother.

"Not right now: we will see how it goes as the evening progresses. I had organised his meal and everything early this morning; he just must microwave some things and he will be alright. He was a little jealous that he wasn't invited but came to accept that girls do like to have the occasional girlies' night. We won't do this too often without him, I sweetly reminded him," Bianca assured Helen.

"Mother dear, your daughter's life seems to be in ruins," Helen began.

You could see Bianca's maternal instinct immediately sprang to attention.

"Why is this, sweetheart? I did notice on your face that something was not right that evening when you dropped by with the invitation for tonight. What is happening in your life, my sweet?" Bianca probed anxiously.

"For about a year now, I have been seeing this young man who swept me off my feet at first sight. Let me come straight to the point. Immediately after I met him, my instinct told me that he was interested in me; maybe not so much in me but certainly, I felt he wanted my body. I put this to the test the first opportunity I had but he played hard to get. He left me frustrated and horny as hell and just laughed and went away to where I did not know."

Bianca listened intently and as though she was reliving a similar experience, as Helen continued.

"That night, I was so humiliated; I became mad as hell. No one, before this 'Samsonite King Cong' of a man had ever managed that feat with me as the subject. After all, I am no run-of-the-mill girl in terms of my physical attributes. I swore then that I would seduce him if it was the last thing I ever did. Mother, that was the error I made," Helen admitted as she mentally and silently recalled what happened just two days later to the 'Samsonite King Cong' when he returned for "just dinner", he had said.

On that second night, 'Samsonite King Cong', as Helen styled him, turned out to be human after all. He could play his game no more, he later admitted. Once, he had dined; he wanted to watch some big football match on the television.

That gave Helen the glorious opportunity to slip quietly outside in the quiet of the night. Her purpose was to ensure that her man would not just bid her goodbye this time and slip away leaving her devalued once more. Helen was prepared. She turned her attention to Gaston's regular car: A white E-Type

Jaguar (TRY 123 B). Bianca had memorised that licence plate number as he drove away the first time. She quickly checked the plate to be sure that she had the right vehicle.

Once she had verified it was his, she got to work and blew out all the air from all four tyres flat as a Jamaican Cassava bammy using a simple matchstick. She hurried back inside, closed the door behind her, and rejoined her man in the TV room to get a report on the progress of the match. His side, 'Spurs', was winning two-nil at the time against Liverpool.

Eventually, the match came to an end and her man became hilarious with joy. At that point, his mobile phone rang, and it was Mavis calling. Helen could see that on the phone just before he retrieved it from the sofa where he had rested it throughout the match. His stomach was now full, his side had the three-nil, a woman had called him and now he was ready to go, still playing hard to get.

'King Cong' pocketed his phone: gently pulled Helen to his bosom pecked her sweetly on her cheek and whispered thank you for a lovely meal. He told her that he had to go to join the boys in celebration of the match. He then reached for his car keys and headed for the front door and the darkness of the night.

When he had pulled Helen close to him, she had felt a warm sexual surge running through her entire body. She wanted to feel this brute of a man inside her even more than on the first night when he had walked away from her lusting exuberance. Tonight, it will be different; she had thought as she headed towards her bedroom where she waited patiently.

In due course, 'King Cong' came knocking. He opened the door to find a demurely beautiful naked woman standing there. He choked on what he was about to tell her about his car. She was too irresistible for him to continue, so, he froze. The tables had turned. She pulled him gently towards her nakedness and helped him to undress whilst still standing in the doorway.

King Cong surrendered and succumbed to the wiles of his conqueror. His whole body had become wearily arrested and domesticated in unconscious slumber. His dream might well be around the essence of Sampson and Delilah, who knows?

He repeated this act three more times throughout the night and each was qualitatively better than the previous. And the next morning, Helen knew she was hooked, and hooked good and proper. At age 24, she had not had many men, but she had had a few; none, however, had ever satisfied her so robustly like this guy has. For this alone, she was his forever.

"I don't understand: what mistake did you make? Tell me about it," Bianca urged.

"Mother, going to bed with this man opened my eyes, my legs, and my mind to the kind of sexual experience that I had never thought possible. The kind which when you find it, you never ever want to let go off it. Mother, but briefly, I became hooked to this man, hooked like a fish to a baited hook. Life after that was so sweet. I could always count on him to be by my side at times when I needed him most.

"Occasionally, he had to slip away on business, but it was never more than for a week. Then he would come back to me bringing perfume, chocolate, and other various types of gifts as presents. He was such a charmer: flowers, in particular roses, were always part of his amour. I had found the man that I had waited all this time to meet.

"Above all, I was never wanting for sex. I had that from him regularly and often repeatedly until one day I caught him red-handedly cheating on me in my own bed. Since then, I have seen less and less of him. He seems to have more and more business trips which are longer in duration. His sexual urges for me are declining.

"All happening at a time when am going to need him even more. Mother, you are about to become a grandmother. I am pregnant, mother. I am three months pregnant," Helen declared the plain truth.

To say that Helen's mother was stunned to have all this dropped upon her just like that and for the first time would be the understatement of the decade. Bianca had always bragged about the daughter and mother relationship which she had with Helen. They were always totally open with each other and certainly never kept secrets from each other.

That she was only now learning about Helen's highly kept secret from her for as long as a year was a major blow to what she had always cherished about the relationship with her only child. Bianca then looked back on herself and became quite frightened as she recognised many elements of hypocrisy in what she was thinking. Did she not keep a secret what had been going on between her and Gaston Burney for a similar length of time?

Wake up, she said to herself. We were dealing with human beings, and we were all subject to changes and variations in our behaviour subject to circumstances. Circumstances could be such that you were forced to abandon normative behaviour as in my present situation, she thought. In view of this, I must not be too harsh with Helen. But what a coincidence; I have been expecting my first child since giving birth to Helen twenty-four years ago, and that child is concurrently announcing the coming into being of her first child.

That fact Bianca considered that to be very good news for her. What mother doesn't look forward to the day when she becomes a grandmother. She wished, though, that the relationship climate was different for Helen. Maybe things will get better for her once the father to be learns that he had procreated.

She did notice, however, that Helen had not told her who the father of her child was. Why is it that she had never met her daughter's beau? Maybe the time wasn't right, Bianca rationalised.

"My daughter, I do not wish to lecture you. You are an adult and must make choices for yourself. However, from personal experiences and those of many others I know, a sound relationship is rarely founded upon 'hot sex'."

Look who was talking, Bianca thought to herself wryly.

"You see, once the sex thing wears off, you are then faced with the realities and hard facts of life. If the relationship can survive these later issues, then you are unto a good thing. So where is your 'Samsonite King Cong' at present? And why do you call him that: does he not have a proper name? In a whole year, you have not mentioned his name, even once," Bianca awkwardly grappled with her own hypocrisy and motherly instinct.

"Where is my 'Samsonite King Cong' right now? Who knows? The last message I got from him; he was in Switzerland gallivanting with friends."

Bianca almost fell off the chair on which she was sitting. This cannot be a coincidence. It was far too close to home.

"Say that again, did you say Switzerland? Where in Switzerland? And when was this?" Bianca nervously fired off a barrage of questions at her daughter in rapid quick-fire fashion.

"He was moving from one city to the other which gave me the feeling that he was gallivanting. I think he was in Geneva when he called last Saturday night. But, according to him, he was going to be moving on to Zurich and some other place which I cannot recall. I have heard nothing since," Helen replied.

Bianca remembered the identical story her husband, Carlos, received from his son, Gaston, the same Saturday night in question. Same night, same places in Switzerland.

She even remembered debunking that story as being rigged to look like a conference call, though she could not find a reason why it needed to be doubted.

She had, however, found some reinforcement for her belief because the contents of the secret compartment in Gaston's room were missing as was the Sunday paper which Carlos wanted so very much to read by the time, she got back from the working lunch with the headteacher on the following Sunday.

This whole thing stinks of Gaston Burney. Bianca was, by this, bracing herself for what she believed she was about to hear: that Gaston Burney, her husband's blue-eyed son, both literally and figuratively, had impregnated both mother and daughter in roughly the same period.

"You still have not told me who this 'Samsonite King Cong' is. I would truly like to know and to learn how you came to meet him. Don't keep me in suspense any longer. Who is this man?" Bianca urged her daughter to be forthright in her revelations.

"Mother, I have never told you his name or introduced you to him because you already knew his name and had already met him and, in many senses of the word, I was seriously ashamed of the relationship, but heavens know that I was captivated and captured so irrevocably by this man, I could not help myself until it was far too late. I thought you might have guessed when I insisted that I needed to talk with you alone.

"You see, I would have choked up if I had to tell you all this about Gaston Burney in the presence of his father. Mother, I realised that this is a tangled web; but to be true to yours and my custom and practice of sharing truthfully and openly with each other, I just had to share it all with you even if cowardice and shame forced a delay upon me.

"I am sorry for the delay and for the music you will now face when you must disclose it to your husband in your way. I cannot imagine what Carlos 'reaction will be when you have to tell him he is to be a grandfather because his beloved son has had a union with your beloved daughter," Helen breathes a sigh of relief as she gets it off her chest completely.

For Bianca, this must be the end of the road for her and Gaston. There was no foul adjective—or noun, for that matter—that was too low to call Gaston. This man was so low he would have to look up to see the gutter. Her resentment was total and complete. She was feeling only revenge of the highest order for this cold-blooded skunk. She swore she would find a way to get even and do him harm.

She was now wondering whether it was time to share with her daughter what she had discovered at the working luncheon. At the time of the discovery, she thought it had implications only for her. Today it was a different matter: it now included her only daughter. She thought better of sharing it. Her daughter's state of mind was somewhat delicate at present and, should she learn another woman in Sweden were betrothed to Gaston Burney, it could be the straw that pushed her over the edge.

She decided against this. She also decided against sharing her own pregnancy situation with her only daughter for the same reason she would not say anything about the Swedish engagement. There was the added reason of whether she would lose the respect of her wonderful daughter, friend, and companion over many trying years given the adulterous picture she would have had to paint of herself to her own daughter in these awful times.

Her resolve, therefore, was to follow up on two of her earlier probes which Helen either overlooked or deliberately ignored.

"Helen, how did it all begin with Gaston? How did you meet? Please enlighten me," Bianca vehemently insisted.

"Mother, I first met Gaston Burney the day you married his father. I think that was the day you met him for the first time too. At least, that is what he told me. You were far too wrapped up in the happiness of the day to even notice that someone had eyes for your only child. It didn't matter where I went that day; he would somehow find himself next to me.

"He had little interest in what was taking place between you and his father. He just wanted to make small talk with me and was making it very clear that he wanted my body that same night, but your reception got in the way of his mental plans. I wanted him too but that could wait whilst I celebrated your joyous occasion with you. At the end of the day, we became separated for various reasons.

"Then, you might recall, Jo and Jacky joined me in preparing a grand supper for you and Carlos. Gaston was part of that. During the evening, Gaston tricked me into parting with my mobile number. He was quite open about it so you might remember him saying to me that evening that his phone didn't seem to be working and as a result he gave me his number in the presence of everyone and asked me to test his phone by dialling the number.

"Nothing was wrong with Gaston's phone; I would subsequently discover. It was all a ploy to get my number registered on his as a missed call. That night, soon after I did the test on his phone he retired to the bathroom, you might recall.

The true purpose of that bathroom visit was to save my number to his phone, he later confessed.

"Why he went to such great lengths just to get my number, I will never know. He had only to ask for it and I would have gladly given it to him and hoped he would make use of it. That was how sold I was on him. Perhaps he was secretive and sneaky because of your and his dad's presence. Or should I have seen this ploy as a reason to question his confidence?

"Anyway, the very next day, he called me just out of the blue. I didn't recognise who it was and that was when he confessed how he came by my number and then I placed him. He wanted to know if he could see me that night if I lived on my own. I assured him that I was a single girl, and I could hear him mumble to himself 'what a waste'.

"He made no bones about it: he made it clear that he wanted my body there and then. I told him to give me five minutes and then call me back. During those five minutes, I saved his number to my phone for future use. This I should have done when he first gave it to me for testing purposes at the grand supper. I had had a previous arrangement for that night with Jo and Jacky.

"I didn't think the arrangement was important, but I needed a few minutes to alert the girls that I would be dropping out of the plan for the evening rather than just not turning up and having them interrupt the evening, with Gaston, by telephone to find out why I didn't show up. No sooner than this was done: Gaston was back on the line. Without hesitation, I gave him my address and told him it was fine for him to come around. From that point on, I was in a daze. I didn't think it would happen so soon. I was over the moon with lustful desires, my head also whirling with loads of romantic projects. And, mother, you know the story from here. It was appalling how coldly he treated me that first evening and this is where it all led to another human being on the way," Helen said, pointing to her slightly bulging tummy.

A confused and terribly hurt Bianca from this point seemed inclined to want to blame Helen for leading on Gaston Burney just so that she could get him into her bed. Why did she have to hunt in her mother's husband's garden? Though she really meant her mother's garden, she had neither the audacity nor moral uprightness to say so.

She implied that Helen had acted with such moral turpitude she really wasn't a fit person for a polite society. She was so unladylike and common; it was very much contrary to her upbringing. She had no idea how the rest of decent society would react when all this was out in the light of day. What was also so bad about the whole affair was that she was not just her mother but also her friend and confidante.

Yet, she had no opportunity to offer a guiding hand because Helen acted so secretively.

"As for Gaston, he never let on that he was having an affair with you or anyone else for that matter. I am almost certain that his father is as much in the dark about this matter as I was until today. Oh, well, his father's wish for his son is that he should *"...start a family with a sensible and respectable young lady"."*

He certainly had started a family but which, if any of us two can be considered sensible and respectable? On reflection, Bianca silently thought that she would be disqualified; but how would Helen score?

"Helen, to be frank, I don't think you behave properly in all of this, especially knowing that by virtue of my marriage to Gaston's dad, you are by extension a part of our family. It is almost incestuous what you have done."

In view of Bianca's moral drift in this situation involving her daughter and her son-in-law lover, the officious bystander reader, having some prior insight into Bianca's own behaviour might well conclude that she was living in a completely different reality.

In view of what the reader already knows, surely, this moral outburst and admonishment directed at Helen must make it so much more difficult for Bianca to explain her own predicament when the time comes. She was going to need the shoulders of the very person that she now treats with scornful disdain.

Helen became somewhat taken aback by this holier-than-thou attitude coming from her mother who had never been like that with her over all these years. First, there was intense questioning with hardly any visible understanding or signs of sympathy coming from her mother. Where were the hugs and sympathetic understanding?

Secondly, what, in effect, turned out to be an onslaught of interrogation was soon followed by the passing of judgment and condemnation. This was not the mother she knew. Something clearly had gone wrong.

Bianca, sensing that she was helplessly drowning in a sea of hypocrisy whilst mercilessly doing considerable mental harm to her only child, looked anxiously at her watch and began gathering her belongings as though she was ready to go. Helen noted the restlessness in her mother's actions and questioned whether she was ready to depart.

"It appears as though you are ready to go home mother?"

"Yes, dear, it is getting quite late. Carlos will soon be wondering what we are up to so late."

"OK, I will just gather up the dishes and I will take you home as planned," Helen assured her mother.

By this Bianca was feeling that the journey home with Helen might be very awkward. Deep down, she knew it would be no fault of Helen's, but she was feeling so hopelessly trapped and entangled, that she realised that she would not be good company for anyone. She needed to avoid this trip with Helen at all costs.

"Sweetheart, you have too much on your plate to be planning on doing the journey to Camper at this time of the night and then having to travel back on your own. That is ridiculous. Why don't you just call me a taxi? I have enough cash with me; I will be able to pay the fare. This way it will be easier for everyone," Bianca conveniently suggested.

Helen would not hear of it and forcefully responded, "Mother, my word is my bond. We agreed in the beginning that I would fetch you from school at the end of the school day, we would have supper here whilst we chatted about the terrible situation in which I had found myself and then I would take you back before Carlos goes to sleep. All other parts of this agreement have been fulfilled and I intend to fulfil this last part too."

Then there was a plea from Bianca.

"To be quite truthful, Helen, the way I am feeling right now I will be extremely selfish and would make very bad company. I just need the solitude of the ride home to be alone with my thoughts for a little while.

"With you in the car, I will not get that and, certainly, when I get home, I will not get that either because Carlos will be wanting to know what we did tonight, and I am in no mood or shape to relay the essence of your story to him as we know it. Please, please call me a taxi, it is getting late, and I have school tomorrow."

Helen's heart rushed to a state of melting and so, she reached into her desk drawer and produced several cards—all bearing the names of different taxi firms and their telephone numbers. The very first one that Helen dialled said they would have a car sent to her address in just five minutes and they did.

Helen and her mother recaptured some of their usual rapport: embraced each other and said their good night salutations. Bianca got aboard the waiting taxi and as the vehicle was out of sight Helen shut the door behind her and cried herself bitterly to the emptiness of her bed.

The evening traffic was beginning to die down and so the drive over the five or so miles to Camper would be shorter in time than otherwise, it would be. However, some time saving would still be lost because the rain had begun to fall with the consequential effect of slowing the traffic down somewhat.

At the same time, the rain shower was constantly beating on the roof of the moving vehicle and some of its drops sliding down the windows as if to epitomise the bitter tears that were Helen's at the said moment in time.

The rain drops also gave some solace to the distressed Bianca Burney, now in a daze miserably gazing from the moving vehicle. The neon lights from dazzling advertisement boards across town seemed more colourful and attractive against the background of the falling night rain. This made Bianca much more relaxed and opened to her now much more reasonable analysis of Helen's predicament.

Across the road, she could see dozens of pedestrians dodging the spouts of neighbouring umbrellas as they hurried to escape the rain before getting soaked and drenched. One person caught Bianca's eye. This was a young lady that seemed to be around Helen's age, height, and builds. She was holding her umbrella in her right hand as she used her left to give protection and guidance to her child about four years old.

The scene was both awkward and uncomfortable in the rain with passing vehicles unwittingly and unintentionally splashing the pedestrians including the mother and child. This imagery prompted Bianca to indulge in a flashback to an almost identical situation long ago on an awfully wet night with Helen when she was about four years of age just like this little girl was now; the picture was of importance to Bianca because of another reason too. She was imagining Helen being in a similar situation in the not-too-distant future and wondered how she would cope.

The taxi had by this reached less lit vicinities and so there were fewer interesting sights to dominate Bianca's mind. This brought back the earlier situation with her daughter, herself, Gaston, and Carlos, never mind Sweden and possibly beyond, in much sharper focus for the remainder of the journey to Camper.

The almost hopelessness of the unimaginable tangled web made her recall some old literature she once read with limited understanding then. It was becoming so much clearer in the present context.

"Heaven has no rage like love to hatred turned, nor Hell a fury like a woman scorned," Bianca was now revisiting William Congreve's 'The Mourning Bride' (1697).

"Watch out, Gaston Burney, you have something coming your way," Bianca murmured to herself as she alighted from the taxi at Passion Street, in Camper, Birmingham, and the rain now just slightly drizzling allowed her to get inside still mostly dry.

As Bianca entered her home, she looked frantically for Carlos' whereabouts. He was already in bed, it seemed: far too exhausted to wait for her any longer. She checked the cup and saucer sitting almost at the edge of the dining room table with its half-drunken contents. Whatever Carlos had made himself for a nightcap was still warm and probably tasteless, hence its unfinished remainder, so Bianca knew that he wasn't long gone to bed.

She went directly to the bedroom that she shared with Carlos and gently opened the door with the sole intention of announcing her return to Carlos. However, Carlos was already deep in sleep as he normally was in the evening. She quietly drew closer to her sleeping husband in the dim of the bedroom light and gave him a peck on his waiting forehead.

As she turned to visit the bathroom for freshen-up purposes, she noticed a familiar handwritten note on Carlos' bedside table.

It read: "Dad, I am around— no you or Bianca. I will not be home tonight but will check you both in a day or two. Hope you are staying safe from COVID-19 and its numerous variants. See you soon."

The handwriting was unmistakable. Bianca had seen many similar notes before. Gaston, she thought was up to his usual lifestyle and practice: gallivanting, flirting with and effectively ruining the lives of vulnerable women who fall for his charm, sex appeal, and good looks and will let him much to their later regrets.

The note was not timed so there was no way of knowing what time Gaston was here today. Carlos must have slipped out for one of his brisk walks when Gaston came and subsequently left his true form and character note.

On the way out of her in-suite bathroom she thought further to herself as she crept into the sheets next to her lightly snoring husband:

"I have a plan about which I will consult with my daughter, Helen, as soon as possible."

Chapter 8

Monday the twenty-fourth of May had arrived. This day signalled those two members of Dixon Pen School will be seen by the police in connection with the brutal murder under their investigation. Both interviews were to be conducted at Harbourne Police Station in the afternoon of that day. Throughout the course of the usual, busy morning, Bianca Burney was mentally preoccupied trying to anticipate what the questions to be directed at her would be.

She was still stubbornly of the view that there was nothing that she could tell the police that could in any way be useful to them. She timely remembered that the other person to be interviewed at the same station today was Frankie Watson and he would be accompanied by both his parents. In fact, it was she who had made all the arrangements for the interview with the Watsons.

It was even more difficult for her to understand what role Frankie could be playing in this saga; but then, she thought that the police ought to know best; and, maybe, she would see Frankie and his parents at the station sharing feelings. These thoughts now helped her to resign herself to what seemed to her to be a pre-destined groove with no way out of it.

At the station, Bianca got the feeling that, from the inside, this blue and white imposing monstrosity for a police den was much more friendly and harmless than she had hitherto assumed when on many previous other unrelated trips, she had gone past it.

Whilst Bianca waited in the reception area for her interviewing personnel to appear, she noticed both uniformed and non-uniformed male and female police officers milling about on the inside. There were also many civilians like her arriving for their differing purposes. What was noticeable was that none of the officers passed her by without acknowledging her presence and querying whether she was being seen to or in need of assistance. Indeed, twice she was asked if she would like a drink of some sort whilst she waited.

Just as her interview panel arrived, she observed Frankie Watson and his mum and dad arriving through the front door. A reception officer greeted them and directed them to the seating area which Bianca had just vacated on her way to the interviewing room reserved for her.

Bianca's interviewing personnel explained that the Watsons will be taken to another room for their interview. As it turned out, Bianca was deprived of that 'sharing of feeling' moment that she had anticipated with the Watsons.

It was later learned that the police interviewing personnel, there were two of them, really wanted to know whether there was any animosity between Bianca and Elaine Bridgewater. Bianca had explained that at first, she mildly resented the fact that an outsider had been appointed over her.

This was largely to do with the fact that, from the records, she, Bianca, had longer and more relevant experience for the job which was advertised. The police were very interested to know whether Elaine's colour and younger age made a difference in how she was accepted. Bianca was quick to reject any such idea of racial difficulties. She was also very emphatic that age played no part in her earlier responses to Elaine.

The officers also wanted to know about the responses of the other team members to Mr Bridgewater's appointment. Bianca was quick to assure the officers that the other team members were very quick to accept their new boss. In just a matter of a few days, it had become obvious that the team was going to knit together much more warmly and quickly than when it was under the leadership of the outgoing Chief Administrative Officer, Mrs Barron, on retirement.

Perhaps what brought the team together so quickly was the speed with which Elaine mastered the job. Additionally, she was kind, very considerate about the feelings of the members of her team, and above all her willingness to listen to the concerns of her team members.

That ring that had permanently adorned Elaine's left hand was a great conversational piece among them. None of them had ever seen a ring like that. Its uniqueness and apparent high price tag made them wonder why Elaine was always wearing that ring. They thought that it should have been something that was suitably insured and vaulted for special occasions. But Elaine had assured them that for sentimental reasons, she would not part company with that ring, not even for a minute.

Bianca could remember very clearly that it was that ring that broke the ice between Elaine and the rest of the team members; and since then, there was never any looking back until some nasty hoodlum came along and did what had now preoccupied the school, the police, and almost everyone.

The police thought that Bianca's account of hers and the team's reaction to Elaine's appointment was so sufficiently and convincingly told, that they could just let go of that line of investigation. But somewhere in the back of their mind, they just wondered whether Bianca might just be a brilliant actress and that some of her unsuspecting telephone conversations with team members, or friends and relatives might just show otherwise.

The chief interviewing officer then turned to Bianca and said:

"Mrs Burney, we shall bring this meeting to a close right now but to be tidy, we would like you to leave your mobile phone with us for a day or two, no longer. Your headteacher will testify to the fact that we kept our word and got his phone back to him in just two days. We have the facility; we can make it happen. We hope you don't mind and please forgive the short-term inconvenience this will cause?"

And suddenly Bianca remembered that she was unable to reach Mr Austin on his mobile phone all that Saturday, the day after the murder. Yes, the police had interviewed him on the evening of the murder and must have taken his mobile phone from him as they were doing to her right now.

"It is not something that I am going to accommodate very easily right now; but if you think it will assist you in your investigation, here it is," Bianca said as she handed her phone to the officers.

Meanwhile and elsewhere in the station under the silent participation but watchful eye of his mum and dad, the young fifteen-year-old Frankie Watson was talking to two other police officers about the day before the murder took place at Dixon Pen School.

The officers, Chief Inspector Harding, and Detective Corporal Brown, who had interviewed the headteacher on the night of the murder, had detected several unexplained hesitations on the part of the headteacher when he had to recall his encounter with Frankie on the day before the murder took place.

It was the hesitancies on the part of the headteacher which made them want to hear the story directly from Frankie under the supervision of his parents.

Detective Corporal Brown thanked the Watsons for their cooperation with his investigation. He ascertained whether the family needed a drink before getting started. The day was very warm and so, all three requested a cold drink of orange juice. The niceties now over, the detective and his colleague got down to the business of the afternoon.

"Frankie, you do know that there was a very serious crime committed at your school on Friday thirteenth of this month, do you?" The detective gently asked Frankie in opening the interview.

Frankie furtively glanced in the direction of both his parents as if to seek approval before answering the question. Having found no disapproval indicated, he turned to the questioner and replied.

"Yes, sir, I know about it".

"We do not want to ask you anything about the day of the murder or anything about the murder itself. We are only concerned with your activities on the day before. That is your movement on Thursday twelfth day of May. We are given to understand that you had an encounter with your headteacher that morning sometime after your morning break had ended and you should have been in your math lesson. Is that correct, Frankie"? The detective pointedly followed up.

This time with greater and growing confidence, Frankie did not bother with the glancing consultation of his parents. He replied with certainty; the kind that belies honesty.

"Yes, sir, on the way back from Mrs Edgewater's office, the headteacher saw me and wanted to know why I was late for the lesson. I told him that Mrs Edgewater's brother had asked me to show him where her office is because he wanted to surprise her because he hadn't seen her for a very long time. So, I quickly took him there and was hurrying to my lesson when the headteacher saw me," Frankie explained.

At this point, it could be observed that Frankie's parents nodded their heads in acknowledgment of their son's consistency in his story. That was exactly what he had said at the meeting in the headteacher's office on the day of the murder and before the murder was committed.

"Did you meet this stranger in the reception area after he had reported to reception?" The detective's colleague enquired.

"No, sir, I met him at the side entrance that leads down to the school canteens. I was at that gate doing my hobby for a competition when I saw him pull up in one of the cars that I was interested in," Frankie explained.

"Tell us a little more about this hobby of yours. What is it about"? The detective probed.

"My scout group from time to time runs competitions among the scouts and cubs to see who can collect the highest number of licence plate numbers of a specified make of cars. On this day the make was Toyota Celica.

"I wasn't having much luck when this guy showed up in a green one with the number plate HPH 344V. He got out of the car and asked me if I was from this school. When I told him 'Yes', he told me about his sister Mrs Edgewater who works here. I told him that I knew her, and it was then that he asked me to show him to her office," Frankie explained.

On the faces of the police officers, positive hope was written all over. As Frankie was speaking, they took copious notes, intervening only to seek clarity.

"Frankie, do you remember what this stranger looked like and what was he wearing"? the detective asked.

"I didn't take much notice of what he was wearing but I remember that he was tall with blond hair and piercing blue eyes," Frankie added for the benefit of the officers.

"I just want to ask you one final question, Frankie. After you showed him to Mrs Edgewater's office, did you see where he went? Did he enter the office?" The detective's colleague probed finally.

"No sir, I was getting late and so I ran off and left him looking at the office door and that was when I ran into the headteacher, as I told you before," Frankie sighed in relief as he gave his last response and he and his parents were advised that they could now leave for their home.

Chapter 9

A couple of days later, the twenty-sixth of May, once the police forensic department had completed their examination of Mrs Burney's mobile phone, Chief Inspector Harding—the officer in charge of the homicide at Dixon Pen, and his colleague, Detective Corporal Brown, felt it necessary to hold police only conference to ascertain what they had so far found out and to determine where they would go next.

The conference noted:

1. That the headteacher was the person who discovered Mrs Elaine Edgewater's dead body in her office and raised the alarm by reporting it to the police. This was not, so far, considered suspicious given the reported circumstances which led to the discovery. The police line of inquiry regarding this factual situation had now been paused.
2. Forensics had found the headteacher's fresh fingerprints on the external doorknob to the deceased office. Forensics had also taken swabs of the headteacher's foot tracks leading from the deceased office directly to the headteacher's office and had established conclusively that there were traces of the deceased blood on the soles of the headteacher's shoes. It remains the view that these facts were consistent with the headteacher's actions which led to the discovery of the crime. Here too, a pause on this aspect of the investigation had been advised.
3. It had been much rumoured and stated that the deceased should and would have been wearing a precious ring at the time of her demise. The police cannot establish or deny that allegation except to confirm that postmortem and forensic examination of the body revealed that marks on the third finger of the deceased's left hand indicated that it was

accustomed to being banded with a ring. This matter remains open to further inquiries.

4. The police have information to suggest with a fair degree of certainty that the deceased was not who she said she was. However, the deceased was employed at Dixon Pen Comprehensive School on the National Insurance Number of Mrs Elaine Edgewater who, though also is dead, had been long dead and was a much older person at the time than the deceased whose death we were currently investigating.

5. The true Mrs Elaine Edgewater died leaving identical twin girls. They were thirteen-year-old Gloria and Hazel Upton at the time of their mother's death. And it appears that their father, (Mr John Upton) from an earlier marriage that lasted only three years, died from a motor car racing accident when the girls were just two years old. Their adopted father, Parker Bridgewater, came on the scene when the girls were just five years, and he was gone again from cancer by the time the girls were ten years old. And, as already mentioned, by the time the girls had just reached their teens, they suffered the loss of their then forty-year-old mother, too from cancer. No one is yet sure of what became of the girls. The team needs answers here and will remain in focused pursuit of them.

6. The police carried out a very thorough search of the dead 'faked' Mrs Elaine Edgewater's home and found just two items of interest. One of these items is a note that looks like it was scribbled hurriedly on a bit of brown paper. It was found hidden at the bottom of a drawer containing the faked and dead Mrs Edgewater's lingerie. It simply read: **"They are in Box A"**. The second item of interest is a folder containing cuttings of an unsolved murder of many years ago (December 3rd, 2016). The names: Mustafa Banks, Robert Reid, and Gloria Upton were mentioned somewhat inconsistently throughout some of the cuttings from different News Papers. It had not been possible to see what any of the characters mentioned had to do with the unsolved case. The police, however, needed more information on this unsolved case which we understand had gone cold if for no other reason, the method of slaughter, in that case, bears a close resemblance to our current case. This area of investigation is still very wide open for us.

7. Because of the examination of Mrs Bianca Burney's mobile phone, the police were now interested in some photographic documentary material

found on her phone. Nothing else found on that phone was of any interest to the police.
8. Following the interview of the young lad, Frankie Watson in the presence of his parents, two very interesting angles have emerged. Firstly, who was the stranger who visited the school the day before the murder and claimed to be the murdered victim's brother? Secondly, we know that the stranger in question drove a green Toyota Celica with licence plate number: HPH 344V. It stands to reason that these issues will be vigorously pursued.

Some two days, on Wednesday the twenty-sixth of May, after the interview with Mrs Burney, the police kept their word and returned to the school to return her mobile phone. Very conveniently, the school had just been dismissed and in the throng of a dismissed school at home time, the police were hardly noticed as they headed for Mrs Burney's office. They rapped on her office door and were invited in almost instantly.

"Hello, Mrs Burney, It appears we caught you just in time. You were just in the act of leaving for home, it seems. We hope we can delay you for just a few more minutes whilst we return your phone and clarify just a few minor matters," Detective Corporal Brown said by way of greetings on entering Mrs Burney's office.

Mrs Burney, who was not quite sure whether Gaston, who normally chauffeurs her to and from school when he was around, would be collecting her, was somewhat hesitant. Normally, she would have received a message via her mobile phone from Gaston to say what was happening.

This was not possible today because the police had had her phone for the last couple of days. Hearing, however, that her phone was about to be returned to her, she acquiesced to the detective's desires.

"Officers, it is very good to see you. You have absolutely no idea about how inconvenient it has been for me not to have use of my phone. Right now, I am not even sure about how I am getting home because my stepson who sometimes takes me home would normally have communicated his intention via my phone.

"As it is, it is all guessed work without my phone. However, yes, I will cooperate with your wishes even if I must struggle on the buses getting home in the evening rush traffic once you are through with me," Bianca strenuously outlined.

"Oh no, Mrs Burney, don't you worry about getting home. We will drop you at home if need be. It is the least we can do after causing you all such inconveniences. Just let us know what the situation is at the end, and we will comply," The detective stressed compassionately.

At this point, the detective returned Mrs Burney's mobile phone in a transparent casing and neatly labelled.

"I thank you, officers, for the return of my phone and I do notice that you have kept your word in terms of the amount of time you would keep it. Now, how else can I be of help?" Bianca asked.

"Mrs Burney, we have examined your phone very thoroughly and could find nothing whatsoever that could possibly assist us in our investigations. However, we did notice that you had taken some recent photographs of two people's passports and a certificate and or receipt of sale for what looked like a very expensive ring and a couple of ornamental fans purchased in Jamaica a long time ago.

"We would like you to enlighten our darkness concerning these documents. First, who are the characters on the passports? Are they twin brothers, identical twins, maybe? They look so very much alike?"

"One of the characters is my stepson. He is the one on the British Passport. You might even see him tonight if he turns up to take me home. The other is his Swedish look-alike friend who came to stay with us for a few days but has now returned home to Sweden.

"Whilst he was doing his tourism thing, they both thought it wise to have a photograph of their passports just in case they lost them. It would be easier to trace or replace them. It was just a sensible precaution, officers. Concerning the other document, it is a recording of an old souvenir I once had, that is, this fan from Jamaica," Bianca untruthfully told the police officer as she produced her ornamental fan from her handbag.

"And, please, may I ask what about the other fan and the ring, Mrs Burney?" The other officer asked.

"Officer, I always wanted to know the answer to that question: but I will never know because he died in an accident abroad before I could get the chance to ask him. He had, whether intentionally or mistakenly, enclosed the receipt with my fan and that made me extremely curious to no avail in the end."

"May we share the name of the person who gave you the souvenir and who unfortunately died where and what date?" The second officer probed.

"Oh, officer, it was given to me by Lance Dunkley for my birthday which is the fourteenth of May if you ever wanted to buy me a gift. It was given to me for my birthday at twenty-fifteen. Lance died in Brazil that same year in a car accident in June that year. He was a good friend," Bianca further lied facetiously to the officers.

The need to lie to the police officers arose from the fact that Bianca was very uncertain about Gaston's involvement in anything untoward. She feared saying anything that might be detrimental to her lover even though there was boiling hatred in her for him following what she discovered about Gaston and her daughter Helen never mind his Swedish connections.

She wanted to avoid any more questions the answers to which might implicate Gaston in anything that she knows or does not know about until she, herself, becomes clearer about several outstanding issues. Lying in such a way as to evade probing by the police, she thought, would be the best way to get the police to move on to other business. She was partially successful.

"My colleague and I wish to thank you most kindly for your very helpful cooperation and we will call it a day at this point. Perhaps you could ascertain the situation regarding your ride home and let us know how it is. We stand ready to deliver on our promise to take you home should you need it," The detective reiterated.

"Thank you, officers. Shall we walk to the reception area where my stepson would be waiting if his service is available? If he is not waiting there, then I will gladly accept your very kind offer of a ride back to 50 Passion Street in Camper," Bianca stressed cautiously as she and the two officers walked to the school's reception waiting area.

In the waiting area, there was no one waiting. Gaston had either not come or had given up waiting; so, Bianca gladly accepted the ride home from the police officers. She learned then that it does make a difference to be travelling in a vehicle with flashing blue lights. You somehow seem to arrive at your destination a great deal faster.

The three people drove the entire journey to Camper in relative silence. In Bianca's mind was the issue of her lying to the police and what consequences could be served up as a result if she was found out later?

In the officer's mind was the same issue. They knew that Bianca was not all truthful. The date on the receipt which was issued in Jamaica at an in-bond store (SATISFACTION IN-BOND) in Ocho Rios, was posted after the time of her souvenir giver's death. Did Lance Dunkley's ghost conduct the shopping in Ocho Rios, St. Ann, Jamaica, they wondered, or was it a memory failure on Bianca's part?

The flashing blue lights had ceased when the officers pulled up at number fifty Passion Street in the Camper. Bianca thanked the officers very warmly for the ride home. The officers politely acknowledged her gratitude and then sped away into the fading evening light believing that they had much to do.

As Bianca turned the key to her front door, she couldn't help wondering if Carlos saw her coming out of the police car. She recalled the hell there was the last time Carlos saw her cuddling in some 'character's' car. This time, it was not Carlos who saw her alighting from the police car. It was Gaston who was waiting on the inside to greet her.

Bianca looked at Gaston quizzically. He also returned a similar gaze. They needed different answers, however. Bianca knew he had been around since Wednesday the nineteenth of this month. That was the day she had dinner with her daughter, Helen, and stumbled upon the revelation concerning Helen's pregnancy and Gaston's role in the sordid affair. His own handwritten note found on his father's bedside table that night had stated that.

He might even have been around earlier than that. Who knows? Did he go to spend the missing time with Helen? Bianca had telephoned Helen three times since that dinner and revelation to see how she was getting on. But there was no mention of Gaston from either of them. What did he do with his week? Bianca wondered. She was clearly losing trust in Gaston.

Why was it a whole week later that she was seeing him for the first time since he did a disappearing act on Friday thirteenth May, the same day of the murder at Dixon Pen? Bianca, who by this was fuming painfully inside, wanted to openly confront Gaston on many issues; but their location placed a restraining hold on her. She could not let loose as the situation demanded without giving the whole sordid thing away with Carlos's presence in the home.

Gaston had other ideas. He was clearly interested in raw sex. It had been some time now since he had had a tumble between the sheets with his father's wife: a fact which seems to excite him beyond imagination. Bianca recognised the looks and the shade of his come-to-bed eyes. She knew he wanted tonight to be one of those nights when they would both take advantage of Carlos's early to bed, deep sleeping, and total reluctance to climb the stairs that lead to Gaston's den.

The more she took in Gaston's demeanour and body language, the more willing she became to allow her questioning anger to become domesticated by her own lustful desires. She knew that, as on countless occasions, she would find a way to mount those stairs to give and receive what their bodies dictate.

"How are you, Gaston? What have you been up to?" Bianca reluctantly greeted Gaston in plain surrender.

Gaston knew that his father was temporarily out of sight and hearing. So, he answered by pulling Bianca roughly but sexily to his person. His eager hands found her bra straps and loosened them so quickly like the professional that he is. His fingers then found her freed-up nipples as he planted a hungry kiss, inserting a searching tongue in her receptive and willing mouth. Thinking about his father, he judged the time and withdrew.

As he did so, he whispered, "I will tell you later."

Bianca knew what was now inevitable, she too, whispered back, "OK" as they pulled apart to allow her to go in search of Carlos elsewhere in the home.

As Bianca headed towards their suite of rooms in search of Carlos, she saw Carlos just emerging from the bathroom where he had spent the last ten minutes. They greeted each other with an embrace that said I missed you, darling. Bianca quickly enquired about Carlos's state of hunger, which was positive.

She apologised for being a little late and explained that the police brought back her phone and kept her behind at school to clarify a few things. In the end, they brought her home with the aid of their flashing blue lights against the rush hour traffic otherwise she might have been somewhat later.

Carlos said that he understood and was glad to see her. She then let it be known that she would change off into something more comfortable and suitable and then turn to the preparation of supper for three since she had met Gaston at the door on her arrival.

"Oh yes, I forgot to mention that Gaston is back and has spent almost the entire day with me for a change. We had a good old natter about Switzerland and his activities there. Of course, the old thing about him settling down came up and as usual, I seemed to lose the argument. I will be the happiest man alive when that boy of mine settles down soberly," Carlos declared disappointingly.

Once supper was out of the way, the family of three sat around lazily for the next hour or so enjoying idle gossip or the latest issues in the news media. Both the amount and the frequency of appearance of the Dixon Pen murder seemed to be lessening. Therefore, the family of three touched on that issue only barely and then only on the periphery since, to date, there have been no hard facts to report bar that of the actus reus of murder.

Bianca, still somewhat obsessed with not knowing anything about Gaston's missing week, tried cleverly though unsuccessfully, even with the aid of his father, to get Gaston to account. Gaston, just as cleverly, subtly changed the topic of conversation to something much more mundane. The idea was to create an aura of boredom that would drive everyone, his dad, into sleeping mode because, until that happened, he could not get his lecherous way with his dad's wife.

Bianca astutely read and accurately interpreted Gaston's evasive shift in the conversation and so suggested to her husband that they might retire to bed soon. Carlos needed no further prompting. He didn't even want a nightcap when asked and so the conversation ended, and Gaston headed upstairs for his apartment whilst the older Burney couple retired to their suite.

Gaston had to wait for much longer than was normal to have Bianca in his bed. For some reason or the other, perhaps intuition, Carlos wouldn't fall asleep and kept talking about the kind of decent woman he would wish to see his son settle down with soon. The kind of woman who would be fateful to him and give him children legitimately thus making him, Carlos a grandfather sooner rather than later.

Bianca just lies there pretending to be sleeping off in the hope that Carlos would fall asleep deeply to facilitate her intended sexual pilgrimage. Little did Carlos realise how close, both metaphorically and in real terms, his grand fatherhood (in double quantity) was to him.

She was feeling sharp pangs of pain from the expressed desire for a decent woman for his son. However, the sexual indulgence which awaits her provided an anaesthetic that helped her to tolerate the pains generated by her conscience.

At last, sleep had the better of Carlos and his deep sleep snoring was recognisable to Bianca. It was now time to satisfy her amorous desires. She crept out of the bed softly. She already had nothing on, so she reached for the purposely close-by skimpiest of the dressing gown to barely cover her nakedness.

She then tiptoed to and through the bedroom door, closing it quietly behind her. Her overwhelming urges dictating the speed with which she ascended the stairs to the waiting Gaston Burney—one Burney to another, she arrived at his door in the shortest of time.

He instantly took her in with a single pull. He ripped off her flimsy covering before throwing her across his bed and began satisfying her desires. Soon, he too was satisfied and tumbled off her to a resting position.

Now was the most auspicious time to let Gaston know that he was to be a daddy, Bianca began thinking. But should she tell him about Helen's conception too or, for the time being just leave it to hers? Bianca wondered. She resolved that she would mind her own business which was heavy enough.

It was Helen's prerogative, after all, to inform Gaston of her own pregnancy. Besides, if she was to let on that Helen had shared their secret, it may well create the kind of verbal explosion that would wake Carlos from his deepest slumber and that would not be good for anyone. This kind of rationale settled her into just disclosing the truth about her situation.

"Sweetheart, are you awake?" Bianca sheepishly whispered in his right ear whilst he curled up in her arms.

"Hmmm, yes, I am," Gaston exhaustedly acknowledged that he was awake.

"I have something wonderful to share with you," Bianca whispered further.

"What is that wonderful something that you have to tell me?" Gaston inquired sleepily.

"You are going to be a daddy, darling. I am very much pregnant," Bianca confidently disclosed to the dozy Gaston.

"What the hell are you saying to me?" Gaston coming awake exploded in astonishment.

"Calm down, sweetheart, you will wake your dad and we will all be in difficulties, and you don't want that, do you?" Bianca beseeched her lover.

"Calm down! Is that all you can say? You have just ruined my bloody life. You were not supposed to get pregnant, remember? This was just our sport. You will have to get rid of it or do something sensible!" Gaston yelled at her in absolute disgust.

"You have just advanced two options: get rid of it or do something sensible. The first one, you know, is not possible. I am a devoted Catholic, remember? And what do you mean by doing something sensible?" Bianca defiantly reminded Gaston.

"All this religious stuff when it suits you. What does Catholicism have to say about you having an affair with your husband's only son? Why does it draw its brakes only at abortion? If that can't work, under the present circumstances, you will just have to tell dad that the baby is his. You hear me?" Gaston furiously questioned.

"You are forgetting one important thing. Your dad can no longer procreate, remember? He would immediately divorce me for adultery once I told him that lie. You have no idea what hell I went through with your father that Friday when you dropped me home in the borrowed green car—the same day the murder was discovered at Dixon Pen School—he had observed our passionate love scene in the car before you drove off.

"He mistook the strange car for being driven by some lover of mine. He did not recognise you from his friend's window across the street where he just happened to be at the time. The result was that it came close to the end for us, and you were nowhere to lend me some solace; off I suppose, gallivanting with your other women. How many are there besides me, Gaston Burney, how many are there?" Bianca repeatedly demanded.

"You are driving me mad! I cannot take this; I am going out for a ride," Gaston declared as he jumped out of the bed and reached for trousers and shirt, pulled on his loafers, and scrambled down the carpeted stairs.

Soon after he exited the front door, the engine of his E-Type Jaguar roared into readiness and sped off into the uncertainty of the night, just after midnight on the morning of the twenty-seventh of May.

Chapter 10

Bianca, truly stunned at this unpredictable reaction from Gaston, was left hurrying to return to her husband's bed before her absence was detected by a waking husband. She had just managed to slide back into the sheets when Carlos stirred with his hand, feeling for her.

She knew what that meant. Oh my, she thought, two times in one night, how will I cope with that? Before she could answer her own question, she found herself coping.

As Carlos naturally obeyed the slumbering effects of after sex, Bianca lay there contemplating the earlier actions of her stepson lover and dad-to-be for her expecting child. She wondered where he could have gone. Then it occurred to her that Helen might be a fit candidate to receive him in his moment of paternal distress.

She then recalled the vow that she had made to herself that she would do something to Gaston. Remember the thing about "Heaven has no rage like love to neither hatred turned, nor hell a fury like a woman scorned"? William Congreve lives on.

Bianca was right in her summation. Gaston in the loneliness of the night roamed aimlessly for a while before decisively pointing his car in the direction of Pineapple Road in Kings Heath, Birmingham. When he arrived at number thirty at around two-thirty in the wee hours of Thursday the twenty-seventh of May, the lights were still on.

Helen had not long returned from a night out with Jo and Jacky. She was now preparing for bed when she heard the bell at her front door sounding. Helen was curious but extremely cautious. She did not go immediately to the front door but took a surreptitious peep from a slightly shifted bedroom curtain which enabled her to see the relevant section of the road outside.

The caller at the door was growing impatient. He or she sounded the bell twice before Helen noticed a familiar picture across the road from her bedroom window. The picture she was seeing was Gaston's White E-Type Jaguar with the number plate: TRY 123 B. She was now certain who the caller was and hurried to open the door fearing that the persistent ringing might disturb the close-by sleeping neighbours.

"Honey, you look dreadful. Where are you coming from this late? Come on inside let me get you a warm beverage," Helen coaxed as she attempted to rescue her lover, stepbrother, and father of her child to be all in one, just one person, from the imagined wolves that have chased him relentlessly to her waiting sanctuary.

Helen performed the loving miracle with her female knowhow and Gaston soon became almost his old self again. At least, his sexual interest was as obvious as ever. Like her mum, but unknown to each other, Helen was very curious as to why her man was away from her for such a long time. She anticipated that he would, at least, stay the rest of the night with her.

This would give her the opportunity to give Gaston Burney the good news about his fatherhood; and, maybe, just maybe, she might learn something about both his straying tendencies and nocturnal habits.

Helen predicted correctly. Gaston, once so refreshed, uninvitingly moved directly to Helen's bedroom seemingly ready for the kind of actions that usually happen in bedrooms, especially at night. As usual, he was sure of his ground.

Helen joined him very shortly smelling like a rose and as gleeful as a child at Christmas around the Christmas tree.

They wasted no time. The unquenched passion of almost two weeks took total control of the twenty-three-year-old Helen Smith. It led her into a head-on sexual collision with the twenty-five-year-old stallion known as Gaston Burney.

The night and the pleasures were just all they cared for: the rest of the world could pass them by who cares? But all good things have a nasty habit of coming abruptly to an end. Even this did.

Now, they need to talk. It was remarkable how level-headed the participants in sexual indulgence can be once their urges have been satiated and earth was where reality was for them once more. Helen's mind was now intently focused on what had been the realities of life for some time. Since she found out that she was pregnant, she began to realise that the way she had been with Gaston can no longer remain that way.

She will have to insist on Gaston being a great deal more responsible in getting ready for fatherhood. She didn't want to bring a child into the world and there was no father to lend support in bringing up the young human being. The question then becomes how does she approach Gaston Burney who had never shown any inclination to settle down? She thought.

His dad had never missed an opportunity to counsel him in the right directions regarding finding a steady and responsible job and finding the right girl to settle with. Yet, Gaston had never taken heed of any of that, much to his father's disappointment. Maybe, now that a child was on the way, Gaston will see things from a different angle, Helen thought to herself as she lies next to the subject. She decided to broach the issue out of concern for Gaston himself.

"My darling, please tell me why you were so upset earlier tonight? You seemed awfully lost," Helen asked by way of an expression of concern for Gaston.

"Please don't go there, sweetheart. It is water under the bridge. I don't want to go back there. Suffice it to say that my dad made me terribly upset. He is always pressuring me to find a steady and responsible job. He seems to think that my life will not be mine unless I find a sensible, decent, and caring woman that I can settle down with.

"Tonight, he was heavier than usual and that made me terribly upset. I could not take it anymore, so I left and here I am with you. Let us just enjoy the rest of the night. Tomorrow will be another day," Gaston untruthfully evaded the real issue.

Helen did not believe a word of any of that. She had heard so much about Carlos's sleep patterns from her mother to know that Carlos was never going to be up at that time of night discussing Gaston's wayward habits. Something else must be playing on Gaston's mind but he doesn't want to let on.

Helen, remembering how he was and looked when she first opened the door to him earlier, decided that she would not take that line of concern any further. She would just let it rest and gently tackle the main issue dominating her mind.

"I imagine that fathers can be overbearing at times. They think they know best for their children; never pause to realise that children do grow up and make sensible choices for themselves—unfortunately, some of them are not so sensible. I agree with you, just leave it and time will get you two back in sync," Helen started to pacify Gaston and withdraw from the line of thought that she had opened initially.

"Let us change the subject. I have an easier and more interesting question for you. So, do you want to hear it?" Helen asked in tones demure.

"Yes, go ahead, ask it," Gaston said.

Now, he would regret giving her the green light to ask her question.

"Why did you go away and leave **us** for so long this last time honey?" Helen asked whilst taking great care to emphasise the 'plural' in the question.

Despite the obvious emphasis on the word 'us', Gaston almost overlooked that reference. He was just about to answer the question when suddenly he paused and asked a counter-question instead.

"Did you say 'us' just now? What do you mean by 'us' in this case?"

Furthest from Gaston's mind was what he was about to hear. The thought had occurred to him that Bianca might have been talking to her daughter about him. He was asking himself the question of whether the reference to 'us' could be about Bianca and Helen. His darkness was about to be illuminated.

"Well, there is me to start with and there is your baby on the way," Helen very calmly stated.

And still, Gaston read this wrongly. He was now certain that Bianca and Helen had been talking about him and that Bianca had told her about her pregnancy for him. Then he hesitated. Why would Bianca do that? No one is supposed to know about his sexual excursions with his father's wife. And that would include even her only daughter.

Has there been betrayal by both women? He pondered. Gaston both blindly and conceitedly mindfully rambled off in every direction except the obvious. He could find no answers and was now running the risk of saying too much himself. Surely, it would be safer to seek clarity about this reference to 'us', he thought.

"Helen, have you been talking to anyone at all about our affair, for example, your mother?" This was as direct as Gaston dared go without kicking his own goal.

Helen replied: "I have certainly not, darling. I couldn't do that before telling the father to be. Sweetheart, you are going to be the father of our child. I am carrying your baby."

"You guys cannot do this to me! I am going back to Stockholm where I can be safe from baby pranksters," Gaston angrily and carelessly declared.

Gaston fled the bed with swiftness only seen when people are ditching a burning building. He reached for his clothing for the second time in one night as he prepared to flee the scene to nowhere in particular. His exit was so hurriedly done; it was definite that he left his under pants and a foot of sock behind. Helen would find these no sooner than Gaston was gone into the dawning morning.

Helen became frightened. She could not have anticipated such a reaction from a man who was in line for becoming a father. She was finding the whole thing inexplicable. However, two aspects of Gaston's remarks became of immediate interest to her.

What did Gaston mean by, "You guys cannot do this to me" and he stated that immediately after querying her mother's involvement? The other thing of interest was his use of the plural form when referring to "baby pranksters".

Helen was now having a flashback to the night she told her mother about her affair with her stepson and of the resulting baby on the way.

Mum's response was not what she had expected from the mother she had known all these years. There were none of the maternal sympathies which she was accustomed to from her childhood until that night. Her mother's reaction to learning that she was to become a grandmother was more bitter than the expected joy. Her mother acted more like a jealous woman in her condemnation of the other woman.

Her mother's attitude to her since that night and the revelation she shared with her had been less than warm. Was her mother a baby prankster too? Was my mother one of the 'guys' doing this to Gaston? What was the real reason why Gaston arrived at my door looking so dishevelled and upset at that time in the morning? And what was this entire thing about going back to Stockholm? Mother and I needed to talk and very soon, Helen resolved.

The motorist usually thinks that because the roads tend to be comparatively free of traffic in the early mornings, it was an opportunity to sink their accelerators to the floor. Gaston Burney was having that kind of thought the moment he was outside of Helen's house and had set the engine of his E-Type Jaguar roaring. He had remembered that he had a flask of the best and strongest Jamaican Wray and Nephew white rum in the glove compartment of the car and so he reached for it.

Whilst driving, he placed the bottle between his legs and with his left hand unscrewed the bottle of rum and turned the bottle to his head and drank three good mouthfuls of the potent stuff. The pressures of the day had driven him to near madness. It isn't every day that one learns that one impregnates one's father's wife and the daughter of that said wife in roughly the same period. Before long, the Jaguar was heading along the A38 highway, its speed unknown and uncontrolled.

The signs for the M6 motorway northward and southward and for the M1 towards London suddenly appeared in his forward vision and simultaneously he could see flashing blue lights adorning his rear-view mirror. Gaston, now high on liquor, tensed from the stress of his fertility issues, he could not bother to interpret the meaning of the flashing blue lights behind him. The result was that he avoided the motorway turn-offs, took the first slip road heading in the direction of Sutton Cold Field, and drove both recklessly and carelessly until he was overtaken and forced to a halt by the chasing police vehicle.

The officers gingerly and very cautiously approached the now stationary Jaguar, whilst Gaston sheepishly observed their approach from his rear mirror. Tactfully, the two police officers divided as they reached the tail-end of the car and each continued to approach the car from separate sides.

"Good morning, sir", said the police officer at the driver's window.

"Going somewhere in a hurry, sir? You have been showing total disregard for the Road Traffic Act as far as we could see, sir. Please kindly step out of the vehicle and place your hands on top of the car where we can see them, thank you, sir," the officer politely instructed.

Gaston Burney now sobers up in every way because of all that was playing out around him. He obediently stepped out of his vehicle and rested both his hands on top of the Jaguar just as he was instructed.

Gaston was then thoroughly searched by the second officer. His vehicle was similarly thoroughly searched. He was then given a breathalyser test which proved to be positive and way over the prescribed limit.

The resulting charges were many as they were then piled on by the police officer in charge.

These were:

1. evading the police

2. driving beyond the speed limits in built-up areas

3. driving recklessly, and carelessly

4. driving under the influence of alcohol, and

5. being in possession of a dangerous weapon found in his glove compartment.

These were all designated offences for which people can be arrested and so Gaston was taken to the Sutton Cold Field Police Station where he was incarcerated until bail could be arranged. In this circumstance, it would be necessary to conduct bail arrangements in the presence of a local Justice of the Peace.

The search of the Justices of the Peace Register revealed that the nearest available Justice was none other than Mr Allan Austin J.P.—the headteacher of Dixon Pen Comprehensive School in Edgbaston, Birmingham. He was duly summoned, and he promptly arrived at the station shortly afterward.

These two men had never met though there were circumstances where they could have met. Gaston, on numerous occasions, chauffeured his stepmother and lover from and to Dixon Pen Comprehensive School, and of course, there was that time when Mr Austin might have attended the wedding of Gaston's father to Bianca Smith, now Burney.

That attendance did not take place because the headteacher was previously booked on other business and had to excuse himself regrettably, he had explained.

In the circumstances, the bail arrangement was made, the Justice of the Peace executed his documentary role and then departed leaving the police officers to do the rest. Though the men have met on this occasion, they still do not know each other.

On his way back to his home to prepare for school, the headteacher seemed preoccupied with something that was greatly bothering him. He was sure, in his own mind, that he had seen that young man before, but he just could not be sure. The headteacher's thought swung back to the early morning charges placed upon the young man: they were both many and very serious; he is going to have a difficult time in court explaining all these very serious criminal offences.

He might very well get a prison sentence for some of them, subject, of course, to his previous police record. Mr Austin pulled his car up just outside number 10, Lavender Mews, and parked it there. There was no point garaging it since he would soon be on his way to school.

No sooner than Mr Austin entered his reception hall, than he knew why he was so troubled on his way back from the police station. There it was on the centrepiece table. Jason Musgrave in the picture with the headteacher's daughter, Doreen, is the spitting image of Gaston Burney for whom he sanctioned bail at the police station just a few minutes ago.

And what a coincidence, the headteacher further thought, Gaston, shares the same surname as his Chief Administrative Officer and personal assistant (P.A).

Ms. Daniel Johnson, the domestic assistant to the headteacher immediately re-focused his mind on other things more important like breakfast and the need to prepare for the day ahead at Dixon Pen. She was quite accustomed to the burdens and realities of the headteacher's commission as a Justice of the Peace and had become quite skilled in dividing his time appropriately between the two offices.

It was a normal day at Dixon Pen. Everything was ticking over like the metaphorical clockwork. The odd pupil messenger here, a straggler there and the occasional visiting teacher or parent to the school's reception office were parts of the normal scene. There was nothing, absolutely nothing unusual about the school day. The deputy headteachers and other senior teachers seem to have everything under near-perfect control much to the delight of the headteacher.

At times like now, the headteacher feels both confident and comfortable catching up on his administrative workload in the seclusion of his office. He headed there after directing the general office to selectively limit the number of callers and would-be visitors needing to see or speak with him.

The first hour in the privacy of his office was extremely productive, especially in terms of catching up on his correspondence. The headteacher was just feeling proud of himself when he noticed among the pile of papers that he had received a call from his sworn-to-secrecy contact with the Secretary of State Office. It was a request for the headteacher to call back on the number given because it was rather urgent and important.

The headteacher's heart skipped a beat. This could only mean that there was going to be some work on the knighthood issues. As he had promised he would do, he had made secret inquiries regarding the impact and effect of the cancelled education conference which was to have taken place in York on Wednesday nineteenth of May.

He wanted to learn whether the Dixon Pen murder was the true cause of the cancellation, and, if so, where do we go from here. With the media hype about the murder now subsiding, it seems his contact was in a better position to talk with him, the headteacher thought.

Propelled by both eagerness and anxiety, the headteacher abandoned all else and picked up his desk telephone receiver from its resting perch. He was just about to dial the number when, without warning, his mobile phone carried in his breast pocket sounded. He had already decided that whoever it was would have to wait and call back later or wait for him to return the call.

He pulled out the phone to silence it when he noticed that the call was coming in from Umea in Sweden and that it was his daughter Doreen on the line. He quickly re-thought his earlier decision. This time, he postponed calling his secret contact in preference for speaking with his daughter.

Doreen had never called him during school hours. She had always waited for him to be at home before calling him. Clearly, he thought, this call must be important.

"Hi there, my darling daughter, how are you? What is happening in yonder north?"

"Daddy, I am calling to let you know that I am abandoning ship and coming home. I must come home. My flight arrangements will get me into Birmingham Airport at twenty-one hundred this very night. Please be there for me. The world has caved in on me. You will hear all about it once I am home," Doreen said rather tearfully before she was disconnected from her father.

Her world had caved in and now her father's world was turned upside down. What could make such a sweet young girl with all those positive prospects—educationally, professionally, and matrimonially—just give up on everything and just cut and run with just a moment's notice to her daddy, her only pillar of strength? The headteacher began wondering.

He glanced at his watch and verified that it was correct by looking too at the grandfather's antique clock which stands proudly in his office. Confirmed by both instruments of the time, he knows that he had less than seven hours to go before Doreen's flight lands and he can begin to learn about the mess his daughter seems to be coping with at this very moment.

Now the headteacher suddenly lost all his enthusiasm for further work. He decided that his secret contact could wait a day or two longer for a call from him. Nothing seems important any longer. His last and only dependent child seems to be in desperate and life-wrecking trouble. Comes what may, he is determined to be there for her starting with this night at Birmingham Airport. He needed to do just one thing now.

That is, he must call Daniel, his domestic assistant, to alert her to the fact that Doreen will be home tonight. This he did. Daniel was always pleased to have Doreen around, so the news made her joyful but wanted to know why the news was so sudden. Mr Austin could only reassure her that they will know the answer to that question later tonight.

It was often said that time passes quickly when you were enjoying yourself. Well, the reverse was just as true when anxiety rules the roost. Time seems to be at a standstill then. Mr Austin had floated about the school trying to find his deputies to alert them to the fact that he would be leaving school earlier than his usual time and might well be in tomorrow at a time later than usual.

Once so alerted, the deputies will supervise the dismissal of the school at four o'clock and Mr Austin could meander off in the direction of the airport. He would be travelling against the traffic so there would be plenty of time to get there with some ease.

The headteacher got to the airport with plenty of time to spare. Birmingham airport was a very large and complex facility that is seriously congested. There were plenty of parking spaces but getting one close to the arrival building is never easy. Parking was, on this occasion, even more difficult but the headteacher recognised a former pupil who works in the porters' office.

That way, he was given a pledge that there would be a special porter service at the appropriate time to cart any luggage three to four hundred yards away from the arrival building where he had found parking. The flight came in on time and safely. Clearing immigration and customs presented no difficulties and soon Mr Austin could see his daughter, Doreen, strutting forwards toward him.

She was pulling two large pieces of luggage in addition to her hand luggage. It seems that Doreen had brought home the whole of Sweden and had no intention of heading back in that direction any time soon.

She now spotted her father too. They greeted each other with the warmest of hugs that would have made a freezing night melt. The retained porter mobilised into action and soon they were at Mr Austin's waiting BMW parked a fair distance away. Mr Austin rewarded the porter, shook his hand, and then set off for Sutton Cold Field, which was a more direct and shorter route than the one he travelled in getting to the airport in the first place.

The lights along the A45 heading into Birmingham City at night were comparable with those of any other world city. Overhead, the rumble of airplanes either coming into land or taking off was a constant feature in the local vicinity: yet inside the BMW mode of travel, there was a dead hush as both of the people inside the car contemplated how to break the silence. The headteacher was first off, the mark.

"How was your journey, Doreen?" This was a good ice breaker from daddy to a distressed daughter.

"Dad, it was rather good. It went very smoothly, and everything ran on time surprisingly given that it was a connection flight. There was no direct flight from Umea to Birmingham so I flew to Heathrow in London and, luckily, there were two connecting flights from Heathrow that I could have taken. I took the earlier one and everything turned out alright," Doreen explained albeit in a rather sad and worried voice.

"You must be starving: did you manage to eat something on either of those flights?" Mr Austin enquired about Doreen.

"On the flight from Umea to Heathrow it was possible but at the due time I was just not hungry, and I took a pass at mealtime. Frankly, I was so depressed; my appetite had left me all day. There was no opportunity to dine or even snack on the connecting flight to Birmingham. I feel like I could manage a meal now though," Doreen said whilst still in very low spirits.

"We are just about ten minutes from home and if I know Daniel, she will have a great super waiting to welcome you back home. We can dine together since I have not been home to eat since your call earlier today, so I am hungry too. At dinner, you can put me into the picture of what this is all about. I am dreading what you will tell me, I am sure that you know that but please pull no punches," Mr Austin insisted.

"Yes, Dad, I will share everything with you as raw as you will want it and then I will probably have to pick you up off the floor," Doreen said with a smile for the first time since arriving at the airport.

Mr Austin swung the BMW into Lavender Mews and into the garage at number ten. Doreen hurried out of the car and climbed those three decorated stone steps with newly found alacrity from the sight of the welcoming Daniel waiting for her at the front door. These two had always got on together just like a house on fire and now it seemed like that fire was on the verge of rekindling.

Hugs and kisses were in order and the aroma from Daniel's kitchen added to the enchantment. Whilst all this was going on, Mr Austin struggled with the baggage and got it in successfully. Father and daughter, both very tired from their different activities this day, retired to their separate bathroom facilities for freshening up purposes in readiness for Daniel's cuisine.

Just as it was anticipated, Daniel presented a welcome home splash worthy of a King and his daughter at re-union and silently disappeared from the scene for the two to catch up on their stories.

As they dined, Doreen tearfully opened the conversation. And as good fathers will do, Mr Austin listened earnestly and with a very sympathetic ear, intervening only to make prompts and or to seek clarification at key points.

"Dad, let me start at the beginning, just as I did for the police in Umea. I told them everything. I left out nothing. I think it is always the best place to start. You will remember that time, about a year ago when I went on an excursion to Stockholm with the University Preparation School.

"It was at an ice cream parlour whilst on a sightseeing trip that I first met Jason Musgrave. What seemed then to be the most wonderful thing to have ever happened to me has turned out to be a most dangerous nightmare. At our first meeting and for the next six months or thereabout, Jason was both a charmer and a perfect gentleman.

"The only question was about his sexual propensity which would have been craved for by many women including me but could have raised negative questions about this otherwise gentleman. Jason wanted to sleep with me that first meeting in Stockholm, but the inconvenience of the excursion trip assisted me in avoiding him and his obvious intent. He hung around with me for most of the day until just before it was time to board our flight back to Umea.

"He took my entire contact details before saying goodbye. I was so very disappointed that the day had to end but logically assumed that that would be the end of that dream because, from the information Jason gave me, it was going to be geographically not possible to maintain a romantic relationship with someone so far away. You see, Jason had informed me that he was born, educated lived, and work all his life in Stockholm where he was currently working as a laboratory scientist in one of Sweden's most prestigious science laboratories.

"He had mastered the English language since his school days to the extent that no Swedish accent was detected when he spoke, only a slight British accent which could have been gained through the in-depth study of the language. Umea is almost 700 kilometres and approximately seven hours drive northwards from Stockholm.

"He is a full-time employee, and I was in serious preparation for my medical studies at the University of Umea. The idea of romance in this situation was simply not viable; at least that was what I reasoned.

"I could no longer believe my eyes or trust my logic when two days after getting back to Umea, I had an early morning knock on my dormitory door. I opened the door and standing there right before me was Jason Musgrave. I was both surprised and extremely happy to see him. Even though I was still in my overnight garment when he turned up that early, he was so sweet with his flattery about my partially curly hair and tanned skin complexion.

"He made me feel so wanted that I imagined that the world had been suddenly transformed into a much better place. I swiftly and excitedly decided to avoid prep classes that day. Jason and I went hand in hand everywhere in and around Umea that cold wintry day. Yet, we were so warm and comfortable in each other's presence that day. We dined, we laughed, and we caressed and had unimaginable fun together until evening came.

"There was no escaping it this time; Jason wanted to stay the night with me just as I had hoped for throughout the course of the day of leisure. Jason Musgrave finally and repeatedly had his way with me throughout the entire night.

"Gone was my virginity which I had been saving for Mr Right and I didn't even notice or cared. The next morning, much to my regret, Jason had to fly back to Stockholm for an important engagement, he assured me.

"The romance never lost any of its fire over the months ahead except that it didn't seem enough for me. The distance between us did not prove to be a major obstacle because we were so very much in love. Jason would travel to Umea often and he would pay for me to fly down to Stockholm on numerous occasions. There were signs that I ignored.

"For example, each time I visited Jason in Stockholm, he would explain that he wanted me to see somewhere new in Sweden and our lovemaking at those times had to be hotel jobs. Not once was I taken to Jason's home in Stockholm nor was, I ever treated to meeting any of his family members.

"According to him, he was so totally wrapped up in me, that nobody else mattered. Dad, I was consumed with love and affection for this man who made me walk twice my height each time I was in his company.

"I must confess, dear Dad, that your frequent and very sound advice not to let romance get in the way of original purposes largely went unheeded. My prep work has been sadly neglected for what I thought was a price worth paying. I know now that it wasn't. Sex with Jason had dominated every aspect of my life since going to live in Sweden and going on that fatal trip to Stockholm. Jason's response to the several pieces of advice you addressed to us was for us to become engaged and so advised you accordingly.

"He hoped that that way, you would see the seriousness of our intentions and lend us your support and encouragement. Another sign I missed or overlooked was at our special engagement dinner. He had no ring with him even though we had discussed ring sizes etcetera. He claimed that he was so locked in me, that his memory sometimes deserts him. It was some months later that he presented me with a ring that is so rare and beautiful I forgave him for the strange delay.

"I have since discovered that the ring is not new, it was worn before but nevertheless beautiful and up-market. It has a puzzling message inscribed inside a flowery box on the inside of the ring. In the box is the letter 'A'. According to Jason, it meant that I was awesome. The only other present that Jason has ever given me was an ornamental fan which was never needed for functional purposes in Umea.

"The plan was that we would be married as soon as I completed my studies whenever that would have been. There was never any certainty in terms of time as I was taking time out of my studies for the love and sexual demands of this man. A delay in the completion of my studies was going to be inevitable: and we knew that.

"Then the whole house started crumbling when I noticed that my period was well late and applied for an at-home pregnancy test. I found out that I was pregnant with Jason Musgrave. There has never been another lover in my life. About two weeks ago Jason surprised me once more when he turned up unexpectedly on my doorstep with a bouquet of roses apologising for his long absence.

"I had waited for this moment since I never wanted to break such wonderful and important news on the telephone. I needed to tell Jason to his face that he was to be a father and see the expected pride beam all over his face. It didn't turn out or happen that way, Dad. It was as though I had asked him to consume a dose of potent poison.

"He blew up in a rage the likes of which I have never experienced before and hoped to God I will never see again. I told him he was crazy, and he launched at me in a temper so fierce, I was scared out of my mind.

"I pushed him away and then he came back and slapped me in the face so viciously and forcefully, that the full weight of my head collided with the bedroom wall. I screamed loudly for help, but he was able to stifle further screams by covering my mouth with his right hand whilst his left hand made a choking hook around my neck.

"In the dorm next to me the girl occupant had heard everything, including my first loud scream for help, and, thankfully, summoned the Swedish police.

The police were quick in response and that may have saved my life. After taking his contact details, they threw him out of my dorm and sternly warned him not to return to Umea for any reason. It seemed that they were treating the incident as a minor domestic matter.

"Two nights later, the Umea police paid me a return visit to explore the origins of my link with Jason Musgrave and to warn me to be careful with this man. Their records had shown no such person was ever born in Sweden and there is no record of him ever attending school in the country or working at the laboratory in Stockholm.

"The Police assured me that this man is now on their list of imposters who will be pulled into account for his links and purposes in Sweden on sight.

"Last night, I received an anonymous call. I could not tell from where the call was coming because there are ways to disguise that, and it was. The caller also disguised his voice, but I was almost sure that I knew that voice. The caller told me to get out of Umea and have no contact with the police because it would be a shame if anything terrible should happen to me in Umea.

"The people who are interested in your departure have slashed throats before and then the line went dead.

"Dad, I am sure that you now understand why you received that frantic call from me today and as a result, here I am with my pregnant self," Doreen ended her very sad tale at this convenient point.

"My dear girl, you have been through hell and back. The first thing I shall do tomorrow is to be in contact with the Registrar of the University of Umea. I will be seeking on your behalf, a student extended leave of absence. Life begins with pregnancy; it does not end with it even if the putative father seems likely to dodge his responsibilities.

"Tomorrow, we must take you to a private doctor for a complete health checkup and in due course get you an appointment at the family clinic so that we know what the baby is.

"You will be given the best care and support that I can afford right up to the birth of your child and beyond, at which point arrangements can be made to enable you to have a second bite of your medical ambition at the same school as your original choice. Right now, you need to have some rest and we can pick up the reins tomorrow," Mr Austin said in terminating the awful story recounted by his daughter, Doreen, just then.

Doreen sighed in relief. Getting all that off her mind and into the open as far as her dad goes felt like the lifting of a major burden off the mind of one so young. And given her dad's caring, understanding, and, above all, non-judgmental response, it was like the icing on the cake.

She knows very clearly that she will not be alone in all this mess. What was even greater news was her father's determination that she should be given the chance to try again for her great ambition to be successful at medical school and at the top place—The University of Umea.

Her father departed the dining room for his bedroom quarters, and she followed him but diverted to the reception room area to go to her chambers—the one she always uses whenever she is at home. On the centre table hers and Jason's, or whoever he truly is, the picture remains standing as proudly as her father wanted it to be. Now that picture is no more because Doreen had seen to that as she retired to her bedroom quarters.

Doreen's pre-sleep thoughts focused on what a wonderful daddy she has, and how lucky she was to be his daughter. Someday, she hoped she would be able to make him very proud, so much so, that the present embarrassments that he must be experiencing will simply fade into insignificance. As to Jason, other than his memory, she wants very little of him around her. She will destroy all pictures and texts from and of him starting with the one she just removed from the reception room centre table.

The engagement ring and souvenir fan together with her child when he or she comes will be the only tangibles to remind her of Jason Musgrave. The ring will also be a useful deterrent to other 'would-be' prowlers at a time when she will need no distraction from her focus on getting back on the rails.

Chapter 11

The next morning, Mr Austin found the time to look in on his daughter who was still soundly sleeping after the previous day's travel and the stressful mental preoccupation which had been overwhelming her for several days. He then summoned Daniel and told her that Doreen was going to be home for quite some time and that he would like her to chaperon her to Doctor Jones where he had an account as soon as possible, preferably today.

He gave the minimum of reasons for all these changes whilst broadly hinting that Doreen would let her know what is going on in her life. Daniel politely acknowledged the additional responsibility just placed on her and then returned to the kitchen where she was busy preparing breakfast for an extra person.

By the time breakfast was served, Doreen was up and able to join her dad before he was off for school. They greeted each other and sat down to eat. As Doreen reached for her knife and fork, Mr Austin had his first glimpse of her engagement ring.

His reaction openly expressed to his daughter was, "Oh, my, that is some ring you have there. I wouldn't return it even if he asked you to. It is probably worth a fortune".

Silently, though, he thought that if the admin girls at school ever saw this ring, they would think Elaine's was rather commonplace. This was a baseless assumption from a man who had not ever noticed the ring Elaine wore so constantly by all reports.

Breakfast, small talks, and the morning's niceties now over, Mr Austin was able to set off for school where he must accomplish two things, be in contact with the Registrar of the University of Umea and make yesterday's aborted call to his secret contact for the Secretary of State for education office if nothing else is accomplished for the day.

At Austin's home, things had taken on the shape of normality over a period. Some two weeks had passed since Doreen was home from Sweden. As Mr Austin had hinted would happen, Doreen had confided in her old pal, Daniel.

She told her everything that had happened to her throughout her time in Sweden—all of it came flooding in Daniel's direction at the prompt of a missing picture of the couple from the centre table in the reception room. Daniel had queried its disappearance. The story behind Doreen's experiences in Sweden was heart-rending for Daniel but, somehow, it brought two people who were already closed, a great deal closer.

The medical report on Doreen from Mr Jones' surgery was very good. Following a thorough and detailed examination, as was requested, Mr Jones found no health issues. She is a very strong young woman.

Doreen was found to be in top form. He, however, recommended that Doreen should make an appointment to see the Consultant Obstetrician at the family clinic as soon as possible in the interest of her developing child.

Over the same two-week period, several significant developments were taking place.

Although Mr Austin had alerted his deputies and other senior teachers to expect his late arrival at school the day after Doreen had returned from Sweden, that precaution was not necessary. The headteacher had managed to be at school that morning with much time to spare. Since Umea was one hour ahead of the United Kingdom, he was able to get the Registrar of the University of Umea online whilst it was still eight o'clock in the morning in Birmingham and not yet for school to commence.

The Swedish gentleman at the other end was delightful and delighted to be speaking on the phone with Allan Austin. He had heard of Dixon Pen Comprehensive and the pioneering work it was doing in the field of equality in education. He told the headteacher that it was a great honour to be speaking to the leader of such an esteemed project. As they were speaking the register said, an idea had just occurred to him.

The University of Umea could greatly benefit from the kind of work for which Dixon Pen is renowned. He would be very happy to put a proposal to his governing body to invite the headteacher to Umea, all expenses paid, of course, to be a lead speaker on race equality in education if the headteacher would agree at least initially.

What was more, whilst the headteacher is in Umea, the extended leave of absence for his daughter could be sorted out there and then, thus eliminating paper communication from the various interested departments? This would be a massive affair here in Sweden because the media would want to be involved in a big way.

The subject had been toyed around throughout Sweden but, frankly, only by way of lip service. That we could bring you here would mean an accolade for our university. No doubt you would like to think about this, and I could call you back, we have your numbers, in a few days to see if we can get this going.

It was not necessary to call back the headteacher who had seen the glorious opportunity to revive his pioneering status from an international platform. Nevertheless, he agreed to have the time to consider the surprise proposal.

It was exactly two days after, and the Swedish Registrar was back on the phone sounding even more enthusiastic about an answer. The headteacher agreed to play the stated role and the ball was set rolling with all the pertinent details to follow on the fax machine.

In the meantime, that same day, the headteacher had made the pledged contact with his secret informer from the Secretary of State for education office. Still, under high secret, the headteacher had learned that although the murder at Dixon Pen was a factor in cancelling the York education conference, it did not adversely affect his chance of knighthood.

He was encouraged to soldier on and expect good things to be announced up ahead. The informant was not allowed to say more. Both matters had been with him since that day. Doreen had raised the issue of the extended leave of absence once or twice to which the headteacher had replied that it was very advanced in the making and that she just had to be patient.

Very importantly, Mr Austin had met with his PA to finalise and place the advertisement relating to the permanent post of Chief Administrative Officer which was currently held by Bianca Burney herself in an acting capacity. The adverts were placed in the Education Guardian, in the Times Educational Supplement, and the local Birmingham Readership newspaper.

This day was also when the headteacher and the Acting Chief Administrative Officer had met to appoint Marjorie Phillips as the temporary addition to the admin team. The rest of the day was spent completing the outstanding correspondence which was so abruptly interrupted on the day of Doreen's return.

Following the blowout that Gaston had had at Helen's early Thursday morning on the twenty-seventh of May, Helen had been demanding an audience with her mother to iron out several strange feelings which she was having since that night when she disclosed the fact of her pregnancy to her mother. That meeting was eventually scheduled for Saturday the third of July.

Bianca really didn't feel ready to face her daughter with anything to do with Gaston Burney in the present circumstances and so kept making a variety of excuses, against the meeting taking place, mainly about the pressures of work. Helen was fiercely determined that the meeting should happen. Eventually, Bianca had run out of evasive tactics and finally gave in to her daughter's persistent demand.

The atmosphere at the home of the Burney's had become measurably strange. Communication between Bianca and Gaston was almost non-existent since he found out about her pregnancy and had thrown that huge temper tantrum and walked out of the home that said morning. Everything was made considerably worst following what happened at Helen's that same morning.

The double paternity whammy of that morning had sent him at breakneck speed disastrously into serious legal entanglement with law enforcement. Thanks to the Bail Act, he was not incarcerated for very long. However, the conditions of bail were so onerous that they were having the same effects as though he was imprisoned.

Gaston was (a) confined to his home, leaving it only to fulfil condition (b) which requires him to report once daily to the nearest police station; (c) he had had to surrender his passport pending the adjudication of his charges in a recognised court of law, and (d) his driver's licence had been suspended pending the outcome of the case which is scheduled for Wednesday, June thirtieth. He was effectively grounded. This was never going to be a pretty situation for one whose love of freedom was likened to that of a bird.

That Gaston could not talk to either his father or Bianca about the entanglement with Helen was a major burden of his own making. He had yet to realise that Bianca is already in the know about his and Helen's affair.

He remained in some doubt as to whether Helen had shared their affair with her mother and vice versa. If that ever happened, he would consider himself to be inextricably in deep waters, he was thinking.

Bianca is a working woman and so she is out of the way for most of the day and most days of the week. This fact in the circumstance had given Gaston a lot of lawfully enforced time with his father, Carlos. Carlos is beginning to think that he has, at last, tamed his only son. Gaston is no longer roaming near and far but is giving much of his time to his daddy.

All that is needed now is for Gaston to find a steady job and a decent and loving woman to settle in family pursuit. Though Carlos was ignorant of the true reasons for Gaston's presence at home, Gaston's presence at home was considered a blessing from above and a welcome change for Carlos who had grown accustomed to being left alone by son and wife very frequently.

The police overseeing the Dixon Pen murder had revisited the Upton murder case which had gone cold and now had some good reasons to have another stock-taking conference regarding the two cases. And this could take place any day now. However, the date is yet to be announced.

Bianca Burney had not stopped thinking about her pregnancy from the day the pregnancy test established that factual reality for her. Even though she had not been able to share the joy with anyone except Gaston, because of the highly unusual circumstances, she, herself, had remained super conscious and mindful that a developing child will need to be watched medically.

It was for this reason that Bianca had arranged with a very accommodating Mr Austin to have the afternoon off on Friday the eleventh of June so that she could keep a previously made appointment with the obstetrician at the family clinic in Hampstead. Ostensibly, she was having an annual genealogical checkup.

At the clinic, Bianca's eyes focused on two other females in the same waiting area as she was. Bianca was convinced that she knew these people but could not immediately place them. What was even more intriguing was the fact that one of these ladies, the older one, kept staring at her as if she too had recognised someone she knew.

Bianca was early for her appointment, and it turned out that her appointment was scheduled to follow that of the two ladies who were clearly together, perhaps mother and her beautiful mixed-race daughter. Bianca thought, gosh, I am sure I have seen that heavenly beauty before, but where?

She kept wondering that if their appointment is before hers, she might recognise their names when the receptionist calls for them. She wondered who was accompanying who. Neither of them seemed obviously pregnant.

That time came and the receptionist came forward and duly announced that Ms. Johnson should step forward, please. This left Bianca none the wiser; but as the two ladies passed Bianca on their way in to see the specialist, the older lady said, "Hello Bianca", they both smiled at her and went in to see the doctor.

It was then that Bianca realised who Ms. Johnson was. Surely it is Daniel Johnson! It is none other than the domestic helper at Mr Allan Austin's home. What a coincidence, she thought.

Mr Austin had given two women in his life the time off to attend the same clinic on the same day. But who was the accompanying beauty with Daniel? It was not until the two ladies were on their way out of the doctor's office that Daniel once more stopped and said hello to Bianca and at the same time introduced Doreen.

"Doreen, this lady is your father's personal assistant and Acting Chief Administrative Officer at his school. Bianca, this is Doreen: she is your boss's daughter. She has come back home to live."

Bianca, somewhat amazed, shook hands with Doreen as they both respectfully acknowledged each other. It had become exceedingly clear to Bianca by this that Doreen is that beauty in the photograph on the centre table in Mr Austin's reception room—the same young lady who is betrothed to be married to the Swedish native, Jason Musgrave.

Now Bianca was left with her mind whirling with inquisitive thoughts.

Before Daniel and Doreen departed for home, however, Bianca's body language gave away very clearly the fact that she would like to know more about Doreen's Swedish scholastic endeavour.

Daniel, observing Bianca's body language, mentioned that she and Doreen had planned to be in the Birmingham City Centre tomorrow and suggested that, maybe Bianca could join them for coffee. She was sure that Doreen would appreciate hearing how a school is run by someone other than her father.

"Oh, and by the way, you could give us both an update on how things are advancing on the murder situation if you are anymore in the know. Mr Austin has been far too busy to do that," Daniel suggested tactfully.

Bianca thought that that idea was a great one and said so. The result was that they agreed to meet at eleven o'clock on Saturday, the next day, the twelfth of June, at the Occasional Coffee Joint on New Street.

It was now Bianca's turn to see the doctor so she bade the ladies goodbye until tomorrow when they would get a chance to talk and catch up.

That night, two things preoccupied Bianca's thoughts. What had become of the planned marriage between Doreen and her Swedish beau, Jason Musgrave?

Who was seeing the specialist at the clinic today? She finally gave up thinking about these two issues as she remembered that Gaston was going to be at home but as he wasn't too talkative, he might not be willing to drop her in town tomorrow.

She checked in her handbag and found the card of a nearby taxi firm, so she pre-booked a taxi for ten o'clock tomorrow morning. To hell with Gaston, Burney, she thought before joining her husband for the rest of the night.

Chapter 12

The next morning, Bianca sorted out her usual Saturday morning chores and shared with Carlos that she would be out for a couple of hours or so meeting with the headteacher's daughter and his domestic assistant for coffee in the centre of Birmingham. Gaston was present and would have heard everything but made no offer to chauffeur her as he would normally have done.

Bianca thought it both strange and vindictive on the part of Gaston. She, of course, had no knowledge of the fact that Gaston was legally grounded at home. She just put it down to Gaston still being terribly upset with her for getting pregnant.

On the stroke of ten o'clock, the pre-arranged taxi arrived. Bianca bade the two men goodbye and off she went to keep her appointment with the ladies from Austin's home. The morning was somewhat murky, damp, and a bit sticky. The sun did not bother to come out but nevertheless, the heat was uncomfortable for this time of the year in Birmingham.

On arrival at the Occasional Coffee Joint on New Street, Bianca found the other two ladies already seated and a waitress hovering to take their order. She was not late. It was Daniel and Doreen that was a bit early. As the two ladies saw Bianca entering the joint, they politely asked the waitress to let them have a little more time so that their guest could be settled.

Bianca greeted the two ladies and they reciprocated and beckoned to the waitress. They ordered their coffee and cake; grumbled about the unpleasant weather conditions and then settled into more purposeful conversations.

By the end of the three ladies' coffee session, Bianca had learned many useful things, the importance most of which she could not share with the other two ladies. Doreen did not hold back.

She recounted a very romantic tale, if a little lascivious, that went horribly wrong. She was encouraged in her openness by the supporting presence of Daniel who could have been mistaken for a mother figure.

The first of these revelations was that just as she, Bianca, had previously thought, the young man in the picture on Austin's centre table at their home was not Jason Musgrave as Mr Austin and, indeed, Daniel boasted that day she had a working lunch with the headteacher at his home.

This strongly held view by Bianca had now been confirmed by the Swedish police as reported by Doreen.

Secondly, whoever this guy is, he beats women and had a very nasty temper. Doreen had the marks to show for it even with some make-up coverage.

Thirdly, this guy seems to have some kind of awful phobia about pregnancy where it involves him. Consider the extreme reaction to what should have been wonderful news, especially in the context of a planned marriage. Poor Doreen, she must have been frightened beyond imagination. She was extremely lucky to have had a near neighbour who acted quickly and sensibly.

Fourthly, Bianca can no longer talk about Elaine Edgewater's ring being unique because Doreen was wearing a ring that looks identical. Her father had discovered Elaine's corpse.

Did he somehow find that ring and passed it on to Doreen? Highly unlikely, but it is possible. Pictures taken of the deceased at the time the body was discovered showed no ring on her finger. Elaine had never gone anywhere without that ring.

Lastly, and perhaps most telling of all, Doreen, in response to the warm weather they were having in Birmingham, produced a fan that was identical to the one Bianca had, there and then, in her handbag.

Bianca could not help wondering whether Doreen's fan was the other fan which according to the receipt from Ocho Rios in St. Ann, Jamaica, was bought at the same time as Bianca's together with a rather expensive up-market ring.

The other ladies took away what they wanted from the coffee session too. Doreen had remembered schools very much from the standpoint of a pupil. She was pleasantly surprised to learn that the people who run and managed them have rules to follow and many, sometimes huge, responsibilities like the occasional murder inquiry.

Daniel thought that she will be more understanding about Mr Austin's different moods given what she had learned about the pressures of the job. In all, each of the three was very happy that the event took place, and all looked forward to the next occasion when that opportunity presents itself. The ladies then split up and went their separate ways for home.

Chief Inspector Harding, Detective Corporal Brown, and other involved police officers felt it necessary to have yet another updating conference on the matters relating to the Dixon Pen murder. They chose Sunday the thirteenth of June for this purpose.

The two chief officers had instigated a revisit of the Upton unsolved murder that had gone cold. Following their search of Elaine Edgewater's accommodation and what they had found, it had become prudent to revisit that cold case.

Chief Inspector Harding on opening the second conference explained that the London police who was in charge of all investigations pertaining to the unsolved Upton murder at the time, December 3rd, 2016, was extremely cooperative and made all the shelved documentation immediately available to the Birmingham officers in accordance with their request. The media fraternity was no less cooperative.

The various tabloids, evening and Sunday papers made a concerted effort to present a collective library of relevant publications at the time of the murder. From the voluminous amount of paperwork, it could be clearly gleaned that the case was a high-profile one that attracted deep interest from all the political parties as well as from most of the residents within a five miles radius of Tower Hamlets where the murder was committed.

The London police investigators recorded that after their extensive inquiries and a most thorough investigation, the case went cold for lack of hard evidence and explained to Chief Inspector Harding, that we could see why.

Most of what was reported in the various media outlets were speculative with no confirmed truth.

One interesting theory, and the one that seemed the most popular with most of the media at the time, was that the victim died because she knew too much. It was at a time when drugs and gun smuggling were rife in London, the United States of America, and the entire Caribbean region. The trade was a very lucrative one albeit criminal in all its aspects. Many players lost their lives to prevent them from spilling vital information which could cripple the trade.

For example, it was reported that AK-47 rifles could fetch upwards of US$400,000 with 9mm Gluck pistols or 45-calibre handguns fetching US$250,000—US$300,000.

Weapons from the guns-for-drugs business have flooded many parts of the Caribbean in return for ganja, cocaine, and other hard illegal drugs which find their way to high-paying customers in the United Kingdom and the United States. Of course, the activities of these traders and their reach were not confined to the areas mentioned. At the time of the Upton murder case, however, the media seemed certain that the players had business links with these specified areas and our victim had become too wise.

The police were aware of this phenomenon and, with or without the aid of informers, had mounted many successful raids and made numerous arrests; but all that seemed to have happened was that the trade became more secretive, went underground, and, indeed, became far more dangerous in more ways than one.

The proliferation of guns in the poorer areas of the world had facilitated gang wars, and murderous slaughter on the streets, in places such as the United Kingdom and the United States the numbers of drug addicts and those dying from the substances were growing seriously out of control and, if we were to believe the media, many die because they had to be silenced before they become informers and aids to the authorities, thus threatening this lucrative trade.

Several names of people unidentified were liberally paraded in the media at the time of Gloria Upton's murder, but none of them was ever positively linked to the murder. The names Robert Reid and Mustafa Banks received constant mention in the media and even found their way into police reporting.

The view expressed at the time was that these two characters were senior trading operators with definite overseeing links with the gang that made a ghost of Gloria Upton. There was simply no substantial lead that could have unravelled the case, the conference heard.

As far away as Yorkshire, the reporting of the Upton murder took on a more definite tone. The view stated with more than ninety-five percent of certainty was that the wrong person was killed. Gloria Upton was an identical twin sister of Madge Upton. She had left the village of Wake in West Yorkshire early on the day she was killed.

The story went that she had gone to visit her twin sister whom she had not seen for over three years and who lived in Tower Hamlets in East London. The view was strongly held that Gloria took what was coming to Madge simply because even people, who have known the twins for many years, find it exceptionally difficult to tell them apart.

The reporting was as definite as it was because Gloria was known to be a model of uprightness in her part of the world in Yorkshire. She had absolutely no connection with the world of drugs and gun smugglers as were the hints being peddled in the south. Her death, therefore, had to be an unfortunate error.

There seemed to have been some substance to the Yorkshire media angle; though, without more, it was difficult to base a case on that view at the time. The conference is of this view because firstly the murder took place at the temporary home of Madge Upton and secondly, Madge was the person who discovered the body of her gruesomely murdered twin sister just about an hour after she had welcomed her and left her for a while.

According to the extensive report that Madge made to the police at the time, she Madge, had just left to get a pizza takeaway so she and Gloria could nostalgically indulge in their childhood delicacy.

Madge had recently met this guy who introduced himself as Robby. Robby and his friend Bunny were at a lavishly organised party to which she was invited by a girlfriend. This party, she recalled in her report was where and when she met these two chaps. Robby was a charmer. He traded with his blue come-to-bed eyes and otherwise good looks. She had found herself in bed with Robby on that same night even before the party had ended. He had easily enticed her up the stairs and away from the dazzling and partially inebriated crowd to the seclusion of one of several empty bedrooms waiting upstairs.

The man was some man in bed: a woman could not have asked for or wished for more. The end of his repeat session with me coincided with the winding down of the party. Bunny went off with a girl assumed to be his regular and Robby invited me to spend the night with him at his nearby rented apartment. Madge reported that that ground-floor apartment became her home for the next two weeks to the day her sister was killed.

The apartment was expensively decorated. It was spacious and accommodating. It was for this reason why she had rung her sister Gloria who she had not seen for some years and invited her to come to London and spend a few days with her. Robby and Bunny were very busy people, she reported. They were always entertaining strangers and frequently away from the apartment which meant that she was often alone and lonely.

Having her sister with her for a few days would reduce the ennui she sometimes experienced when she was alone, she thought.

On one occasion she overheard a telephone conversation that she was certain she should not have heard.

Robby was in conversation with some unidentified female person who wanted "the stuff on the next flight out of London otherwise Parker cannot collect the shooters in Haiti. Your reward, as usual, will be in Stockholm and I can have back Box A which I know is still with you. I need to see that beauty on my finger again where it rightly belongs."

Madge reported remembering hurriedly scribbling down Box A on a brown paper bag that had some rubbish waiting to go in a disposal bin. She had then torn off the scribbled-on edge of the paper bag and palmed it as she continued to eavesdrop. Robby had replied to the female, don't you worry baby, Box A is safe and secured in my drawer as we speak but will be in a safe deposit where you can personally retrieve it with your bonus of US$10, 000 in cash when next you were here.

She was so carried away with this eavesdropping, her ears up against the tiny crack in the door, that she didn't notice Robby entering the room from the other side of the room. She tried to pretend that she was just going to the bathroom, but she knew that she was good and truly caught in the act of spying. Robby behaved as though nothing was wrong and came to bed with the same sexual vigour that he had treated her to on the first night they had met. The next day Robby was gone as usual.

It was not of any major concern to Madge since she was expecting company from Yorkshire that same day. On her return from the pizza joint, she found Gloria with her throat adroitly severed and left sprawled out in a pool of blood across the dining room table in the kitchen. She panicked and for several minutes she knew not what to do. As she slowly returned to her senses, she began to realise two very important things.

Firstly, she might be a suspect in this case and secondly, her own life might now be in danger. She dialled 999 and waited for the police to arrive, hence the report she subsequently gave them.

No one ever saw or heard from Madge Upton again. The police wanted to make follow-up inquiries on her original report but were never able to locate her. They had conducted a thorough search of the rented apartment but had never found Box A and the US$10,000 referred to in Madge's report.

The landlady for the rented premises had no real knowledge of any significance about Robby. According to her, she had really liked the white fellow, the one they call Robby but had genuinely disliked Bunny because he was too black and seemed to be dishonest. For this reason, she didn't trust him.

They have now disgraced her premises and she bitterly regrets having had anything to do with those characters. She clearly thought they were responsible for the killing.

The case went cold from there on.

However, we here in Birmingham have noted several parallels between the Upton case and the Edgewater case.

The first thing that caught the eyes and attention of our boys is the method and skill used to kill the victims in both the n's case and the water. In Upton's case, the victim's throat was adroitly slashed by a sharp instrument which also seemed to have had a jagged edge towards the rear. There was a clear similarity with the imposter Edgewater's case.

Her throat, too, was slashed with the same brutal proficiency with an instrument of similar description. In both cases, the victims were left sprawled across some wooden surface and lying in a pool of blood. The murderer had fled the scene unnoticed.

The paper records also showed that there was little to no struggle and that in both cases the victims would have been taken by surprise by someone appearing to be friendly. At Upton's murder, some inference was drawn to the effect that the victim knew too much. The same conclusion is likely to be drawn in Dixon Pen's case.

Fingerprint experts in Upton's case had found dozens of different prints on the rented premises. That was very much expected in circumstances of frequent short-term lettings. There were no matches even if these prints were subjected to computerised scrutiny. The fingerprints were, however, kept safely on file.

Similarly, the fingerprints taken from Edgewater's case were many in numbers but not unusual for a building that entertains frequent visitors. Apart from the prints of the person pretending to be Elaine Edgewater and those of the headteacher, no other prints made a match-up via the computer. So, here too we were left in a most unhelpful limbo.

The conference will however recall that some of us met with a fifteen-year-old pupil, Frankie Watson, from the school in the presence of his parents. Although the headteacher was somewhat doubtful about the veracity of the boy's report, (apparently, recalcitrant pupils frequently concoct wildly imaginary stories to avoid accountability), he had told the headteacher of a stranger visitor to the school the day before the murder.

At our meeting with Frankie, we followed up on this report. Frankie was adamant that he was relating the absolute truth as far as that issue was concerned. He was not just fabricating a story just to escape his headteacher's wrath for not being in his lesson at the right time. The lead we got from this meeting with Frankie was that the stranger, who, at the time, claimed to be Mrs Elaine Edgewater's brother, was tall, blond, and muscular and had remarkable blue eyes.

He drove a green Toyota Celica with registration plate HPH 344V. Frankie on the day in question was collecting licence plate numbers of Toyota Celica's for a special project and the stranger was one of very few he spotted that day. When we had this licence plate checked out, the computer told us that the owner of that vehicle was Mustafa Banks.

We thought this was an important breakthrough and wasted no time in giving Mr Banks a social visit with the clear intention of inviting him to super at the station and perhaps to stay at Her Majesty's pleasure for some time. Mustafa was extremely cooperative when we got to his home. He took us to the garage where the vehicle was kept and our examination revealed that that was the car we were seeking. It was the right car but the wrong driver according to the eyewitness report.

Mustafa was VERIFIABLY out of the country both on the day Frankie saw his vehicle and on the day of the murder. In fact, Mustafa was attending a major five days Rastafarian festival in Ghana where he had speaking engagements on both days and was a guest on all other days.

In any case, he is not blond with blue eyes and certainly not tall and muscular. This is, in fact, a black man with Rastafarian locks. Mustafa swore that he did not lend his car to anyone and that as far as he knows; no one had access to his car. Mustafa could help us no further, except to verify that he was born in Jamaica and still had established links there.

The rendezvous with Mrs Bianca Burney and her mobile telephone had not been very helpful either. We had become very interested in some recent WhatsApp pictures found on her phone. These were pictures of the passports of her stepson, Gaston Burney, and his Swedish friend, Jason Musgrave who had stayed with her family for a short while.

Apparently, photographing those documents made it easier to recover them in the event of theft or loss. There was another photo, said to be sentimental, of a receipt issued to a friend of hers for the purchase of a ring and a couple of ornamental fans from a shop in Ocho Rios, Jamaica. She needed a souvenir of the receipt for sentimental reasons. The officers were not convinced that Mr Burney was altogether truthful about that photo as far as the dates were concerned. It is possible, however, that her memory might have been unreliable in places.

Now, Conference might be thinking that we were no further forward with this case. I beg to disagree, said the chief inspector. We have made some small but very significant steps forward. We had already established beyond doubt that the murdered Mrs Elaine Edgewater was an imposter. We know that the person being impersonated was Mrs Elaine Edgewater in reality with the National Insurance number: YA 66 10 53 B.

This number was also being used by the imposter. This real person however was much older and was married twice and had identical twin girls. The girls were not named Edgewater because they were the product of their mother's first marriage to one John Upton who died in a motor car racing accident when the twins were just two years old. Their mother also, unfortunately, died when they were just thirteen years old.

From that time onwards, not much can be traced about the twin girls. It is believed that they went their separate ways. However, somewhere in this world, there were two identical twin girls going under the surname 'Upton' or nee Upton if a marriage had intervened. **On the other hand, they could both be dead**. Colleagues, we all know that not all 'Smiths' were necessarily related. Neither were all 'Uptons'. But the Upton murder had brought into play some issues which would be rightly considered extra-ordinary were they to vie as mere coincidences.

Let us for a moment forget about the name 'Upton'. We shall just focus on the report that Madge gave to the police when she found her sister Gloria good and truly butchered. In her report, there was a reference to **'Box A'** being hurriedly written on the edge of a brown paper bag and then torn off and palmed. Let us fast forward now to the death of the imposter, Elaine Bridgewater.

Did we not find references to the Upton unsolved murder and very significantly, did we not find a scrappy piece of brown paper with **'Box A'** written on it? Surely, we can now claim to have moved forward. The Upton sisters of the December 3rd 2016 murder are, in fact, the identical twin sisters of whom we have lost track since they were thirteen years of age.

At the conference, we still needed to know what '**Box A**' all is about and why Madge Upton disappeared after lodging her report with the London police following the murder of her sister, Gloria, that awful day. Chief Inspector Harding then signalled the end of his reporting to the conference with these closing remarks:

"Colleagues, I think I know where to find Madge Upton: but I won't be so brave so as to make that announcement just yet without more. However, I will say this, if you tell us what '**Box A**' is all about, I will show you the murderer of Gloria Upton and of the imposter Elaine Bridgewater. I thank you, Conference."

Chapter 13

It is Wednesday, June thirty and Gaston Burney had to appear in the Birmingham Crown court on many serious charges. The arrogance of the man: he had done nothing to defend his case. One would have expected that he would have reached out to a qualified and experienced solicitor or a combination of solicitor and Barrister to assist him in his plight.

He did not. Whether this was done out of confidence or because he really didn't care no one really knows, but here he is arriving at court determined to manage his own defence.

The case had been listed a few days to be before the Honourable Justice Sheila Brown who had a reputation for being hardnosed and unforgiving. It was all the more reason for the defendant to be properly prepared and don't take chances with charges such as:

1. evading the police when told to stop.
2. driving beyond the speed limits in built-up areas;
3. driving recklessly, and carelessly.
4. driving under the influence of alcohol and
5. being in possession of a dangerous weapon found in his glove compartment.

Gaston Burney entered a plea of guilty with the explanation on all counts. The court heard that his otherwise previously unblemished record was impulsively ruined because of an inordinate amount of stress that had come unexpectedly tumbling down on him in one fell swoop in the early morning of Thursday twenty-sixth of May.

He went on to explain to the court that his two girlfriends that do not know of each other had quite separately on that same morning announced that they were pregnant and that he was the father. The announcements confounded him and made him resort to drinking and the rest followed on from there.

As a result of his stupidity, he was now standing humbly in front of Her Honour trying to atone for his sins. As he explained all this, Gaston Burney was in uncontrollable tears. He asked the court for mercy and forgiveness and assured the court that he would never be caught doing these breaches ever again.

If playing for the court's sympathy was Gaston's aim all along, it partially worked. The Honourable Justice Sheila Brown ratified his plea of guilty on counts 1 to 4 and imposed fines totalling £500.00. On count 5, the learned judge insisted on knowing more. She asked for detailed reports on Mr Burney, the purpose of such a dangerous knife, and why it was in Mr Burney's car.

She also ordered the return of Mr Burney's licence and lifted the curfew and reporting that were parts of his bail conditions. However, she ordered the continued retention of his passport pending the hearing and outcome of the case concerning the possession of a dangerous weapon. The hearing was set for Wednesday 27th of October 2021 at ten o'clock.

On his way out of court, Gaston Burney stopped by the court's office, paid his fine, and then left for home a relatively free man once more.

Bianca was dreading today. She had been very reluctantly persuaded by her daughter, Helen, to meet with her today, Saturday the third of July at a neutral location in the Birmingham City Centre, the exact place and time were to be fixed nearer the date. Two nights ago, Helen had called her mother and they jointly agreed that the Pepper Candy Restaurant on Charles Street would be a suitable meeting place.

They would get there at noon in time for lunch in one of the restaurant's private rooms upstairs in the building. Carlos was duly briefed last night that Bianca would be meeting Helen today and that he would be expected to fend for himself if Gaston was not around.

There was no need for a taxi, since the number eleven buses that stop across the road from the Burney's pass close to the **Pepper Candy Restaurant.** As luck would have it, Bianca's bus arrived in good time. And as coincidence would further have it, she and her daughter arrived at the restaurant at the same time.

As Bianca was walking from the bus stop towards the restaurant, she saw Helen parking her car in the huge car park that serves the restaurant. They met and greeted each other not so warmly but semi-cordial. The **Pepper Candy Restaurant** was warmly welcoming. Its décor is splendidly put together by decorators with magnificent artistic taste, reflected style, and charm in every way.

The waiter that received the ladies at the top of the steps escorted them to a private room to be seated and served. Both these women enjoy a good Lasagna Verdi al Forno so they ordered that with a bottle of Curacao's green pale wine to go with it and then got down to business as they waited to be served.

Helen opened the conversation with a deeply felt historical set of questions.

"Mother, dear, do you remember when, at ten years of age, I foolishly played with a match and accidentally burnt the kitchen down three days before Christmas? And do you remember that when I was fifteen years old my girlfriend, Sally, and I were caught shoplifting at the corner store and how that single instance had brought disgrace and stigma upon our home: so much so that we had to sell up and moved away?"

"I sure do, Helen, I remember both incidents and how dreadful they were for us especially not having your father around to share in the consequences. But why are you asking me about these long-ago matters? They have long been forgotten. You are almost twenty-four years of age now?"

"I have never forgotten them, my dear mother. Those incidents, together with countless more minor others, have remained indelibly stamped in my memory for one single reason. That reason is how you remained my friend throughout all the agony you suffered at the time and for as long as those episodes lasted. I remember how humanely yet firmly I was admonished for doing wrong.

"I had always told myself that one day when I would have children of my own, I would follow the example which you had set me right up until the night of Wednesday eighteenth of May. That was the night, I believe, I lost the mother I knew. And it was for that reason why I pestered you for this meeting. Having to pester you for a meeting was another reason that reinforced my determination to have this meeting.

"Normally, we never needed pestering to meet. There are certain matters that I must get to the bottom of before I can fully understand your behaviour, or should I say your attitude towards me, on that said night. Are you ready for this, mother?"

"Helen, I wasn't ready for any of this on the night of the eighteenth, I am absolutely sure of that, but I think I am now, and I pray to the heavens that some of that old-time chemistry which we had as mother and daughter whilst you were growing up is either still in place or will hurriedly return. I know for sure that what I am about to share with you will disgust you and might drive you away from me in terms of space and time.

"You see, my daughter, listening to you as you recounted your experiences with Gaston Burney from the beginning to your pregnant state, I was not only listening but reliving it. Your story could have been an exact photograph or photocopy of mine. The only difference was I was a married woman when it all began and what is worst, I was married to Gaston Burney's dad.

"Sweetheart, I can tell you truthfully that my attitude on that night was the direct product of combined shame, jealousy, and entrapment. There was a shame because what I was involved in is just what I would have advised others not to do. I had fallen for Gaston Burney on the first day I met him. That day was the day of my marriage to his father.

"Throughout the course of that day, I had eyes only for him. On just the second day after I was married, the same night of the 'grand super' which you and your friends Jo and Jacky had so thoughtfully and kindly treated us to, I found myself willingly in bed with Gaston Burney who had already worked out that I was his for the taking.

"This kind of clandestine affair has been happening all along until he walked out on me in the early hours of Wednesday 26th May soon after he had had a mad passionate sex with me. He walked out in a huge huff because I had gently broken the news to him that he was going to be a daddy. I never mentioned you and your pregnancy because I felt that was your news to break.

"He doesn't know that I am in the know about his affair and subsequent development with you. I simply explained to him that he had made me pregnant. He suddenly lost his cool and, had it not been for his father sleeping downstairs, he would have blown the roof off with his anger. I was so glad when he chose to leave the house. Where he went, I cannot say, but since that he speaks to me only reluctantly.

"What I can say for him, though, is that since that walk out on me, he has been spending a great deal of his time with his father, much to the partial delight of Carlos, who, as you probably know, won't ever be completely happy with Gaston until he finds 'a decent girl' with whom to settle down; and he wants that sooner rather than later. There was jealousy because I wasn't at that moment seeing you as my daughter and only child that I love so much.

"Truthfully, that evening, you were the rival awful cheating woman who had been sharing my man and now claiming to have a hold on him forever with your pregnant self. I wanted to call you every derogative adjective in the dictionary and others I could make up. At one point I wanted to scream at you that I too was carrying Gaston Burney's child, but I could not find the courage.

"It was then that I needed to get away from you and get back home. You made it so hard for me when you insisted on taking me home. That would have been the most awkward journey together had you had your own way. That you had honourably promised to take me back that night was of no value to me at the time. The promise had become irrelevant and unnecessary once I had heard of the good times that you had been having and still were having with my man.

"I felt entrapped because I could not end the relationship. There was no way out. It had gone too far. Even now my lust for that man has not been quenched. The worst part of all this is that I had no one with whom to share my mental agony. I could talk to no one about it. I had often thought of sharing with you but the cloud of shame and the thought of losing you forbade me from sharing with you.

"All I could do leading up to this moment was to try and lose myself in my schoolwork. This only worked in the daytime and then only for five out of seven days.

"My reluctance in meeting you had solely to do with the fact that I could not face you without deep remorse and I am sure that that would have been written all over me, especially in my body language. I was afraid that I would lose your respect which would be further damaging blows to me. Over these last few days, I have finally come to terms with what I had already known was your concern.

"I mustered up the courage to confront you and to be totally candid with you. Admittedly, I didn't reach this position without some assistance from a story that I will share with you today and from a plan which I have hatched and hoped that we can execute together. All of that I will share with you today."

At this point, they were interrupted by the arrival of the steaming hot lunch. The waiter poured them a glass of wine each and departed wishing them a very good appetite.

"Mother, I do understand your predicament. I see why there was a temporary loss in your usual sympathetic understanding. Gaston is a brute. How dare he do this to you? How dare he do this to my mother? Did I understand you to be saying that Gaston had you in his bed on the morning of Wednesday twenty-sixth of May?

"And then he walked out on you? Did you know that he came to my home and fucked me silly like a ravenous bull that same morning? I too took the opportunity to let him know that I was with child for him. He became instantly boisterous and stroppy. You could see the temper surging from his every part.

"I had never seen anyone so angry as when I gave Gaston what should have been happy news. He took off from me in a rage too. So mad was he, he left his underwear behind and one foot of his sock. Where he went, I do not know but I have not seen him since. And you know, mother, I am not sure that I would ever want to see that shit again: at least, not in loving terms."

"Sweetheart, I see that you are beginning to feel like I do about Gaston Burney. 'Shit' is too decent a word to describe him. Now, I am going to share with you a true story that I found out about our man Gaston Burney only recently.

"I cannot go too publicly about it as yet because it links my boss and could have very serious repercussions for a lot of people if he finds out: not if he finds out, but when he does, because find out he will. Our man, Gaston, has unwittingly, but with his usual callousness, linked Mr Austin into all of this mess that we are currently experiencing by impregnating Mr Austin's daughter, Doreen, too.

"It seems that Gaston is involved in something illicit that takes him to various parts of the world including Sweden which is where he stumbled upon Doreen. Doreen is my headteacher's last child. She was on a preparation course for the University of Umea where it was her plan to study medicine. Not long after she got to Umea, by way of initiation, the university ran an excursion to the Capital City of Stockholm.

"It coincided with a day when Gaston (who was masquerading as one Jason Musgrave, a born and bred Swedish national and who was gainfully employed as a scientist at a prestigious laboratory in Stockholm) was also in Stockholm for whatever reason. Fate brought the two together at an ice cream parlour. What happened to you when you first met Gaston, and what happened to me when I first met Gaston, also happened to Doreen who was just seventeen years old and very inexperienced having led a very sheltered life.

"She suffered the exact terrible experiences we did. We dare not criticise her. If she was foolish and weak, then what were we older women, especially me? In just a day or two after meeting Doreen in Stockholm, Jason found himself at her doorstep in Umea some seven hundred kilometres or seven hours away. That same day he spent the day sightseeing in Umea and its surrounds. In keeping with Doreen's unexpressed desire, he spent that night with her.

"He took the young girl's virginity and left Doreen suitably hooked on him just as he did us. He then made it a regular habit to meet Doreen either in Umea or in Stockholm or its surrounds for their sexual rampages. In the end, like us, Doreen became pregnant.

"Doreen had proudly boasted to her father about this fabulous Swedish national she had met. The wise father that he is, Mr Austin had cautioned his daughter and by extension, Jason Musgrave, that her studies should be prioritised above romance.

"According to Doreen, her father's advice went mostly unheeded but to appease her father she and Jason Musgrave became engaged with their marriage planned for the end of her studies sometime in the drawn-out future given that the highly charged sexual relationship had caused her to seriously neglect her program of studies.

"On the day I was promoted to the Acting Chief Administrative Officer (incidentally, the substantive post for my job is now nationally advertised and I have applied for it: wish me luck), I was visiting the headteacher's home for the very first time. One of the first things I noticed about his home was a stunning picture of a couple posing so proudly on a centre table in the headteacher's reception room.

"At that time, I had not met or even known of Doreen. However, I was certain that I knew the male figure in the picture. In my mind that was Gaston Burney. The same come-to-bed blue eyes; shoulder-length blond hair and irresistible physique were unmistakably much in evidence. I must have been lost in a daze and only snapped out of it when the housekeeper came along and saw me staring so intensely at the picture.

"She explained that the couple had recently become engaged, and that the beautiful young lady was in fact Mr Austin's last child now studying in Sweden and that the young man was Jason. Not long after that Mr Austin came along with mounting pride in his voice and demeanour and not only confirmed Daniel's explanation, but he also unsuspectingly enlarged upon the details pertaining to the supposedly happy couple.

"You can imagine my feeling. I was burning anxiously inside but could not raise the issue in contra-diction. I simply left it there. It did, however, jolt me into checking out why my period was several days late. It was so that I came to realise that I was pregnant for Gaston. Gaston, Carlos, and I know that Carlos can no longer have children since the removal of his prostate.

"There was simply no point going down that road as Gaston had suggested. And I told him categorically no way when he suggested abortion as a way out. My Catholic upbringing was steadfast against that, I told him much to his chagrin.

"In the meantime, I had become absorbed by the murder inquiry at the school and the challenging responsibilities of my new post.

"So, you might be rightfully wondering how I have come by this horrendous piece of information. Well, Gaston Burney was at it again; he also treated Doreen to the same kind of response, when he heard that she was carrying his child, as he gave us when we told him about our pregnancies. Only, in her case, he violently slapped her about and the Swedish police had to become involved.

"Jason Musgrave was checked out by the Swedish police, and they could find no such person having ever been born in the entire country. As a result, the cops are on the lookout for him. They want him to account for his presence and activities in the Swedish Kingdom.

"Subsequent to this development, Doreen was the recipient of death and other sinister threats telling her to get out of Umea before something unpleasant should happen to her. The young girl panicked and fled the country only telling her father when her flight back to Birmingham was already booked.

"Sometime after she was back, Mr Austin had arranged with Daniel, his housekeeper to ensure that Doreen made a visit to the family clinic. I, too, being very aware that a child was developing inside me, had sought, and obtained permission from Mr Austin to go for a medical checkup.

"Low and behold, the day I chose to visit the family clinic, was the very same day that Daniel had taken Doreen there. Daniel immediately recognised me from that day I visited Mr Austin's home. She introduced Doreen to me and said that Doreen was back from Sweden and living at home now.

"I was curious, bearing in mind the photo which I had seen at the headteacher's home and, indeed, what both Daniel and Mr Austin had told me about Doreen's marital prospects and her medical studies. Before leaving the clinic, all three of us had managed to agree on a meeting the following Saturday morning in Birmingham Town Centre where we had coffee and a bite to eat at the Occasional Coffee Joint on New Street and Doreen, herself, told this story in all its details.

"So far, only you and I, and, indeed, Gaston Burney know about all three pregnancies. Mr Austin knows, obviously, about his daughter's situation but as far as he is concerned the connecting man is one Jason Musgrave who is best forgotten and relinquished to the Swedish graveyard of unknown citizens. Doreen has yet to know of your existence.

"She has met and spoken with me but as far as our pregnancies, yours and mine, and the name Gaston Burney are concerned, she is totally unaware. Carlos knows nothing about his son's carrying on with any of the three women in all of this. Can you visualise the shock it will be for him when he does find out?

"Despite Gaston's knowledge of the three pregnancies which will make him a father three times over in the same month next February, he has remained silent about everything thus indicating that he is unaware that at least you and I are fully aware of what is going on. What on earth will he do when he does realise that all three women are in conversation about the result of his sexual prowess"?

"Mother, this is so shocking: I am ashamed to be a part of it. What do you mean by 'when he does realise that all three women are in conversation'? Do you intend to tell Doreen about us and who Jason Musgrave is?" Helen queried in total astonishment.

"Yes, Helen, and this is where my plan comes in. It will require your complete cooperation and that of Doreen's for it to be the shocker I intend. Doreen is temporarily out of the country so I will have to await her return before I can put it to her".

"Where is Doreen, now then?" Helen interrupted her mother.

"She has accompanied her father back to Umea for an international conference being planned by the University of Umea. The university had heard of Mr Austin's pioneering role in 'Equality in Education' and persuaded him to play the leading role at this conference and his daughter has gone back with him so that, with her knowledge of Umea, she can be a useful guide to her father whilst they are there.

"I believe, too, that whilst they are there, Mr Austin plans to refresh Doreen's interest in medicine at the university. The media Headlines about this conference and Mr Austin's role and achievements in its agenda are already being splashed all over the globe, you will have noticed," Bianca explained with some pride for having known the man and is, in fact, working for him.

"Can you share that plan with me, in the meantime mother? I hope it is something that will sink that brute and I can be a part of it."

"This is it, my beloved daughter. We need to find a way for Gaston to unwittingly walk into some place by compelling arrangements and suddenly come face to face with all three of us strategically spaced out so he cannot fail to see each of us. Knowing his tendency to lose his temper, we would need to make sure that there are many people present and have some security built in just in case we need it.

"Unless there are other developments that we could incorporate later, we, all three of us, would link our arms in sisterly friendship and make our exit, thereby, leaving Gaston Burney frightened in shock having found out for the first time that all three are in the know. What do you think of this plan, Helen? Do you think it could have the desired effect?" Bianca asked anxiously.

"My view is that something like this can work. It will require Doreen to sign on just as you said and, of course, it will require a good organisation which should not be beyond the skills and determination of three callously abused women. When is Doreen due back, do you know?" Helen asked.

"I am not quite sure, but I can give Daniel a tinkle tonight and see what I can learn. Otherwise, I would have to wait until I am back in school on Monday. The deputies will know of the entire headteacher's movement. They will be high-spirited now; what with all the collateral beneficial publicity Dixon Pen is having because of the head's involvement in the Scandinavian International Conference. They will readily divulge everything," Bianca joyfully speculated as she realised that Helen was on board with her scheme.

"Mother, as soon as we can get all three of us together, we will organise this whopper. We have both a moral and social responsibility to call a halt to this criminal behaviour that characterises this man. We also owe it to women everywhere to neutralise uncaring sexual beasts such as Gaston Burney so that women can be safe," Helen declared with a noticeable amount of vengeance in the tone of her voice.

The two women hugged each other and declared that it, once again, felt like old times. They were a team once more. This time, Bianca was happy to accept the offer of a lift from Helen on their way back home. She dropped Bianca two minutes from her door at Passion Street, Camper, Birmingham by arrangements because Gaston was expected to be home and they didn't want to alert him of their plan before it could leap up and bite him on the ass at the appropriate time.

"Heaven has no rage like love to hatred turned, nor Hell a fury like a woman scorned."

Right on William Congreve—Three times over! Bianca smiled a broad grin to herself as she went inside her precious home.

Inside the home, everything seemed alright and quite normal. Carlos was seated on the sofa reading the papers as usual. There was a muffled sound of Reggae music drifting down the stairs coming from Gaston's domiciliary quarters signalling the fact that he is at home. Bianca had just greeted Carlos and sat down beside him for a general chat when his mobile phone sounded.

It was Chief Inspector Harding on the phone. He broke the news that the gang at Headquarters had carefully reviewed the meeting the police had with her following the return of her mobile telephone. In the main, they were happy with her responses, but the view prevailed that as far as the picture of the receipt from a Jamaican establishment was concerned, some statements were either untrue or there was a memory failure.

If the latter, then it must be officially admitted for the records. To this end, the inspector is seeking a return visit on Monday, to tie up the loose ends.

Bianca who was no longer being protective of Gaston agreed to see the inspector on the morning of Monday the fifth of July at ten o'clock. She knew exactly where the doubts lie and she was now determined to be candid with the police, no matter where it took them.

Chapter 14

Inspector Harding was punctual. On the dot of ten Monday morning, he arrived at Bianca's office where he received a warm welcome. He, however, respectfully declined the offer of some freshly brewed coffee. The two officers then sat down in business-like fashion for a review of Bianca's earlier statements. The inspector handed Mrs Burney a written copy of her replies to the questions which were asked of her at the time the police had returned her mobile phone.

The document was dated: 26 May 2021. Bianca was asked to look through the document and say whether it truly reflected what had taken place at the Meeting in May. After about five minutes, or thereabouts, Bianca confirmed the accuracy of the copy document.

"Good," said the inspector. "This makes for a good starting point".

The inspector then continued to engage Mrs Burney.

"Concerning the photo on your phone of the two passports, we had asked you to tell us who are the passport holders? We needed to know if they were twin brothers, identical twins, maybe because they looked so very much alike."

"Your reply was: 'One of the characters is my stepson. He is the one on the British Passport. You might even see him tonight if he turns up to take me home. The other is his Swedish look-alike friend who came to stay with us for a few days but has now returned home to Sweden. Whilst he was doing his tourism thing, they both thought it wise to have a photograph of their passports just in case they lose them. It would be easier to trace or replace them. It was just a sensible precaution, officers.'"

The inspector then asked: "Do you still stand by that reply, Mrs Burney?"

To this question, Bianca then replied: "Inspector, that reply was not truthful. Both passports are held by my stepson, but I was afraid of admitting that since I did not know the reason for the two different names on the different passports. The Swedish lookalike was a fiction that I created to avoid unwittingly causing a problem for Gaston Burney. The thing about photographing your important documents in case there is loss or theft is truly a sensible proposition."

"With regard to the Jamaican receipt, you told us that it is a recording of an old souvenir you once had, in reference to the fan from Jamaica. What is the truth about this matter, Mrs Burney?" The inspector probed as he moved on to the other photo that was seen on Bianca's phone.

"That too, Inspector, isn't exactly truthful. The truth about all of this is that I was snooping on the affairs of my stepson with limited time with which to do so when the opportunity presented itself. He had all these documents together in one place so I made photographs of all of them so that I could go through them to find out what he was up to at my leisure and with more time," Mrs Burney truthfully answered.

"We also do not believe that we got a proper answer from you when we asked you to account for the missing fan and what seemed like a very expensive ring. Did we, Mrs Burney?" The inspector asked rather forcefully.

"Honestly, Inspector, at the time, I truly did not know anything about that ring and the second fan. To this day, I still do not know their whereabouts. The only thing I know is that they were bought in Jamaica several years ago and that the receipt was a verification of purchase by the person (Robert Reid), whose passport number, A1238760 is recorded on the receipt.

"However, I intend to find out more about these items, especially where the white gold ring with a ruby, opal, and diamond cluster went because I am very puzzled why my stepson gave me a simple fan as a present and is hoarding a receipt that testifies to more products being purchased for what seems like a great deal of money in Jamaican foreign currency terms.

"J$3m in any currency sounds like a lot to me. I hope that this explains why I was, and remain, so inquisitive enough to make photographs of everything so that I could study them in my own time. All the crap I told you about Lance Dunkley giving me a souvenir gift for my birthday was all nonsense intended to mislead you. I now realise how unwise that was and sincerely beg of your forgiveness," Bianca explained as she tried desperately to disguise her obvious jealousy.

Chief Inspector Harding signalled that the interview was now over. He remarked that the responses which Mrs Burney had given the second time round very definitely have a better feel to them. He indicated that he had noticed that there was a worry on Mrs Burney's part that she might unwittingly land her stepson in some form of trouble even though she doesn't appear to know what that might be.

That was neither unreasonable nor uncommon in situations like this one. However, he feared that her fear might yet be realised because, whilst there is nothing in what she had told the police that could assist them in their murder inquiries, there were enough suspicious circumstances here that will cause him to make references to, at least, Passports controller and, indeed, Narcotics Departments.

A man can lawfully have many passports in his name but one person having many passports in different names seems very irregular and worthy of urgent investigation.

Before the inspector departed, Mrs Burney asked him whether the police were making good progress on the Dixon Pen murder inquiries. The inspector replied that there were still a few knots to disentangle before they will know for sure where they were heading. He instanced the need to determine who was impersonating Mrs Elaine Bridgewater; that they need to find the missing Upton sister, (Madge); and, very importantly, determine the significance of the reference to **Box A** found at the imposter's residence.

Once we find the answers to these, we will know who murdered the imposter Mrs Elaine Bridgewater. You were at liberty to share that information with your headteacher when he returns from Scandinavia. The inspector also shared that they were following all the news in the media, at home and abroad, about Mr Austin and his achievements. She should kindly pass on the police department's congratulations on his return.

On Wednesday the seventh of July, the Austins flew back to Britain after what was a tremendously successful international conference was conducted under the leadership of Mr Austin. At Birmingham Airport, there was a fanfare of Scottish pipers and buglers and a lavishly organised welcome home reception.

This was funded and organised by the city's education department in honour of one of their heroes. The media was present in profusion to welcome and applaud the man who had brought home so much prestige to the city. In the resulting mêlée, the young lady accompanying her father was good and truly overlooked except where she was, on the odd occasion, caught in pictures being taken of her father.

When she was leaving her home on her way to school the morning following the return of the headteacher and his daughter, Bianca caught sight of the front page of one of Birmingham's daily papers. The paper boy had stuffed it, among others, through the letter box and it lay where it fell on the door mat. Prominently displayed were the headteacher and his daughter whose name was also in the caption.

This picture if left there could blow Bianca's and her daughter's plan asunder. Bianca quickly retrieved the paper from the door mat and slipped it into her school bag. During the lengthy journey to school, she remained very worried. She was lucky just now, she thought, but what if Carlos goes to fetch another paper?

Gaston is at home, and he would be bound to recognise Doreen and subsequently make all the pertinent connections. This would take all the shocking whammy out of the blow she was planning with Helen for this guy. Luck attended Bianca once more. By mid-afternoon, all the papers had disappeared from the shelves in the areas where it was likely that Carlos might have gone.

A number of strategic phone calls to newsagents had brought her that information. That particular paper was not seen by her household and will not be seen since Bianca made sure of that. She left that paper behind at school at the end of school.

On the pretext of wanting to welcome back Doreen after her father's international acclaim, Bianca telephoned Daniel that same night. She had obtained Daniel's number on the day that they had met at the family clinic.

After some friendly greetings and some chit-chat exchange, Bianca asked how Doreen was and was she able to come to the phone.

"Doreen is fine if a little tired after her trip. She is standing not too far from me: I will get her for you," Daniel responded as she walked over to where Doreen was standing and handed her the phone.

"Hello, who is it"? Doreen in a friendly manner enquired.

"Doreen, it is Bianca, your father's personal assistant. I have seen and read a lot about your father's success in Scandinavia and just wanted to personally say welcome back and pass on your share of the congratulations for the key role you must have also played. It is good to have a famous daddy, isn't it?" Bianca thus tactfully explained why she was calling.

"Oh, thank you so much. I am glad someone recognises that I was part of that trip too," Doreen replied with a cheeky chuckle.

"You are welcome, Doreen, most welcome. How is the baby bulge coming along? Is the morning sickness subsiding by now?" Bianca asked as she resorted to smaller talk.

"The bulge is not all that noticeable as yet but the morning sickness ensures that I don't forget that a little human is on the way into our odd world," Doreen responded cynically.

"Doreen, I have a daughter. Her name is Helen. She is my only child and is in her mid-twenties; and, like you and I, she is very much pregnant at the present time. Maybe we could all three meet sometime to compare the development of our bulges. That could be useful—kind of a pregnant women's club. What do you think?" Bianca bravely enquired as she found the courage to disclose a fact that could be an impediment at her upcoming interview for the substantive post of the acting post she currently holds.

What was even braver, she was making this disclosure to none other than the esteemed daughter of the man whose views at the interview will be exceedingly influential.

"Bianca, I am not sure that I understand you correctly. Who is pregnant, you or your daughter, Helen?" Doreen, now in a state of surprise, sorted clarity.

"Doreen, it is both of us. That is why, like you, I was at the family clinic the day I first met you," Bianca clarified Doreen's probe.

"But, according to Dad, you were there at the clinic for other medical purposes. Something about an annual genealogical checkup, I believe. Daniel and I did mention to Dad that we saw you at the clinic that time. I don't think he knows that you were there because of a pregnancy.

"From my point of view, I would dearly love to meet with you and your daughter and hear more about your experiences. Maybe, that could help me in my situation. Who is the father of Helen's child to be? Are both your hubbies very happy about their oncoming fatherhood? Are they supportive?" Doreen guardedly, but searchingly inquired as she reflected upon her own answers to some of these questions.

"Doreen, there is so much to share. Some of it might surprise you. This coming Saturday, the tenth, we could meet where we met for coffee that Saturday following our clinic appointments. It was at the Occasional Coffee Joint on New Street, do you remember? How about eleven o'clock for a repeat?" Bianca cleverly arranged a date that she knows would not conflict with her school working day.

"Consider that we have a date. I am really looking forward to meeting your daughter, Helen, and, of course, you, once more too. It seems like we have plenty in common and much to share." Doreen declared as she handed back the phone to Daniel who was ostensibly doing other things but heard all the arrangement that was lined up for Saturday.

Bianca was now one step closer to getting her three-some scheme against Gaston Burney off the ground and into action. She had convinced Doreen that a meeting with her and Helen was important without giving too much away. And now, Saturday the tenth at eleven o'clock had a meaningful place on the calendar for all three pregnant ladies.

Then it suddenly occurred to Bianca that in her eagerness to tie up that date, she had completely left Helen out of the consultative process. What if Helen cannot manage the day time and place? She really ought to have checked with Helen first before blindly committing her. After all, Helen sometimes works on a Saturday.

No time now to waste, Bianca got out her mobile phone and dialled Helen's number. Helen's line was engaged. Bianca waited two minutes and then dialled once more. This time the call went through. Helen was at the other end of the line.

Bianca clearly outlined to Helen what had been planned with Doreen and apologetically expressed regrets for not consulting her before now. However, she hopes that Helen will find it convenient to fit in with the arrangements. Helen's response was a tonic.

Bianca then realised that her fear was unfounded. Helen was available and gladly agreed to join forces as far as the arrangements for Saturday were concerned.

Mother and daughter then made their own arrangements for getting to and from the **Occasional Coffee Joint.** In fact, Helen will collect her mother from home that morning and will ensure that she is also delivered back safely.

Both Gaston and Carlos were in the dining hall seeming to be minding their own business when Bianca conducted all her conversations with Daniel, Doreen, and subsequently Helen. If they heard anything, they said and asked naught and so Bianca also had nothing to share.

The big day eventually arrived and so all three ladies assembled at the Occasional Coffee Joint as previously planned. The introductions were made, and the greetings had, and so the ladies got down to business as planned over what will be repeatedly replenished pots of decaffeinated beverage.

This was how and when Doreen came to learn that both Bianca and Helen were impregnated by the same man and that that man was the only son of her current husband, Carlos Burney. She learned too, that whilst all this was happening over the many past months, Carlos knew nothing and still does not.

She listened to both mother and daughter describing how they had quite separately fallen for a sexual charmer who at first made them feel so important, loved, and wanted. She learned too how the two ladies had kept all this a secret from each other until their pregnancies blew it all into the open, at least, to the two women, yet remained a total secret to the rest of the world, especially Carlos.

As she listened, Doreen imagined herself being in the position of either woman. She conceded that the sexual aspects could have been hers; in fact, were exactly like her own experience with Jason Musgrave whilst in Sweden.

Doreen imagined that her own story was already known to Helen for her mother must have shared it…she knows that she could not be overly critical of Bianca and Helen for their sexual weakness because the similarities in their stories were so blatant. Instead, Doreen settled for asking serious questions.

"Where is this Gaston Burney now? Where is this hell of a man? Will I ever meet him?"

"Yes, Doreen, part of the reason we are gathered is to arrange for just that to happen. But before we do that, we need to share with you something that will no doubt, surprise you," Bianca interjected.

"I am listening, what might this be, ladies? Helen, do you know what this is about?" Doreen anxiously enquired of the ladies.

"Yes, I do know about what my mother is about to share with you, and I am partially responsible for the subsequent plan we will also be sharing with you today," Helen replied inclusively.

"Well, let's have it, Bianca. What is it?" Doreen eagerly pressed the ladies.

Bianca began by asking Doreen if she had heard anything more from the Swedish police. Bianca wanted to take out some of the obvious anxiety that Doreen was displaying and the best way of doing that, she thought, was to get Doreen talking about her own situation.

"The only thing that I know about that, ladies, given that I am no longer there, is that Jason Musgrave has never been sighted in the Stockholm area and certainly not in Umea since I was last there. Before I left Umea, the police had interviewed me, in particular, about my relationship with Jason leading up to the state of turmoil from which they had rescued me.

"It seemed then that they had other concerns about Jason beyond what I had told them. Consequently, there is now a ticket out for him via The International Criminal Police Organisation (Interpol). I am advised that if he ever attempts to trace me, I should report that to any police station in any part of the world that I happen to be at the relevant time," Doreen said in reply.

"We are not surprised that Jason Musgrave is nowhere to be found in Stockholm or anywhere in the Scandinavia Peninsular for that matter. This is because that rascal is, as we speak, sitting most comfortably at my home at 50 Passion Street, Camper, right here in Birmingham."

At this point, Doreen almost falls off her chair in total disbelief. She wanted to know what kind of game Bianca and her daughter, Helen, were playing with her. She had come out to exchange ideas on pregnancy and to learn from the older women: but so far it had been totally distressing news that she was enduring.

She was on the verge of losing her calm when she insisted that Bianca should explain where she is coming from with this ridiculous statement. Why would she be entertaining Jason Musgrave in her home? Is not her husband, Carlos, at home? How did she meet Jason and what does she know about him other than what Doreen had told her?

Bianca calmly took each question in the order in which it was posed and dealt with each thus:

"You see, Doreen, Jason Musgrave has a legitimate home with me and his father Carlos. Carlos is at home with his son right now. I first met Jason on my wedding day; the very day I married his father. You see, Jason Musgrave is none other than Gaston Burney the philanderer. I had known this for a very long time.

"I visited your father's home for the first and only time on May sixteenth for a working lunch. I could not help but noticed a framed picture of you and the man I knew was Gaston Burney adorning a central place in my boss's home. I was shocked: even more shocked than you must be right now. However, that day, both your dad and Daniel persuaded me that I was looking at someone else called Jason—a name which I had come across before too on a Swedish passport: only, on the passport, it preceded the surname Musgrave.

"Before leaving your father's home that day I had deliberately filled in the missing blank, but I am not sure whether either your father or Daniel had caught on. Neither of them had mentioned Jason's surname to me. But as I was ready to leave, I complimented that picture once more remarking that Jason Musgrave (and emphasising MUSGRAVE) was a most handsome character. The expressions on both Mr Austin's and Daniel's faces were one of puzzlement, but I was soon into my taxi and out of sight," Bianca carefully inserted every detail.

And still a great deal was not clear for Doreen. Tears filled her worried eyes as she yearned for greater understanding.

Helen timely swapped her seat for another closer to Doreen. The closer proximity enabled Helen to put a comforting arm around Doreen in a moment of deepest sorrow.

"We are in this together, my friend and we must support each other and make this brute get what is rightfully coming to him," Helen sympathetically stated.

"How can you be so sure that Jason is in fact, Gaston?" Doreen challengingly asked Bianca and Helen.

"Let us forget that the two men answer the identical description; let us forget the sexual antics of both men; let us forget the sexual charm and attraction of both men; we will just concentrate on both men's reaction to ownership of pregnancies and let us take into consideration times and dates.

"Look at the times and dates which you swore Jason was with you, or you with him, these coincide exactly with those times and dates when neither Helen nor I could account for Gaston's whereabouts. Finally, according to the Swedish police, there is no such Swedish national by the name of Jason Musgrave. What is more telling, there is no trace of the phony Jason Musgrave in that part of the world according to the Swedish police.

"Yet, there is someone answering the same physical description as Jason Musgrave in my home right now but not in Sweden; there is someone of the same sexual inclinations, charm, and brutishness as Jason Musgrave in my home right now and not in the Swedish Peninsular. All that is left for us to do to establish the truth of all this is to confront him and let his reaction confirm what we already know.

"My daughter and I have a plan to do just that. We want you to be a part of it, if for no other reason to avoid other women falling into the same trap as we three did and being left stranded to fend for themselves. Can we count on you, Doreen?" Bianca with open determination tried to entice the very distressed Doreen Austin.

"What is it that we shall do?" Doreen implored.

Bianca and Helen detected a glimmer of hope for their plan in that Doreen was no longer expressing doubts about the single identity of both men. She now wants to know about the plan for confronting the phony Jason Musgrave and thereby firmly establish him as Gaston Burney.

"Here is the plan that Helen and I have been considering. We need to find a way to have Gaston Burney walk into a place with lots of people planted. When he does, he would not fail to notice three people strategically placed. Imagine the triple shock? At present, he thinks he is the only person that knows he has fathered three children on the way. He is thinking that only each individual woman shares her own secret with him.

"As far as he is concerned, you Doreen is some thirty hours or seventeen hundred miles away in Umea. He will be blown apart to see all three of us getting up and walking past him as we hold hands in a united fashion. Yes, we have thought of his uncontrollable temper and will make security arrangements to counter any of that should it arise.

"That is as far as the plan goes at present, if there are any further developments worth building into the plan we can do so as we go along. But even if the plan stops there, the dire shock which he will have experienced will be some payback for what he has so cruelly done to the three of us and possibly others that we do not know about," Bianca thus gave it to Doreen in considerable detail.

"It is all going to come out into the open from that point onwards. How will this affect my father? What about Carlos? Both men are still in the dark about the interchangeable Jason and Gaston and his antics?" Doreen realistically asked.

"Let us be philosophical about this whole matter. As our bellies grow larger it would all be out whether we like it or not. We can either agree to forewarn both men about the imminent future developments or just leave it and cross those bridges when we get there," Helen promptly chimed in realistically.

Doreen needed no further convincing. She threw away the doubtful reluctance and enthusiastically declared her willingness to be on board as a team.

"Count me in on this. Any man, who goes to such length to satisfy his overdeveloped sexual indulgence and, in this way, hurt women so terribly, must be stopped and stopped publicly. Please leave me to handle how I deal with my dad and I expect you two will handle Carlos's situation," Doreen declared in solidarity with the proposed plan.

All three ladies were now fully on board, we're left to contemplate the finer details of the plan and share with one another any suggestions of dates till the plan is firm and ready to go.

Chapter 15

On Monday, July twelfth, Mr Austin arrived at school walking taller than he always had been. The weekend papers were still singing his praises for the recognition he had brought to his school and the wider British society.

The morning was advancing very productively: everyone seemed chirpy and exceedingly bright as nearing the end of a school term always is. The occasional late stragglers hastily made their way to waiting for lessons with just the help of a telling glance from the spirited headteacher.

Mr Austin, on his way back to his office, travelled in the direction of his PA's office and suggested to her that she should join him so that they could, together, set the date and arrangements for the short-listing and interviews for the substantive post of Chief Administrative Officer.

The headteacher wanted this person to be known before the end of the school term on July sixteenth. The person appointed would then be ready to start at the commencement of the Christmas term on Monday the sixth of September. Ten minutes later he was so joined in his office by Mrs Burney.

The meeting was quick. The six candidates long-listed would be invited to arrive at the school at nine o'clock on the morning of Wednesday, July fourteenth when the panel of three interviewers will conduct the short-listing exercise to reduce that number to three. The three so short-listed will go on to the final interviews in the afternoon of the same day. Mrs Burney was soon on her way back to organise all that.

The headteacher now turned to the waiting correspondence sitting on his desk. He immediately noticed the cream-coloured envelope which had Her Majesty's Service written on it. He extracted from among the pile and, hands shaking, slit opened the letter with his usual paperknife.

It was what he had always wanted. Mr Austin would receive a knighthood in the New Year's Honours list from Her Royal Highness the Queen of England.

The headteacher folded over in sweet joys for having reached the pinnacle of his ambition.

Meanwhile, on account of the Interpol connection, some sharp-eyed sleuth who is associated with the British Police inquiry into Mrs Edgewater's murder had observed a commonality between the Swedish police expressed interest in tracing one Jason Musgrave and the local police's revisit to the unsolved Upton murder case which had gone cold.

The officer, on his own initiative, had gone online to research the rationale behind Interpol's request. He was able to read and re-read one of Doreen Austin's statements made to the Swedish police following an altercation with her fiancé in late May. The exact quote from Doreen's report to the Swedish police read:

"Another sign I missed or overlooked was at our special engagement dinner. He had no ring with him even though we had discussed ring sizes etcetera. He claimed that he was so locked into me, his memory sometimes deserts him. It was some months later that he presented me with a ring that is so rare and beautiful I forgave him for the strange delay.

"I have since discovered that the ring is not new, it was worn before but is nevertheless beautiful and up-market. It has a puzzling message inscribed inside a flowery box on the inside of the ring. In the box is the letter 'A'. According to Jason, it meant that I was awesome. The only other present that Jason has ever given me was an ornamental fan which was never needed for functional purposes in Umea."

The sharp-eyed detective did not consider it a mere coincidence when aspects of Doreen Austin's report seemed to be reflecting aspects of a report given to the London police some years ago, albeit in a slightly different form. The report to the London police some years ago was, in fact, referring to the revisit to the Upton unsolved murder case and the report given to the police by one Madge Upton who seemed to have disappeared from the face of the earth ever since.

The relevant section of Madge Upton's report is as quoted here:

"Your reward, as usual, will be in Stockholm and I can have back **Box A** which I know is still with you. I need to see that beauty on my finger again where it rightly belongs," Madge reported remembering hurriedly scribbling down Box A on a brown paper bag that had some rubbish waiting to go in a disposal bin.

She had then torn off the scribbled-on edge of the paper bag and palmed it as she continued to eavesdrop.

Robby had replied to the female, don't you worry baby, **Box A** is safe and secured in my drawer as we speak but will be in a safe deposit where you can personally retrieve it with your bonus of US$10, 000 in cash when next you are here.

Both quotes, in their own way, refer to **'Box A'** in connection with something which is worn on the finger like a ring, perhaps? In fact, Doreen Austin was quite specific. **Box A** was reported to be some form of a decorative inscription on her late-arriving engagement ring. With Upton's murder report, however, the reference was more oblique but did not leave much to the imagination concerning whether it was an instrument for wearing on someone's finger.

Perhaps, though the sharp-eyed sleuth, if either or both of Doreen Austin and Madge Upton could be traced; some light might be thrown on what appears to be a mystery at this moment in time. The sharp-eyed sleuth also remembered that Chief Inspector Harding, at the second review conference, openly stated that the key to the solution of both murders was to identify the significance of **Box A** and locate Madge Upton the other half of the identical twins who mysteriously went missing following her report to the London police on December 3rd, 2016.

The sleuth was not quite sure what it was, but he was almost certain that there was something big in this **Box A** issue which is now appearing like some awkward coincidence. He thus pledged to himself that he would seek a private audience with Chief Inspector Harding and Detective Corporal Brown, the two officers who were leading on the Edgewater's case so that he might magnify their attention on this matter.

In his private meeting with Chief Inspector Harding and Detective Corporal Brown, the sleuth found out that he was in fact, pushing on open doors. The Chief Inspector and Detective Corporal listened very keenly to the sleuth's stated curiosity before informing him that there was a real possibility that in a few days he will come face to face with Doreen Austin, the giver of that report in Umea which had led to the involvement of Interpol.

This, he told the sleuth, was because he had received a request from three ladies, one of them Doreen Austin, for some police assistance when they plan to meet with a male acquaintance who they believe might cause them some trouble.

By way of explaining what the three ladies' request was all about, Chief Inspector Harding introduced the three ladies to the sleuth. First, he explained who Mrs Bianca Burney was and her connection with Dixon Pen School where Mrs Elaine Edgewater was found murdered.

Secondly, the inspector explained that Miss Doreen Austin is, in fact, the daughter and youngest child of the headteacher of Dixon Pen School. She was closely tied in friendship to Mrs Burney. Finally, there was Helen Smith who was the only daughter of Mrs Bianca Burney. She had no personal connection with the school beyond her mother.

These three ladies have jointly decided to stage a surprise birthday party for Mr Carlos Burney, husband of Bianca Burney, during the school's summer break up. Mr Gaston Burney, Carlos Burney's only son will be an active participant in the birthday party.

Showing on the guests' list for this party, there will be some close friends of Carlos, but sworn enemies of Gaston in attendance. However, Gaston is well known to be very erratic sometimes and subject to some terrible mood changes. At such times, Gaston can become very abusive and violent. It is against this happening at the party, that the three ladies were seeking some police security presence.

Inspector Harding then announced that he was committed to providing a small team of discreet security officers in the interest of community safety at Rose Hall Community Centre in Camper, Birmingham on Saturday 31st of July commencing at 2 pm in accordance with the three ladies' expressed wishes.

This occasion, he said, would be a good opportunity for the sleuth to make a workable contact with Doreen Austin to eventually pursue the concerns that he had just shared with the team. You are, therefore, one of the assignees to the small and discreet team for that day, the inspector instructed the sleuth who enthusiastically acknowledged the given assignment.

What neither Chief Inspector Harding nor Detective Corporal Brown did was to inform the young sleuth that the more senior crime operators were a step or two ahead of him in relation to the **Box A** issue, and in fact that the seasoned team had some major interests in Gaston Burney on account of their investigations and information gained therefrom.

They had noted the same **Box A** coincidence as the sleuth's but they had gone further in their calculations to make a suspicious link to Gaston Burney.

The inspector and his immediate senior team had reasoned that given that, according to the Swedish police and now Interpol, there is no recorded Swedish national known as Jason Musgrave; and given that, as coincidence would have it, there was a photo of one Jason Musgrave's passport found on Mrs Burney's mobile phone—said by Mrs Burney to be her step son's look-alike Swedish national, but later admitted by her to be her step son with a different passport in a different name.

These were suspicious circumstances worthy of serious investigation by the relevant departments. The chief inspector had thus passed on these suspicious findings to both the passport control department and the narcotics department. As a result of this reference, word had got back to the Inspector Harding team that the character involved may be part of drugs for guns trading schemes. The team, therefore, wants to question Gaston Burney about this possible link.

Also, Gaston Burney appeared in the Birmingham Crown Court on Wednesday, June thirtieth on numerous charges. All bar one of these charges was settled by fines on the day. However, the judge postponed the hearing on the most serious charge, that of possession of a dangerous weapon for Wednesday 27th of October 2021 for a ten o'clock hearing.

One of the officers, who interviewed Mrs Burney on the first occasion about the photos of Gaston Burney found on her mobile phone, had noticed this dangerous weapon charge whilst checking the charge records at the courthouse for details pertaining to another matter. He recognised the name and thought that we too should become interested in the circumstances which explains why a young man with multiple passports in different names should be in possession of a dangerous weapon.

We have now in our possession some detailed imageries of the dangerous weapon in question. We, therefore, need to talk to Gaston Burney about that too.

Wednesday, July fourteenth finally arrived. This was the day that interviews and selection for the substantive post of Chief Administrative Officer were to be held. Although Bianca had been acting in the said capacity for just about two months now, she was not taking anything for granted.

After all, she had previously competed for this very post a few years ago when, like today, she was also the only internal candidate. She had then put on her best performance but had, nevertheless, lost out to the very person whose demise had created the opportunity for her to compete for the post once more. Bianca is satisfied that over the last two months, she had performed in the post exceedingly well despite all the traumas she had had to endure.

Yet, in the forefront of her mind, the fact of her pregnancy constantly parades itself. The uncertainty as to whether Mr Austin knows about her physical state had tormented her over the last week as this day approached. She could not be sure whether Doreen had discussed this with her father given that she had shared it with her as part of the scheme now planned for Rose Hall Community Centre in Camper, Birmingham on Saturday 31st of July.

She didn't want to withhold essential details that could have a bearing on the decision which is to be made today. But equally, she didn't want to adversely affect her chances and thereby cause her to lose out at this post for the second time. In the end, Bianca decided against voluntary disclosure but reconciled herself with a pledge to answer truthfully if asked about it during the interviews.

The question simply never surfaced and Bianca who survived the short-listing process, later managed to sail through, with some ease, the final interviews in the afternoon and thereby defeating the other two candidates. Mrs Bianca Burney is now officially the chief administrative officer of Dixon Pen Comprehensive School with effect from Monday the 6th of September 2021.

The end of the school year, which beckons the start of the summer holidays (July sixteenth) and its concomitant celebrations, was hugely different from previous years. It was not often that a school had so much to celebrate. This year the headteacher had been crowned the metaphorical champion of equality in education. He gained international recognition and put his school and country on the educational map of equality.

Although there were no official announcements, words had leaked out that the headteacher was to be knighted by Her Majesty the Queen in the New Year as per the New Year's Honours list. Also, and in time for the end of term, the headteacher had announced to the governors, the education authority, and his staff that he would not be returning to the school in the new academic year. This, in fact, meant that he was taking early retirement by approximately three years.

In addition, the acting chief administration officer had announced her ascendancy to the substantive post which called for celebration in every sense of the word. And what a fabulous joint celebration it was!

Yet, even as they popped the champagne corks, poured the softer beverages, and feasted on the most sumptuously prepared cuisine and delicacies, the staff, pupils, parents, invited guests and other school officials knew that there was still a cloud hanging over Dixon Pen Comprehensive School in the form of an unsolved murder inquiry.

The headteacher, himself, referred to this in his farewell speech. He regretted that he would not be "seeing through the removal of that cancerous blot" but he would, however, be following development from a distance.

The celebrations had ended with everyone wishing the anticipated new leadership of Dixon Pen Comprehensive School the courage, determination, strength, and wisdom to continue the part that was so firmly marked out over the last twelve years or so and which had led to the school's recognised greatness and well-earned status in the wider society. Everyone had felt extremely satisfied that she/he had accomplished much over the past year and deserved the well-earned long summer break as each departed for her/his abode.

At Austin's home in Sutton Cold Field, Doreen had been preparing everyone for her intended absence from home for part of Saturday 31st of July. As far as her dad and Daniel knew, she would be attending a birthday party for Bianca's husband, Carlos, who will be sixty-eight years old on that day.

Doreen had still not shared with anyone at home what she had learned about Jason Musgrave being Gaston Burney from Bianca and her daughter, Helen, and therefore, the real reason for the birthday party remained hidden from her dad and domestic helper, Daniel.

Chapter 16

At the Burney's home in Camper, things were somewhat different. Considerable effort had been employed over the last week or so to hype up Carlos's enthusiasm in readiness for his surprise sixty-eighth birthday party. This party was to be at the very posh venue of Rose Hall Community Centre in Camper, Birmingham on Saturday, July thirty-first commencing at two o'clock that day.

Even Gaston, his philandering son who had recently been displaying hermit-like tendencies and the unsuspecting victim to be, was whetting his father's appetite for all the goodies that will flow on the day. He assured his father that he will be his personal chauffeur on his special day.

The seating arrangements which Helen had devised, in agreement with the other two ladies, for the day will be the key factor for the overall success or otherwise of the three ladies' plan. The top table had been arranged to seat six people; Carlos and five guests: two of whom were currently billed as surprise guests. Carlos will be seated on one side of the table between his wife, Bianca, on his left, and his son, Gaston, on his right. On the opposite side of the table, directly opposite Carlos will be the sharp-eyed sleuth, ready for any action.

He was especially identified for this role by Chief Inspector Harding. Directly opposite Bianca will be her daughter, Helen, and directly opposite Gaston Burney, Doreen Austin will sit. Chief Inspector Harding had made a special request of Doreen; that is, she should flaunt her engagement ring all the time she was sitting at the table, and she did agree.

The top table so composed with Carlos facing all his guests will imposingly overlook the rest of the invited guests seated below. Once all guests were seated, another police officer in disguise and acting as the Toast Master for the event would officially announce the entrance of the special guests who will then jointly emerge from a nearby previously identified powder room to take their pre-arranged seats. And that is how the shock, explosion, or both will occur.

A third secret police officer had been charged with the responsibility to give total protection, care, and assistance, whatever that might be necessary, to Carlos Burney in the aftermath of whatever happens.

All these arrangements were negotiated in advance and approved by the three ladies; but the police had other interests, at the party, which were never disclosed to the ladies or even the secretly disguised police officers charged with specific duties. There was also an unexpected police photographer ostensibly there to photograph the special occasion for Carlos Burney's future memories.

In fact, the photographer's main mission was to record Gaston Burney's expressions and body language at key moments during the event. Everything was now all set and the fireworks will start soon.

On the stroke of two o'clock, the pre-invited but unsuspecting guests began to arrive at the palatial Rose Hall Community Centre. There was nothing that appeared conspicuous, yet the venue and its guests were co-mingling with numerous officers from the Criminal Investigation Branch of law enforcement.

The Burney family—Carlos, Bianca, and Gaston—made their grand entrance together and were seated at the signal and guidance of the planted Toast Master. All other guests were now seated; it was time for the surprise guests to appear. With his own improvised fanfare, the Toast Master announced the entry of the special guests coming forward to be seated at the top table.

Gaston Burney momentarily froze and instantly fainted as Doreen Austin sat opposite him flaunting her engagement ring whilst Helen also faced him but opposite her mother looked on with a glimmer of revenge in her watery eyes. The deed was accomplished.

"Heaven has no rage like love to hatred turned, nor hell a fury like [some women] scorned."

With the aid of some readily available first aid in the form of smelling salt, Gaston was brought back to his senses and re-seated.

He had no time to be anything other than calm when Detective Corporal Brown, with Chief Inspector Harding looking on from close by, said, in the hearing of everyone, "Gaston Burney, I am arresting you on suspicion of murder. You need not say anything, but if you do it might be used against you in a court of law," simultaneously snapping secured the pair of handcuffs brought along for the purpose. He had then led away to a waiting car.

The scene and the outcome were far too shocking for Carlos. He fell off his chair and remained motionless for some considerable time before the summoned ambulance came and removed him to the hospital, right there in Camper closest to his home. He was accompanied, in the ambulance, by his partially satisfied but extremely frightened wife, Bianca.

The chief inspector hurriedly took to the platform. His task now is to explain all the kafuffle and, also, how and why the guests were essentially used as props in the interest of fighting crime. The chief accomplished this task with considerable skills and much admiration.

He had obviously done this kind of thing before. He clearly had the support of all the players as, without any prompting, they gave him a long-lasting standing ovation before leaving for their various places of residence on that very sad, but justice-wise, very productive afternoon.

Following the arrest, the police waiting motorcade, lights, and sirens fully operational, swiftly raced through the busy Saturday afternoon traffic. In the second car they were carrying Gaston Burney seated on the back seat in the middle of, and securely handcuffed to, two accompanying officers whilst the driver negotiated the unspecified number of miles to their destination. Did they arrive at Harbourne Police Station in exactly fifteen minutes?

At the station, Gaston Burney, guided by the officers chained to him, was quickly whisked inside the station with his head and face covered with a throw-over blanket. Once inside, the cuffs were removed and for the second time in just a little over two months, Gaston Burney found himself incarcerated in an unwelcoming police cell awaiting expert interrogation.

It would be some two hours before the available team of expert interrogators would be in place ready to question the suspect. During this time Gaston Burney was advised of his rights with regard to having a lawyer present at the interrogation sessions.

He was cautioned again that he didn't have to say anything; but if he, did it would be written down and could, subsequently, be used against him in a properly constituted court of law. He was also advised that should, for whatever reason, he would not be able to engage a lawyer of his choice, there was always a lawyer in residence capable and available to assist him.

With an air of arrogance and unhelpful bravado, Gaston Burney rejected all suggestions and offers of legal aid and assistance whilst declaring that he was a totally innocent man now being persecuted by these corrupt cops. He stated most vehemently that he was absolutely determined to represent himself in all circumstances.

What must have seemed like ages for Gaston Burney, the suspect, the period languishing in the police cell eventually passed by; and now he was seated in a room equipped with recording and audio technology, ready to be interviewed by Chief Inspector Harding, Detective Corporal Brown and one other officer who was specifically imported in for his expertise and for the purpose at hand.

At the commencement of the interrogation, all three officers introduced themselves to the suspect who barely acknowledged them. The officers, nevertheless, began the interrogative exercise. Chief Inspector Harding was first off, the mark having set the recording instrument rolling.

CHIEF INSPECTOR HARDING

"Are you Jason Musgrave or Gaston Burney or Robert Reid, sir"?

But before the suspect could try at answering, the inspector instantly enlarged upon his question using a well-practiced technique designed to forestall any thought of lying on the part of the suspect.

"We are asking you this because we have uncovered three sets of documentation from the British, the Jamaican, and the Swedish passport authorities all bearing photographs which unmistakably correspond with one another and look remarkably like you, sir. Which one are you, sir?"

Gaston Burney was absolutely flabbergasted. He was thinking that this thing isn't going to be the piece of cheese he had arrogantly thought after all. The very first question had almost buried him alive. Especially in the light of what happened a few hours ago at the fake birthday party for his dad, he didn't know what to say.

What have the three impregnated women been saying? Where is all this leading? He knew that there was nothing illegal for having three passports; but how would he explain the three different names without exposing himself to legal jeopardy and all its concomitant perils? He thus decided to play it safe.

THE SUSPECT

"I have nothing to say. I am exercising my right to remain silent, Inspector."

DETECTIVE CORPORAL BROWN

"On this identity issue, would you be willing to assist us with an identification parade when a young student from Dixon Pen Comprehensive School in Edgebaston will be the identifier?"

Very clearly, the planned method of interrogation being employed by the officers was to deliberately drop snippets of information that would be known by the suspect if he was the criminal perpetrator for whom they seek.

The idea was to leave the suspect wondering how much is known by the police and leave him simmering in self-doubt. A criminal weakened in confidence, and engulfed in self-doubt, will eventually crack providing the pressure stays in place.

THE SUSPECT
"Mum is the word."

THE OFFICER IMPORTED
"Are you engaged or ever been engaged to be married, sir"?

The suspect is beginning to realise that he is in very serious trouble. This second question, as was the first, is a very loaded one. Doreen must have been talking to them. But how had Doreen become a part of this? What is the connection?

She, as far as he knew, is studying in Sweden where he last saw her? If only he could figure out her connection with Bianca and Helen, he could put up a sensible fight in terms of his representation.

Damn it, he thought, marriage ceremonies were recorded but informal engagements such as the one he had with Doreen happen every day and were not recorded. He will take a chance and deny this one and see where it is heading.

THE SUSPECT
"No, sir, I am not engaged to be married to anyone and never was, sir".

The questioning officer reached for the file lying in front of him and extracted some photographs: one of them was a ring brochure, and another was a receipt. Both were found on Mrs Bianca's mobile phone several weeks ago. The officer passed both photographs to the suspect stating as he did so that they were not the originals.

THE OFFICER IMPORTED
"I wish to draw your attention to this receipt. This document was issued in Jamaica at an in-bond store in Ocho Rios. The store is SATISFACTION IN-BOND and situated on Main Street, Ocho Rios, Saint Ann, Jamaica. The

document is fully supported with telephone numbers, fax numbers, and the official business e-mail and website details. It was dated five years ago—the third of July 2016.

"The receipt was issued as hard and genuine evidence of the purchase of a white golden ring with a ruby, opal, and diamond cluster with a related brochure (the second photo is of the ring on that brochure) and two ornamental Jamaican hand-made straw fans. The total sum paid was J$3m paid in cash. Written on the receipt was the purchaser's Jamaican passport number: A1238760. The holder of that passport is one, Robert Reid. What was the purpose of that ring, Sir?

"And more importantly, sir, do you know where that ring is at the present time? Or are you still denying that you are Robert Reid whose passport number is recorded on that receipt indicating that you were the purchaser? And can you explain to us how it was that you were able to pay such a large sum in cash whilst in a foreign country?"

THE SUSPECT

"I never denied anything. Please don't put words into my mouth. What I said, and am still saying, is that I wish to exercise my right to remain silent."

CHIEF INSPECTOR HARDING

"Are you the same Gaston Burney who was charged for possession of a dangerous weapon similar to that used in two recorded murders along with several motoring offences and appeared in the Birmingham Court on June thirtieth?

"The records show that all of those charges were settled by substantial fines except for that one pertaining to the dangerous weapon which was ordered to be mentioned in the Birmingham Crown Court on Wednesday 27th of October 2021 at ten o'clock?"

THE SUSPECT

(Remained absolutely silent).

DETECTIVE CORPORAL BROWN

"I think you are stonewalling us, Mr Burney. We are prepared to keep you here as long as it takes for you to become cooperative. When you feel like you wish to have a break, let us know and we will put you back into the cell until you feel able to resume answering our questions. Just let us know. In any case, I have this further question for you. How well do you know Madge Upton, her sister Gloria and Mrs Elaine Edgewater?"

The detective was thinking that a bluff question against a backdrop of an overnight stay in the dungeon in the present circumstances of unknowns and doubts would flush the suspect out into the open. He was right. The suspect realised that these officers might have other questions about entrapment and if he was cooperative it might be better for him in the bitter end.

THE SUSPECT

"OK, you bastards, you have broken me. She had it coming. She turned me into a cold-blooded murderer. Let's begin with the so-called Mrs Elaine Edgewater. She was no more Mrs Elaine Edgewater than I am Jesus Christ. That bitch ruined my life completely and turned me into the wretched killer that I have become twice over.

"You see, I was on a nice little earner which was more than enough for supporting my globetrotting and having exciting sexual affairs with dozens of women wherever I happen to be. My good looks and physical attributes served me well in more ways than one until Madge Upton came along: the same woman you know to be Mrs Elaine Edgewater.

"I had no idea that she was one of the identical twins until I had accidentally murdered her twin sister, Gloria, believing her to be Madge. That day, I expected to find Madge alone in the rented apartment where I had been entertaining her for the past few days. But it turned out that the person I found was Gloria.

"There was no way of telling them apart as I eventually discovered from the massive amount of publicity that attended that case at the time, even in Jamaica where I went to cool off after that dreadful error, the near impossibility of telling the Upton twins apart, dominated the airwaves. The fact that it was so difficult to tell the sisters apart had seemed, to everyone, to be of more compelling importance to the media than was the killing itself.

"My physical attributes, as I said before, serve me in two very important ways—my pleasures and my income. Pleasures because I cannot exist without the steamy pleasures I get from women, lots of them, even my father's wife will tell you. She is currently bearing my child and so is her daughter, Helen, and for that matter, so is Doreen Austin, though I do not know how she managed to link with Bianca and Helen.

"This pleasure aspect of my life is what led to today's fake birthday party in Camper, or so it seemed. At this so-called party, you would have noted, there were three pregnant women who had clearly schemed to confront me publicly to declare that all three conceived for me in the same month. And that had led to my presence here now confronting my sins.

"They are the source of my income because I was able to exploit the racist nature of many international cities, including British ones. Because black people, men, and women are disproportionately targeted by law enforcement in most parts of the world, they are highly unsuitable for the guns for the drug trafficking business in which I was so successful.

"I, with my blond hair, blue eyes, and armed Swedish passport have made my income from trafficking drugs, guns, and funds so derived as an international traveller knowing that the cops and authorities will always go after the black decoy who we always manage to put in place.

"The important thing was to always ensure that the stereotypical decoy was always immaculately clean and, therefore, was never more than temporarily detained until the authorities ascertained that he or she was clean. In the meantime, I am gone through customs or whatever barriers they put in place, unhindered.

"With regards to the ring and fan purchase in Jamaica, '**Box A**' plus, it was my unidentified boss who had me part money laundering and part repaying a pawn debt. She had previously incurred this debt when she was in dire need of some quick funds to make a drug bargain that had come her way but wasn't going to be available for longer than a day.

"She had pawned 'Box A', her prized accoutrement, in order not to miss out on that fleeting bargain. The funds which I used to do the so-called purchase of those fans and that ring in Jamaica were the proceeds of a hot US dollar deal. My instructions were to change enough into Jamaican dollars to reclaim that ring at the pawn facility. That was a way to deceive the trained dogs that detect carriers of large amounts of funds at international airports.

"Dogs do not discriminate and therefore, in such a situation, a decoy traveller could not help. The ring was money had and now taken out of Jamaica despite the damn dogs. Therefore, that so-called purchase was not a true purchase. It was a payback of a previous pawn loan against that ring. Sometimes great bargains just suddenly appear and if you do not have spare liquid cash, you lose out to the more prepared buyers. In this business, dog eats dog.

"This is where the pawn shops can come in handy. The funds so obtained would have been used to purchase drugs in Jamaica. The drugs would then be traded for guns using trained fishermen. And I was to deliver that ring to my controlling boss on her next London trip. Sadly, this did not happen because Madge Upton eve-dropped on one of my conversations with my boss and thereby overheard what she should never have heard.

"I caught her in the act but pretended that I didn't, and she pretended that she was also doing otherwise. However, I knew that from the conversation she had heard, she would have realised that I was involved in the 'drugs for shooters' racket from London to Haiti and that my collection point was Stockholm.

"That night, before bedtime I had to link with our secret operational squad to tell them about the accidental leakage of important information which could be deleterious to the organisation. Without hesitation, the order was given to 'out her out'.

"That was what I thought I did the following day, but, instead, Gloria unfortunately was at the wrong place at the wrong time, and she took the hit because of a case of mistaken identity. It was then that I realised that Madge had heard more than I realised. I quickly gathered together my bare minimum into my traveller's case, and when to a secure drawer to retrieve the boss's ring, fondly referred to as **'Box A'**, but it was gone and with it ten thousand United States dollars. I had killed the wrong bitch, and probably an innocent one.

"I fulfilled the London/Haiti assignment and took off for Stockholm along with Mustafa Banks, alias Bunny, who is the permanently retained travelling decoy for my operations. Bunny is such a great asset, he has been stopped, detained, and searched countless times, and never yet have they ever found any contraband, drugs, or any compromising amount of cash on him: such are the beneficial effects of racism in my line of business.

"You see, I was never stopped because I was always deemed to be the respectable white male traveller; and yet, I was always the one going through unchecked with all the contraband.

"It was almost one month when I received a WhatsApp text from an unknown phone number. The text read: "You murdered my sister, and I will make you pay if it is the last thing I do. And remember, your drugs for guns operation is simply not safe with me. At the right time, I will blow you and it right out of the dirty waters in which you swim". The text was unsigned but reference to 'my sister' gave the author away.

"Since receiving that text, I was under strict orders to find Madge Upton and to eliminate her before she could be harmful to our organisation. Of course, I had a personal interest in her demise too. The search was on for her earnestly, but we never found her. There was simply no trace. Like her sister's murder inquiry, the search for her had gone cold after nearing almost five years. And then, I got lucky.

"For over two years, Madge Upton had been working in the same city in which I live: and even more alarming, she was, suitably disguised as Mrs Elaine Bridgewater, working in the same school as my stepmother and lover work. And yet neither Madge nor I knew of that fact.

"I made numerous trips to and from Dixon Pen Comprehensive School whenever I am in the Birmingham area, mainly dropping off or collecting Bianca but had never come across Madge. Of course, Bianca had often, in general conversations, referred to her boss, Mrs Bridgewater, but that name was of no significance to me.

"Then came the day before she will die, I drove Bianca to school that morning and as I parked near the entrance to the school to let Bianca off, Mrs Edgewater was just coming in too. She greeted Bianca who introduced her as Mrs Edgewater to me and me to her as Gaston.

"Our eyes met in obvious recognition. There was no doubt about it; she knew who I was, and I knew she was no Mrs Elaine Bridgewater. Here before my very eyes was the long-disappeared Madge Upton and there on her left hand was my boss's ring—'**Box A**'.

"There was no time to delay. Madge knew I was about and knew her charade was blown. That same day I abandoned my car and borrowed Mustafa's for a couple of days (I knew he was away at a conference in Africa, but I had the spare key that Mustafa always kept with me just in case there was an emergency) and returned to the school.

"Some kid helped me locate Mrs Edgewater's office. With the minimum amount of reconnaissance, I was able to plan the events of the next day. I had noted that there was a fire glass breakage point on a column to the immediate left of Mrs Edgewater's office and that was going to be helpful.

"The next day was a Friday. I had known from previous conversations with Bianca that Mrs Edgewater was a creature of habits and that most Fridays she is alone in her office following her regular weekly staff meeting with the team. The meetings always end on the dot of one forty-five in the afternoon. I had timed it well.

"On the stroke of two o'clock, I gently knocked on the door with Chief Administrative Officer embossed in golden letters. A voice I knew well had not changed as it invited me in. She was startled as though she knew what was coming: and like her sister five years ago, offered no meaningful resistance. The job was quick and easy, if somewhat bloody.

"I cleaned the knife that had taken two sisters' lives, on the back of Madge's garment. I removed **Box A** from her left hand now dangling over the edge of her desk and I was gone, but not before breaking that glass to sound the fire alarm which sent the entire school scuttling in the opposite direction from my escape route.

"That evening, I returned to collect Bianca as normal, but the news had not been broken up to the time I dropped her home. This time, I would cool off in Switzerland for a few days. Whilst there, I prosecuted inquiries to see who the real Mrs Elaine Edgewater really is and to my amazement, discovered that Madge had been impersonating her dead mother of many years ago.

"Officers, I might not be spot-on in every detail as memory can be sometimes unreliable especially when on the Saturday afternoon of July thirty-first, one finds oneself in such an unbearable and intolerable stressful situation. But the essence is there: and I vow to cooperatively clarify any detail on this certain road to confinement at Her Majesty's pleasure for a very long time."

Meanwhile, back at the hospital in Camper, the three pregnant ladies were having a rendezvous. Their primary concern now was Carlos Burney's health. His condition was very serious, the doctor had told them. It seems he had a double whammy from a stroke and a heart attack and was in an intensive care unit where he is likely to be for some indefinite time.

As the ladies sadly consoled each other, they realised that they were not alone. Standing immediately behind them was none other than Mr Allan Austin the caring daddy of Doreen Austin. He had heard on the news, both television and radio about all the developments regarding the murder at Dixon Pen and how his own daughter as well as his Acting Chief Administrative Officer was instrumental in bringing to justice the perpetrator.

That meant he had to drop all that he was doing and find these women in order to understand in more detail what this was all about. At the Rose Hall Community Centre, he was told that some of the guests had gone to Camper

Hospital and it was believed that his daughter was among them. Mr Austin hurriedly drove the short distance to Camper Hospital where he found the three pregnant ladies who were able to patch together all the pieces for the retired headteacher.

He was stunned, amazed but happy. He thanked them for jointly restoring the good name of Dixon Pen Comprehensive School now that it is being splashed across the nation that the murderer was an outsider and a very bad one too.

The retired headteacher offered to take the ladies home in their hour of mixed blessings. Helen was extremely glad for the offer. She did not bother to drive that day because parking was usually difficult in the area on a Saturdays, and it was imperative that she was punctual for the effectiveness of the plan to confront Gaston Burney.

Mr Austin decided to drop off Helen in Kings Heath first and on his way back he would drop off Bianca and then make his way home, with his daughter, Doreen, where Daniel will be anxiously waiting to understand all that had happened in one short afternoon.

It was on the way to Kings Heath that it dawned on the three pregnant ladies that because of today's development, their children—that will enter this world around the same period—will be fatherless for a mighty long time.

This sounded a bit gloomy, so, Mr Austin decided to share some good news that he received from Umea by phone earlier in the day with written confirmation in the post. He was advised that Doreen can resume her residency in Umea at a time convenient to her and that her place in the medical course at the university was guaranteed.

The atmosphere in the BMW had just started to lighten when, as if to cancel out the good news which was just delivered, Bianca's mobile sounded. It was the hospital advising her that Carlos did not make it. He had passed away four minutes ago.

All the dropping home plans suddenly changed. Neither Helen nor Doreen wanted to leave Bianca on her own for the rest of the evening. It would not be right to leave her alone in these circumstances of mourning, everyone agreed.

Mr Austin turned his BMW around and headed in the direction of Sutton Cold Field with all three ladies aboard. On his way, he buzzed Daniel to let her know that there will be two extra members of the family tonight.

After dinner, which was hardly touched by the increased members of the household for lack of appetite, given the circumstances, the four women gathered for a somewhat impromptu conference. It was in this conference, aptly directed by Daniel, that the idea of making sustained long-term provisions for the three babies due in late spring 2022 was hatched.

The idea of a single nanny for all three children was popular. Even more popular was the suggestion that the nanny should be one of the three mothers. Logically, the idea would allow Doreen to return to her studies as soon as possible after giving birth; it would nicely enable Bianca who, after maternity leave, will still be new to the job, to start afresh in the springtime. Helen whose childhood ambition was to be a nursery nurse seemed the logical choice for the job.

All three women became ecstatically joyful with this refreshingly novel idea. From a distance, Mr Austin readily endorsed what he described as the greatest idea he had heard in a lifetime. He stated that he would guarantee that Helen will be paid an over-the-top salary for the task ahead. Bianca's contribution to her daughter's salary was said to be similarly assured.

Daniel nosily enquired of each of the pregnant ladies if by any chance the clinic had disclosed the sex of their babies. Each woman answered in the positive. The sex of the baby in each case was confirmed to be male.

'All is, therefore, well that ends well. The focus now is to make the future as bright as can be.'

Allan Austin will be knighted; Bianca Burney had been permanently promoted to the substantive post of Chief Administrative Officer at Dixon Pen Comprehensive School; sadly, Carlos Burney had passed away; Gaston Burney, in his own words, will be a very long time behind bars together with his known and traceable accomplices; Doreen will return to her medical studies at the University of Umea; and Helen will spend the next eighteen years nursing, caring for and educating the **THREE LITTLE BOYS**.